MEGALODON RIPTIDE

RUSS WATTS

SEVERED PRESS
HOBART TASMANIA

MEGALODON RIPTIDE

"But more wonderful than the lore of old men and the lore of books, is the secret lore of the ocean."

From "The White Ship" by H.P.Lovecraft

CHAPTER 1

"Pippa, hurry up, we have to go," I shouted. "Get your stuff together and haul ass."

I looked at Chelsea and tried to not give away how nervous I was. The building was creaking and groaning as if it would give way any moment. You could feel it swaying, and the wind howling outside made me shiver. Time was not on our side. I was no architect but even I knew we had to get out.

"It's okay Uncle, don't worry, we'll be fine," said Chelsea calmly.

I don't know how she did it. Pippa's kid was barely sixteen, yet she had more sense than any of us. She rarely freaked out and never threw a tantrum. She was smart, too. It was such a shame she would never get the chance to go to university and realize just how damn smart she really was. That sort of life stopped with my generation. There are no universities to go to anymore. I looked at my niece and wondered how she managed to remain so cool when the building was collapsing around us. I looked into her brown eyes.

"Yeah, as long as your mother gets her ass out here in the next five seconds. If she doesn't, I'll—"

"You'll what?" Pippa hurried into the corridor, closing the front door behind her. She had a backpack slung across her shoulders and flushed cheeks. She looked at me with those big brown eyes of hers that reminded me of mom. "Ready?"

"Pippa, we've been ready for five minutes. You were supposed to have your getaway bag packed and good to go. What took you so long?" I asked, frustrated. We all had an emergency bag by our beds, just in case. Mine was full of food and bottled water, some clothes and a few keepsakes. I had a few things that I wanted to keep: some photographs, a silver chain that had belonged to mom, and a couple of books. I couldn't understand how Pippa could be so disorganized. I suspected that hers consisted of half-eaten chocolate and jewelry. My sister had never been the organized type, but just lately she had gotten worse. Even Chelsea had been ready to go. I don't really blame her. I think what happened shook us all up. Pippa tried to hide how scared she was but I could tell. Chelsea too.

"I had to grab a few things," said Pippa. "It's fine, Luke. Besides, how do you even know he'll be here yet? You said yourself that you couldn't see the boat, so why are you so sure that he'll turn up?"

"He will. He'll be here. I told you that he—"

"And what about Manny? I don't see him," said Pippa looking up and down the corridor. "You told him we were leaving, right, so where is he? I don't see you nagging *him* to hurry up."

"I told you before, we're meeting Manny up on the roof. He'll be there. In fact, he's probably waiting for us, so if you'll just hurry the hell up we can all get out of here. Jeez, could you *be* any more like mom?"

Pippa frowned at me. I knew I shouldn't have said it, but she was beginning to get on my nerves. The comparison to mom wasn't flattering, yet nor was it a lie. She got more and more like her every day. As much as I loved my sister, the building was still creaking and groaning, and I wasn't sure we had much time left. I watched as Pippa fished her keys out of her pocket and then turned to the front door. As she shoved the key into the lock, I couldn't believe what I was seeing.

"Pippa, what the hell are you doing?" I snapped.

"Mom, you don't need to do that," said Chelsea. "We're *not* coming back."

"And what about all our things? I'm not leaving them for old Mr. Johnson to steal. You know what he's like. Crotchety old bastard."

Chelsea looked at me and rolled her eyes as her mother locked the door. I almost burst out laughing except out situation was so dire that if I did I thought I might not stop.

"Pippa, leave it," I said. "Mr. Johnson isn't that bad. And I think he's got more pressing things to worry about than our old TV that hasn't worked for five years and your granny pants."

Pippa drew herself up and put an arm around her daughter. "Luke, don't try to tell me what to do."

She sounded just like mom when she did that. I was quite sure that soon she was simply going to turn into her. Mom had passed away ten years ago, but I still saw some of her in Pippa every day. She had the same short haircut that ringed her neck, the same funny walk, and the same tone in her voice when she was trying to get me to shut up.

"I'm just saying that we need to go," I said to Pippa. "I don't want to be here arguing about Mr. Johnson when this building goes down. And neither do you."

"So let's *go* already," interjected Chelsea. "We don't want to be stuck inside here when it goes like the hotel did." Chelsea put her fingers together and then splayed them apart slowly, making a whooshing noise with her mouth.

We all knew what Chelsea meant. We'd watched it together in horror barely four weeks ago. The Stamford had stood for well over a hundred years. It was a huge ornate building complete with art deco sculptures adorning the exterior, and decorative cornices and balconies on each upper floor. It was a magnificent building that had seen off two world wars and more Presidents than I could name. I think there were close to fifty people living in it when it happened. We had all heard the stories of buildings collapsing into the ocean before, but none of us had actually witnessed it with our own eyes. It sounded unreal, too far-fetched to be true, even though the ocean was all around us now. The streets and roads had long ago been submerged by water and so the lower floors too of all the cities' apartments and buildings were under water. The foundations of the Stamford had been weaker, perhaps because it was such a grand old building. We all heard the groaning sounds it made as it began to list. It had taken a few hours and none of us really thought it was going to go. I remember sitting up on the rooftop of our own complex with Pippa, watching it. The building had listed over a few hours. I saw a couple of occupants get out. A man and a woman. They had a small dinghy and used it to sail away to God knows where. I guess they must have kept it to themselves because they could have fitted another ten people on that little boat.

The others in the hotel converged on the rooftop when the building began to list so badly that they could barely stand upright anymore. There was nothing we could do. The building was across the street from us and too far away to reach. We had no ropes, no boats, nothing to help them with. At first it was only me and Pippa up there, but soon the whole complex joined us. There was old Mr. Johnson and Manny from the floor beneath us. There were half a dozen others who I recognized, but we had little to do with them. They kept to themselves for most of the time. We all lived within a few floors of each other, yet we didn't even know their names. And we all stood on the top of our complex watching fifty people die. It was a communal experience that should have brought us together. After it was over I hardly saw any of them again. It was as if it had driven us further apart.

I shouted to the few survivors, my voice carrying easily across the water. I tried to make them understand that they should swim toward us, but none of them did. I don't think any of them truly expected it to go. In the end it was quick.

The hotel eventually just collapsed in on itself. The lower floors pancaked and within seconds it was gone. A unique piece of history was gone when the hotel disappeared beneath the water. The people on the rooftop pleaded for help and tried to swim away, but they stood no chance. The water sucked them down with the hotel. I waited longer than the others, in case anyone resurfaced, but nobody did. Not a single one.

After that, I think some of the people in our own complex left. People were desperate. I heard them at night, banging and making their makeshift boats. I could understand it, but there was no way we were going out there like that. I had a better deal on the table.

A week after that horrible day I was awoken in the morning by a crashing sound. It was far enough away for me to know it wasn't our own building, but still, it had me panicked. When I pulled the drapes back it took a moment for me to accept what I was seeing. My bedroom window looked out over the city and the spires of St.Patrick's Cathedral were clearly visible – but no longer. The glass skyscraper beside it had been burnt out long ago, and all around it were derelict buildings. That morning I saw more decayed masonry and debris in the water than normal, and the cathedral had finally succumbed to the sea. I couldn't tell if the spires had crumbled or if the foundations had caused the whole building to subside. I thought I spotted one of the spires still breaching the surface, but I couldn't be certain. The Rockefeller was already under water and most of the familiar landmarks I had grown up with were gone. Every time we lost another one, I felt like the sea was claiming a part of me too. I guess I thought the cathedral would be there forever. It was hard to accept it was gone. All around me it felt like the city was falling.

What happened to the Stamford was in all of our minds now, even though nobody was saying it. We all knew how quickly it could happen. We all knew that we had to leave, which was why it was so frustrating waiting for Pippa.

Chelsea took off down the corridor toward the stairwell and Pippa pushed past me to follow her. The elevators had stopped working months ago so the stairwell was the only way out of the building now. The lower five floors of our complex were under water and the upper ten floors were damp but fine. We had sandbags on the sixth floor but only in winter did the water threaten to climb any higher. It seemed to have reached a plateau recently. So the few of us still living inside stayed on the upper floors, well away from the damp and the cold water that sloshed around the bottom of the building. The once white walls of the corridors were a creamy gray now, and damp had crept up the sides and across the ceiling. It spread like a cancer, insidiously eating away at everything, destroying the plasterboard and electrics, weakening the walls and eating at the decaying air. The smell was bad. We didn't leave our apartment often and I'd forgotten just how musty the air was. As I followed Pippa and Chelsea, I couldn't help but feel bad about Mr. Johnson. He lived alone and had nobody looking out for him. Everyone else in the complex had taken off on their own. I tried to make conversation with him occasionally, but Pippa was right: he was a crotchety old bastard. I wasn't sure that meant we should leave him to die.

I banged on his door as we went past. "Mr. Johnson, you up? It's Luke from next door. Mr. Johnson?"

I could feel Pippa's glare from twenty yards away, so I stared at Mr. Johnson's door. The pale blue paint was covered in a fine film and as I trailed my finger down it some of the paint came off on my fingers. Our building was rotting from the inside out. I heard shuffling noises behind the door and then the sound of several locks being tangled with. Finally, he opened the door.

"What?"

Mr. Johnson stood before me looking older than I remembered. His thin brown hair was disheveled and it looked as if I had woken him up. He wore a simple beige sweater and slacks that were at least two sizes too big for him. Dirty brown moccasins completed his ensemble that suggested he hadn't bothered to change in weeks. I was certain that he had been wearing the same thing when I had last seen him up on the roof. The smell emanating from him and his apartment suggested the same.

"Mr. Johnson, we're leaving and I think it's time you did the same. The building is not safe. We have a boat coming to get us and—"

"This is my home, young man. Grace died here and I'll die here with her. Her ashes have sat on my mantelpiece for eight years and I'll be damned if I'm leaving her now. I'm not abandoning her or my apartment just like that, on a *whim*. The building is perfectly safe. Leave me alone."

As he closed the door, I jammed my foot quickly into the frame to stop him from closing it on me. I knew that if he got that door shut he wouldn't open it again.

"What the hell are you doing?" he asked, surprised.

"Mr. Johnson, I'm serious. The complex is going to collapse, just like the Stamford."

I saw fear in his eyes. There was defiance too and I could see he hated how frail he had become. There was a rumor he used to be a cop, although none of us knew the truth about his past. The mentioning of the Stamford seemed to make him pause.

"Garbage. There's nothing wrong with this place."

I put my hand on the door and got him to open it a few more inches. There were piles and piles of books behind him and his apartment was dark. I don't think he had opened the windows in weeks. I wished his apartment only smelt of damp, but there were other smells that I didn't even want to imagine where they had come from.

"Listen to it. Listen to *me*. Please. I'm offering you a chance to get out of here. If I'm wrong, then in a few hours we can all come back and laugh about it. But if I'm right—"

He looked me up and down, and then opened the door a little more. I removed my foot from the doorway as he poked his head into the corridor. "Your sister and her little brat with you?"

I sighed. "Yes, sir. We're all leaving, right now." I looked at Pippa and Chelsea. They were by the stairwell waiting for me. Chelsea patiently, Pippa impatiently. "There's room for you too, if you want."

Mr. Johnson glanced at me. "No. At least with you gone this place will be quieter and I'll be able to get some sleep. Leave me alone."

He slammed the door shut before I had a chance to grab it. I heard him closing it up, sliding the bolts back into place, and I knew I had lost him. I trudged toward Pippa.

"See? Stupid old man would rather die here than accept our help," said Pippa. She tried to sound condescending, as if she knew he would say no. I could tell she was just trying to sound confident though. She wasn't a bad person and she didn't want him to die alone any more than I did.

"Come on, we can't force him. What are you going to do, break down his door?" Chelsea pushed the fire exit open and we moved into the stairwell. She was right. I hated leaving him, but what could I do? He was too stubborn to listen to me or anyone else. The only person he ever listened to, Grace, had died years ago.

"I hate this place," muttered Pippa as we began to climb the dark stairs.

There was no light to see by and I reached into my backpack for a torch. I wound the handle around and generated enough power to give off a little light. It was weak but at least it didn't need batteries. I'd bought it a few years back after a particularly bad storm and never had reason to use it before. I was pleased we had it now though, as without any natural light in the stairwell, we would've only had the handrail to guide us. The electricity had failed a long time ago and there were no windows. The water had filled the bottom of the stairwell and we could smell the salt water.

I hated it too. It was a dark, dank, horrible place. The sound of the water sloshing around fifty feet below us echoed around the concrete stairwell. I wondered what else was down there. In the darkness it was easy to imagine all sorts of things: dead bodies, electric eels, mutant fish and creatures from the deep just waiting to nibble on our carcasses. My torchlight illuminated the way ahead but scarcely reached more than a few feet. I tried to point it upward so Chelsea could see.

"Just keep close," said Chelsea. "We're almost there."

A little light began to illuminate the stairs as we climbed higher. The door to the rooftop was propped open, something I'd done after the hotel had been destroyed. I used an old pedal-bin from the kitchen. We had no use for it anymore but it found a new lease of life as a doorstop. We'd decided it was safer to leave it open, in case we needed a quick escape. The sunlight slipped between the door and the frame, and as the light levels in the stairwell rose, so too did our prospects of getting out alive. I flicked off my torch and stowed it back in my pack.

Chelsea shoved the door open and stepped out onto the roof. Glorious sunlight hit my face and I sucked in fresh air. If there was one upside to the end of the world it was that the streets of New York were no longer clogged with traffic spewing out toxic fumes. The air was clean and pure, and even the sun felt fresher. I followed Pippa out onto the roof and was pleased to see Manny had beaten us to it.

"How you doing?" I could see that he was prepared and had brought some gear with him too. There was a small, black sports bag at his feet and even better, a six-pack of beer. Manny was the only person in the complex we had managed to make friends with. He used to be a chef at some sushi place around the corner. He was ridiculously handsome and I suspected that Chelsea had a crush on him. He was twelve years older than her, but something told me that wouldn't stop her, given the chance. Of course, I had no intention of letting her date anyone for several years yet. She was only sixteen and in my head still tottering around the living room as she learnt how to walk.

"Luke, 'bout time, man." Manny grasped my hand firmly. His dark skin shone in the sunlight and he beamed, despite the danger we were in. "I was just 'bout gonna give up on you."

"How's it going, Manny?" asked Pippa.

He kissed her cheek and looked at Chelsea. "My two favorite ladies in the world. How lucky am I?"

I noticed Chelsea blush but said nothing.

"You see him?" I asked hopefully. "Any sign of the boat?"

Manny looked to the east wistfully. "No. Nothing."

"You said he would be here," snapped Pippa. "What if he doesn't come? He could be miles away. What if..?"

"*He'll come*," I insisted. Jonah wouldn't let us down. He was a good friend and probably the most reliable person in the world. "Let's get ready. He'll be here soon, I'm sure of it."

Crossing the rooftop I noticed that the rope ladder we had secured a couple of weeks ago was still secured in place. After the Stamford collapsed we had to come up with an escape route. Truthfully it wasn't so much of a rope ladder as a length of rope with knots in it. The collapse of the nearby hotel had forced us to think about what we would do in the event of our own building collapsing. With Manny's help, I'd searched the empty rooms of the complex and found some rope in one of the maintenance rooms. We tied it together and took it up onto the roof. One end was wound around a ventilation shaft and the other was draped over the side of the building. We managed to get a few knots in it every few feet, so that when we had to crawl down it there would be some footholds. It wasn't much but it was better than just jumping into the water. With the rope in place, I propped open the door to the roof and made everyone pack a bag of supplies, in case we had to leave in a hurry. The other part of the escape plan was largely out of my hands. It involved a boat, my old friend Jonah and a whole lot of trust.

I approached the edge of the building and looked down. It had to be fifty or sixty feet to the water. It was calm but from up here the impact of hitting the water would probably break a bone or two, at the very least. The rope looked solid and I tugged on it. It held fast and reached down to the water. It would have to do.

"Where is he, Luke?"

Pippa's question made me jump. I turned to see her standing right behind me. Her arms were folded and she was beginning to look a lot like mom again. She leaned in closer. "Where is he?" she hissed.

I had no idea where Jonah was, but I had to trust he would come. I had no other options. If the building went down before he picked us up in his trawler then we would be right out of luck. The only other boats in the vicinity were too far away, and swimming to them was far too dangerous. Plus, I don't think any of us actually knew how to sail. I was relying on Jonah and beginning to worry myself. He had no ties to us, no commitment to rescue us. Hell, we weren't even related. Jonah was an old friend who I would trust with my life. It felt as if I was about to put my trust in him to the test.

"Mom, give Uncle Luke a break. You sound like a stuck record," said Chelsea.

"Chelsea, I told you to wait with Manny. Can you just leave me and your Uncle alone for a minute?"

"Fine, get your argument over with."

I watched Chelsea return to Manny.

"She's not a kid, Pippa. She knows what's going on," I said, trying not to antagonize my sister any further, but knowing whatever I said would do just that. I could've presented her with a million dollars and she still would've bitten my head off for not getting two million.

"She won't be *anything* if your friend, Jonah, doesn't show up soon. We need to get on that boat, Luke."

"I know, I know. Look, he'll be here. He doesn't go far. He probably got caught up with something."

"What is there to get caught up in? There's nothing to do anymore except fish." Pippa threw her hands up in the air. "Jesus, Luke, this is just typical of you. It's just so—"

"I'm sorry, okay?" I lowered my voice. When Pippa got started on one of her rants it could be hard to stop her. I loved her dearly, but a tantrum right now wouldn't help anyone. It amazed me how calm and collected Chelsea always was, whilst Pippa was always flying off the handle. Another common trait she shared with our mother. I started to explain how Jonah could be trusted.

She'd never met him, so she had her doubts. Fair enough. But I knew he would come, and he would have a good reason for being late. We'd made a pact. He would watch out for us and take us onto his boat when the time came. In turn I would supply him with fresh water. We'd laid out a whole bunch of buckets, pots and pans, and even rigged up an old tent we'd found to collect as much as we could. There had been a huge amount of bottled water and drinks left behind in the complex too, so we had more than enough for the few of us left behind. Out on his trawler he had to rely on trading for it, so was more than grateful to set up a deal. I figured he must have the same deal with people up and down the coast, and not just for water but food and gas too.

Jonah had been captain of his boat for longer than I'd known him. When I worked at the fish market down on Dock Seven I got to know him quite well. He had no family of his own and never talked about anything but his trawler and the ocean. I think his crew were the only family he had. Even when I finished up at the docks and moved on, we stayed in touch. I would go down there most weekends and listen to his tales of life out on the ocean. It was romantic but dangerous. I was under no illusions that our lives were about to get a lot harder. I had never actually stepped foot on his boat and certainly not a fishing boat. He had a Beam Trawler, older than even he was. The closest I had gotten to sailing had been a few trips on the Staten Island Ferry.

I knew Pippa was just worried about Chelsea. She'd had it tough bringing her up on her own. I'd helped as much as I could after her ex did a runner, but I hardly had enough money to get by myself. Chelsea was everything to her and I had to admit she was everything to me, too. She and Pippa were my only family since mom and dad died, and I treated Chelsea as if she were my own. Mom had been gone ten years and dad went long before her. I guess we are what you'd call a 'modern' family.

Pippa listened to me tell her about Jonah, explaining how it was going to work, and she calmed down a little bit. All the while I spoke to her she kept looking at Chelsea and Manny. I thought I might detect a hint of jealousy seeing them get along so well, but Pippa had nothing to worry about. Manny was a good man and Chelsea would never do anything stupid.

Suddenly the building rocked violently and Pippa grabbed me. It was as if a bomb had gone off. The roof top lurched and for a moment I thought we were all going to end up in the ocean.

"Chelsea, are you okay?" shouted Pippa.

Manny had hold of her hand.

"Yeah, I'm good," replied Chelsea. There was fear in her voice. She was calm on the outside, but I knew inside she was terrified.

The building seemed to settle after a minute. I looked over the edge at the water. We had several hours until the sun went down but the water would be icy cold already, and I wasn't convinced the building had minutes left, let alone hours. The roof was now stuck at an angle and standing upright was becoming difficult. With Pippa holding onto me, we made our way past the buckets and pans to Chelsea.

"Mom."

Chelsea flung her arms around Pippa and I had to admit it was my turn to feel jealous. Was it wrong to love your niece more than your own sister? I had seen her grow up and spent so much time with her that I felt like a surrogate father.

The door to the stairwell abruptly swung open. Mr. Johnson staggered through it, still wearing his moccasins and looking like he had just wandered in from an all-day bender. The bottom of his pants were wet, and as he made his way across the roof he left wet footprints on the concrete. His eyes were wild and he seemed to be struggling for breath, as if he had run up the stairs to us.

"The water!" he exclaimed. "We've got to get out of here. The water's here… it's coming up the stairs."

CHAPTER 2

"Steady," said Manny, as Mr. Johnson tumbled at his feet.

Manny helped him up, but as soon as he was back on his feet Mr. Johnson ran to the lip of the roof. He stopped quickly when he saw just how far down it was to the surface of the ocean.

"Damn it, I've got to help him," I said to Pippa. "Stay here."

Manny came with me and together we ushered Mr. Johnson away from the edge. One more jolt like the last one and we would all go tumbling over to our deaths.

"Don't you see? We have to go," said Mr. Johnson. "Right away."

So much for staying in his apartment, I thought. The old man had a growing case of the heebie-jeebies. He had scared himself half to death.

"There's a boat coming. You can come with us, but you've got to calm down." I tried to catch his eyes but they were darting all over the place. His pupils danced like a bee around a rose. I wasn't about to drag him along with us in such a state. "Tell me what happened. What about the water?" I asked.

Manny looked at me as if to say he thought the old man had lost his mind. I had to be sure though. I had to know for all our sakes.

"The bang. You felt the bang, right?"

Mr. Johnson pulled on my arm, dragging my face closer to his. His breath smelt no better than the rest of him, and I tried not to breathe in. I nodded. "Sure. A moment ago. Probably one of the lower floors," I suggested. "Or perhaps a car or a bus. You know how they get stirred up sometimes." The abandoned vehicles drift around the submerged streets and occasionally hit a building. One sunny day we were all relaxing on the rooftop when a subway train appeared right beneath us. It burst up and gave us all quite a shock. "What did you see?"

Mr. Johnson pulled me closer. "I wanted to stay. I wanted to stay with Grace."

He looked around and then his face sank. "I left her behind. I didn't have time. When I heard that sound I rushed to my balcony. I thought something had crashed into us again. I remember in the war. The things that I saw. Poor Grace. I shouldn't have left her. Oh, poor Grace. She's lucky she didn't see what I did. That monster below the window. It went right through the walls. It was… it was—"

Mr. Johnson trailed off and I looked at Manny. I really wanted to go and look for Jonah but Mr. Johnson was beginning to ramble. I contemplated leaving him with Manny as I tried to pull myself free of the old man's grip.

"It was… a shark." When Mr. Johnson finally spat it out he let go of me. It was as if he had saved up all his energy to tell us what it was that he had seen.

"Sure you did," said Manny. The skepticism in his voice was obvious. "But that wasn't what crashed through the walls. The noise was the sound of one of the lower floors imploding. It's the building. It's creaking and groaning, and making all kinds of strange noises. Okay, Mr. Johnson? I know this is scary, but we're going to get out of here. Just stay with us and—"

"Get your hands off me. I know what I saw. And I saw a *shark*. It was as big as a submarine. I should know, I served on a Gato class sub' back in '62, so don't test me, young man. My mind might be old but it hasn't completely gone yet. And that shark punched a hole right through the wall. I don't know where it went after that. I thought I was going to have a heart attack."

I sighed and looked at Pippa. I wasn't sure if they had heard him but if they hadn't, I had no intention of telling them about the old man's dementia and visions. "And the water? Your pants are soaked. Is that from the stairwell or did you trip over one of the buckets? I know you have your own stash on your balcony, Mr. Johnson."

He looked at me then with pity and shrugged. "Don't believe me? Go, look for yourself. I don't care anymore. My poor Grace. All alone now. Oh, poor Gracey."

Mr. Johnson's mutterings became inaudible and I looked at Manny. "Do me a favor and go check out the stairwell, will you?"

Manny looked exasperated. "Really?"

"I know, I know, but just to satisfy him and ease my mind. Please? I need to go check on Jonah. If he's close enough we should get moving down the rope. I don't like the way the building is leaning. Any further and it might go."

As Manny departed for the stairwell, I left Mr. Johnson and approached the corner of the building. All around me I could see the ocean. Many of the taller buildings were still protruding above the surface and I wondered how many others still persisted in trying to live in this dying city. How many people had given up and headed inland? Not everyone had been able to leave and we had been unfortunate enough to get cut off, unable to escape. We had stayed one winter too many and as a result the waters had washed in, replacing the roads with rivers. I guess I lived in hope that the waters would recede, that some sort of fragile infrastructure might be rebuilt and we could start over. The government was still out there somewhere, not that we ever heard from them. As I looked out over New York I caught sight of the Statue of Liberty. The torch was still visible but the lower half of her was gone. Most of the city was the same. As I looked around I realized I couldn't even see any land. In the past I had been able to see a patch on the horizon, somewhere over toward Newark. Yet all I could see now was the ocean, encroaching over the land. The waters weren't receding at all, but taking over our domain, rising and rising until one day there would be nothing left.

As a loud groaning sound echoed through the building, I finally caught sight of movement. About three blocks away something glinted in the sunlight and moved between the buildings. I watched carefully, daring to hope that it was Jonah. I knew I had to be sure before I got everyone down the rope. A lot of boats drifted aimlessly, unsecured with nobody on board to steer them. A lot of other things floated around the city too. Anything that hadn't been tied down before the waters came was free to roam the world now: cars, furniture, office desks, garbage; worst of all was the bodies. We didn't see very many anymore. I think the fish ate them or they got swept out by the currents further down the coast. But sometimes a body would surface. It wasn't pleasant.

Finally, the thing that had caught my eye came around the block and I saw it. It was his trawler all right. Jonah was waving at me and I saw a couple of his crew milling around the deck. The boat moved slowly, but surely, navigating the difficult streets. There were lots of hidden objects, street-lamps and trucks that could cause a serious problem if he wasn't careful. He had been around here before though and knew the safest passage. We were lucky in that our complex was close to the ocean anyway, only a few blocks away. I turned to the others.

"Pippa, Chelsea, he's here. Grab your stuff. It's time to check out."

As they picked up their gear I saw Manny come out of the stairwell. He scooped up his bag as he ran over to me. The look in his eyes told me all was not well.

"The old coot's right. Water's gushing up the stairwell. It'll be here any second."

"Shoot. I thought we had more time," I replied. "Jonah's close but it'll take him a few more minutes to get here. We have to wait."

Manny looked over the edge. "We could use the rope now, get down to one of the lower balconies and wait there. It should buy us enough time for Jonah to get here."

"Right." I looked at Mr. Johnson. He was on his knees, still muttering, his legs wet and his eyes tearing up. "What are we going to do about him?"

"I'll get him," replied Manny. "You make sure your sister and Chelsea get on that boat. *They* are your priority."

"Thanks, man." Before Manny could go and get the old man I stopped him. Ever since Mr. Johnson had mentioned seeing a shark I had an uneasy feeling. I had to know. "Manny, what else did you see? Was there... you know, anything else in the stairwell?"

"You mean, did I see a shark?" Manny looked at me plainly. "No, no I didn't see shit. It's dark and nasty in there, but I didn't see any shark. I think the old bastard's lost it."

I nodded as Manny left me. Our only concern was the building lasting another five minutes. I knew that there could be sharks out there somewhere, would be, but none that could bring a building down. And there wasn't one swimming up the stairwell. I couldn't believe I had almost fallen for it. The idea was ridiculous.

"What's so funny?" asked Chelsea.

"Nothing. Just something Mr. Johnson said." I pointed out Jonah's boat. It was already much closer. "There's our ride."

"About time." Pippa tugged on Chelsea's shirt and ensured her backpack was on tight. "Chelsea, just make sure you hold on tight to that rope. You'll be between me and Uncle Luke, so any problems you just stop and yell. Okay, honey? It's not a race. We just need to get down safely and—"

"I got it, mom." Chelsea smiled politely, but she hated being fussed over. She was more of an adult than a child these days. She had to be. I suppose to Pippa she would always be her little girl.

"Manny's going to bring Mr. Johnson," I explained. "Let's get started. Pippa, you go first. Make your way down as far as you can. If Jonah isn't here by the time you reach the water just wait on the nearest balcony. Chelsea, you're next and I'll be right behind you. If you get into any trouble just yell. We can—"

I stopped. I realized I was sounding just like her mother and I could see Chelsea's eyes glaze over. She didn't need another lecture.

"Let's just go shall we?" I grabbed the rope and gave it one last tug. It wasn't going anywhere. As long as the building held up we'd be fine. "Pippa?"

She took it and jumped up onto the ledge. Turning around so her back was to the ocean she wrapped the rope loosely around one arm and then leant back as she braced her feet against the wall.

"You can do it, mom. Focus on me," said Chelsea.

That kid was so brave I couldn't believe it. As Pippa nervously disappeared over the edge of the building Chelsea scooped up the rope and followed her without hesitation. It was as if she had been abseiling her whole life. There was a faint breeze bringing with it the smell of salt and sunshine, tinged with diesel from Jonah's trawler. I was confident we would make it. Chelsea's head dipped below the ledge as she followed her mother, and I picked up the rope ready to follow. As I braced myself and turned my back to the ocean I saw the door to the stairwell. Water was pouring steadily out and onto the rooftop. Manny was right. The water was coming. I guess the structure of the building had been compromised. The water must have breached the sandbags and begun to churn upwards, forced up as the building sank down into its own foundations.

"Manny, you set?" I called out. He had an arm around Mr. Johnson and was slowly making his way over to me. He nodded.

"Right behind you," Manny said through gritted teeth.

I wanted to help him, but he was right; I had to make sure Pippa and Chelsea got to that boat before anything or anyone else.

I gripped the cold rope and took a step back. It was an odd feeling and a strain putting my body weight on my arms. We hardly ate well and I immediately felt weak. I could only imagine how Pippa felt. She ate even less than me and our muscles hadn't had a good work out in months. I saw Manny look at me and then suddenly there was a rushing sound from behind him. The weather was calm and I couldn't figure out what it was. Mr. Johnson yelped and he broke away from Manny. I saw water surging through the open door then, pouring from the stairwell and onto the rooftop. It was like a flash flood as the torrent of water knocked over buckets and the tarpaulin we'd set up to collect rainwater. I saw Mr. Johnson lose his footing as the water washed over him and I called out to Manny. He was struggling to stand as the water began to fill the roof. It was already up to his ankles and would soon reach the ledge. If it came over onto us as we abseiled down the side of the building we would have difficulty holding onto our makeshift rope ladder.

"Hurry up. Get over here!" I hesitated, wondering if I should go back up to help. I hated myself for doing it, but I had my own family to think about. I continued my downward trajectory slowly, carefully, until I heard Chelsea call out from below me.

"Wait, Uncle. Hold on."

"What is it?" I asked. I lowered my head to see, but my arms were aching and I was focusing on saving my energy for the descent. I managed to get a clear view of Chelsea, finally. "What's happened?"

There was a terrible cracking sound before she could answer. It reverberated around the whole building and I knew it was going to collapse. I still had a few feet between me and Chelsea so I lowered myself down a bit more. There was a window in front of me and I saw the contents of the room beyond it floating in six feet of water. The whole building was flooding. I began to feel a trickle of cold water running down the nape of my neck and I glanced up to see Manny clambering over the side of the roof. Water was trickling around him and I suspected the rooftop had been flooded. There was nowhere left to go. There was no way back.

"Chelsea?"

"It's okay. I'm okay. I thought I saw something in the water. It's okay. It's nothing."

She began to lower herself and I twisted my neck around to look for Jonah. His boat was almost within reach now. The trawler was on our street, barely fifty yards away. It looked as if he had made it to us in the nick of time.

I kept going, the trickle of water hitting my head and splashing over my shoulders. I daren't look up for fear of seeing the water become a raging river, yet I daren't look down for fear of seeing how far I still had to go. So, I kept slipping down the rope, using the intermittent footholds and holding on for dear life. The building continued to lurch as I climbed down, swaying as if it was caught in a hurricane. My fingers ached, and the skin on my hands was sore from gripping the rope so tightly. I kept seeing visions of the Stamford collapsing, of all those people sucked down into the water. I didn't want to go the same way. I didn't want Pippa or Chelsea to die, not when rescue was so close.

"Ouch!"

I stopped as my foot connected with Chelsea's head. We'd reached the end of the rope.

"Hold on a second."

I heard Pippa's voice and then the rumble of an engine. The trawler was right beside us. I pushed my feet back against the wall and turned myself around. I saw Jonah looking right at me.

"You going to hang around all day, Luke, or are you going to come aboard?"

CHAPTER 3

Relief washed over me as I planted both feet onto the deck of Jonah's trawler. Pippa and Chelsea helped me down and I looked around me. Two of the crew had hold of the rope and had it stretched out so it hung over the boat. I saw another man in the wheelhouse, but that was it. I'd assumed it took a lot of men to operate the trawler, but there was only Jonah and three others.

"Luke." Jonah shook my hand and I instantly felt safer. His hands were thick and strong, and the skin was calloused. He smelt of the ocean and he looked briefly at Pippa and Chelsea. There was no malice in his eyes, but I sensed a certain uneasiness. I put it down to the fact he wasn't used to having strangers on his ship, least of all a teenage girl and her mother. "We'll save the introductions for later. You good to go?"

I looked up at Manny. He was still halfway down the building and the water rushing over him made it look as if he was underneath a waterfall.

"Almost. Manny's still up there."

"Luke, we ain't got much time, you know that, right?" Jonah licked his lips and looked at me. "That building of yours is on its way out and when it goes we need to be far away from here. I can't risk it hitting my boat. The *Tukino* has been through a lot. She's seen off hurricanes and squalls bigger than you could imagine, but I've never had a building fall on her. I don't intend to start today."

"Just give him a chance, please," I implored. "Manny will make it. He's almost here."

"And what about him?" Jonah raised an arm and pointed to the roof.

At first I couldn't see who he was pointing at. Then, at the corner of the building, holding onto the building, I saw Mr. Johnson. The old fool hadn't followed Manny and I'd forgotten about him. It looked as if he had got himself cornered.

"Damn it," I muttered. "That stupid old man." I didn't mean it. I was just frustrated. I should've gone back to help when I'd had the chance. What could I do from down on the boat?

"There's no way we're going to be able to get up there and help him," said Pippa. "What can we do?"

"Manny, hurry up," shouted Chelsea. "The boat's right beneath you."

The trawler listed to one side and I felt the water tugging at it. I heard glass breaking and looked up to see one side of the building cave in. Every window shattered as the walls buckled. Masonry began to tumble down and I was grateful it was far enough away not to affect us. I knew what it meant though. The building was sinking.

The man from inside the wheelhouse called out. "We gotta go, Captain!"

I saw doubt on Jonah's face. It was a face that usually held nothing but happiness. He was old enough to be my father, but as lively and spritely as anyone half his age. He wore traditional fisherman's oilskins and I don't think I've ever seen him in anything else. Jonah scratched at the white stubble around his chin.

"Time to go," he said abruptly.

"But—"

"Sorry, Luke. We have to go or this damn building will take the whole boat down with it. Then you and yours are done for."

"Manny!" I shouted to him and he stopped descending. He looked at me as the window next to him shattered. "Manny, jump!"

He was still several feet above the boat, but I was sure he could make it. The rope was beginning to sway and he was struggling to hold on. His hands and clothes were wet, and even as I looked up at him I could feel the boat turning away.

"Manny, please." Chelsea ran to the railings at the boat's edge. "There's no more time."

I felt like I was watching it on television. It felt surreal, as if I wasn't even there. Manny let go of the rope and pushed himself away from the building. His legs and arms swung through the air and he fell quickly. I waited for the impact, for him to land on the deck, and just hoped he wouldn't break anything. None of us had any medical knowledge and even the most innocent of accidents had lethal consequences these days.

Then something happened that none of us expected.

The boat suddenly swerved away from the building and I turned around, cursing at Jonah for not giving us a few more seconds.

"Hold on!"

Jonah was inside the wheelhouse, standing next to the man I had seen earlier. It was only a few feet away and quite small. Both men wore the same sort of oilskins, but the other man was a lot taller and fairer in complexion. Both men also wore the same look of confusion on their faces and I realized they hadn't turned the boat at all. They were trying to keep the wheel steady, yet it was being forced out of their hands as if an invisible force was steering the boat.

"Weir, full throttle, you bastard," shouted Jonah.

Whoever Weir was and whatever he was supposedly doing, nothing happened. The engine whined and roared, but the boat refused to budge. I heard Chelsea scream and turned back to see a shape flash by the boat and hit the water.

"Manny?" I raced to Chelsea's side just as Pippa began to pull her away.

"He's in the water, he's in the water," shouted Chelsea, as Pippa dragged her kicking and screaming to the safety of the deck.

I peered over the wooden railing and saw nothing. The water was churning all around us, but I couldn't see Manny anywhere. Pieces of glass and parts of the building were falling now, splashing into the water.

"It's pulling us down!" screamed Pippa.

The building let out one final breath. More windows exploded and I searched the water desperately for Manny. I heard another voice, faint and pleading for help. I heard Pippa and Chelsea crying, imploring me to get away from the edge, but I couldn't leave Manny like that.

"Hold tight." I heard Jonah's voice and felt the boat begin to move slowly through the water. We were finally heading away from the crumbling building and then I saw him. Manny resurfaced several feet away. His sports bag was gone, lost forever in the water, but he was alive. I frantically looked around me for something to fish him out with. There was a life saver on the other side of the deck and I raced to get it, ducking under the winch and around the A-frame. The trawler was cold and buried in shadow.

"Let me help," said Chelsea, as I sprinted past her.

"No, it's too dangerous. Stay with your mother," I ordered. I knew Pippa wouldn't let go of her, and I grabbed the orange ring. The deck was slippery and I was grateful I had a pair of sneakers on. As I pulled the life saver free I felt a hand on my shoulders.

"I'll help you."

The voice belonged to one of the crew I had spotted earlier. I didn't know who he was, but I was grateful for the assistance. I wasn't sure how long Manny would be able to hold on. The water was churning and frothing as if bubbling atop a volcano. The man took the life saver from me and came back with me to the other side of the boat. He was a tall man, dark like Manny, and wore a tattered old green beanie on his head. His thick gray jersey smelt of the sea and I imagined he'd worked with Jonah for a long time. The sleeves were rolled up revealing tattoos that ran up both arms. I was intimidated for a moment, until I saw the kindness in his eyes.

"Manny, grab it. We'll pull you up," I shouted, as the man threw the ring into the sea. It landed barely six feet away from Manny.

"Grab it and—"

I heard the boat's engine whining, as if it were being mangled, and felt the boat rise up. It actually rose up out of the water a full two or three feet and I heard Jonah shouting orders at his crew. He was yelling about the rudder and tacking, sensors and channels; I had no idea what he was talking about. The man next to me ran back to Jonah, leaving me with the task of saving Manny. I couldn't understand why the boat was rising. The water level seemed to be the same and as I watched Manny reach for the ring I saw something in the water alongside him that made my heart skip a beat.

Beneath Manny there was something gray, shiny, and long, and it was moving. The skin was smooth like a dolphin. This was no submerged vehicle and I was sure it wasn't part of the building.

It wasn't just beneath Manny, but the boat too. What was even odder was that there was no end to it. I couldn't see a tail or a head. The thing was huge, longer than the trawler. I guessed it was a whale, lost in this new world and now stuck in the underwater streets of New York. Whatever it was, it had got itself stuck under the trawler. That was what was forcing us up out of the water and putting so much pressure on the engine. I had to trust Jonah would figure it out while I got Manny.

"There. I told you. It's there!"

Startled, I looked up to see old Mr. Johnson standing on the corner of the building. He was pointing down at us.

"It's come for us!"

I had no time for his delusional rants again, and looked back at Manny. He had his hands around the life saver thankfully and I began to pull him up. It felt like trying to drag concrete through quicksand, and it was slow work. Pieces of the building kept falling around us and I was all too aware of how perilous it was to be so close to it as it disintegrated. Our apartment complex wasn't going like the hotel. The Stamford had gone quickly, pulled into its own foundations without warning. By contrast, our building was falling to pieces around us. I felt tiny shards of glass shower over me as another large window shattered. A balcony a few feet away broke free of its moorings and plummeted to the water below, landing worryingly close to Manny. He held on though as I continued to pull him closer to the boat.

The trawler suddenly dropped as the whale-creature disappeared. I lost my footing on the deck and fell on my ass, but I kept hold of the rope. I wasn't about to let Manny go that easily.

There was an almighty booming sound and then I saw the complex, our home for the last twenty years, begin to subside. The whole thing was shaking and sinking.

"Quickly, Manny." He was right alongside the boat now and as I tried to heave him around to where he could climb up, the crewman from earlier appeared next to me. He held a shepherd's crook, and reached over the side of the boat. Manny grabbed it as the man pulled him up.

As the *Tukino* pulled away from the building, a shadow flitted across my eyes and I saw Mr. Johnson leap from the crumbling building. He literally jumped into the air and said nothing as he fell. I felt so sorry for him, yet I had to remind myself that we had tried to help. He was going to hit the water with such force that I wasn't sure he would make it. Could he even swim? There was every likelihood that he would hit the water with such force that he would break his neck and I winced as I watched him plummet to his death.

As Manny clambered into the trawler I heard Chelsea and Pippa rush to help him. I couldn't take my eyes off Mr. Johnson though.

Before he hit the water I caught his eyes. I wish I hadn't. I wish I could get rid of that image, of him looking at me so full of terror and hatred. I wish I hadn't seen what happened to him next but I can't deny what I saw.

It wasn't a whale. It wasn't stuck beneath the boat either. What rose up out of the water didn't seem real. I had never seen anything like it. I recognized that same silvery smooth skin instantly. This time I saw its head. Mr. Johnson was right. It was a shark, only bigger. A *lot* bigger. The shark's head had to be as big as a bus, its two black eyes as large as hubcaps; the creature's jaws were wide open revealing two rows of razor sharp teeth. There was a scar on its head, a nasty looking cut about four feet in length that must have left it close to being blind in one eye. The shark rose up out of the water silently. Mr. Johnson never hit the water. He simply plummeted right into the gaping maw of that terrifying beast without a sound. I saw the shark snap its jaws shut and then disappear beneath the ocean.

"Jesus," I whispered.

"Everyone, get back to the bridge, now!"

I was aware of Jonah shouting orders, but I couldn't take it in. I was still trying to process what I'd seen. The shark had to be three or four times larger than any shark I'd ever heard of. I'd only ever seen sharks on documentaries or in cheesy horror films, yet I was sure this was not like them. It had to be related and it looked like a Great White. But how could it be so impossibly *big*? It had swallowed Mr. Johnson whole with ease. What kind of animal was it?

It was only when Pippa pressed her face up against mine and hauled me to my feet that I snapped out of it. Suddenly, I realized that we were pulling away from the building and I was sat on the deck with water spewing over me. Our apartment was gone. Where the building had been I saw sunlight streaming through the gap in the city buildings. The complex was gone and so was Mr. Johnson.

"You saw it, right?" I asked her, as she led me to Jonah.

"Saw what? Our home collapse? Manny almost die? Yeah, I saw it. Stop messing around, Luke. Jonah wants everyone inside, in that cabin thing and off the deck. He said it's too dangerous with all these buildings around us."

"Okay, okay." I let Pippa drag me toward the wheelhouse. Manny was there, safe, alive, and Chelsea was throwing a dark gray blanket around him, rubbing life back into his freezing joints. I saw the other crew members and made a mental note to thank whoever it was that had helped me. I never would have got Manny aboard on my own. I had to know that I wasn't losing my mind though and before Pippa could pull me into the cabin I stopped.

"Wait. You saw it, didn't you? You saw the shark?"

Incredulity was written across Pippa's face. "What shark? We hit a truck. Jonah said we were caught on it and he managed to break us free just before the building came down. What are you on about?"

"The shark. Didn't you see it? It was right beside us."

Pippa shook her head. "No, Luke, I did not see any damn shark. I was too busy trying to help Manny like all of us were. Who cares if there was a shark anyway? The main thing is we're all here, we're alive; Chelsea is alive. And I want to get inside, so quit talking like an idiot and be thankful we're all still breathing. Stop going on about sharks will you, you'll just scare Chelsea and she's been through enough today."

Pippa left me on the deck and went into the wheelhouse. She was right. I couldn't say anything to her or Chelsea. They had enough to worry about. It was true that they were all helping Manny, and maybe they hadn't seen it. The only one who might have was Jonah, but he was trying to keep the trawler upright. If he hadn't seen it then he had to know. He had to know what was in the water around us. Pippa held the door open and I followed her into the cabin. With all of us inside it was way too cramped. There was a small set of stairs leading down into the bowels of the ship, where I assumed we would find sleeping quarters, a galley and the hold.

"Jonah. Thanks." I approached the wheel where Jonah was sweating, turning us away from where our building had been.

"Luke." He acknowledged me, but didn't look at me. He seemed preoccupied and I could see he was concentrating on managing his boat.

"Can I help?" I offered. "Can I do anything?"

"Just get inside, Luke. With your building collapsing it might have a knock on effect and bring down others. It's not safe out here. I want everyone, *including you*, downstairs. In a few minutes we'll be out of here and out on the open ocean. We can talk then."

I hesitated. If he had seen it then surely he would've said something. I had to know.

"Jonah, what about..?"

"*Now*, Luke. We can talk later."

I knew when to follow orders. It was Jonah's boat and I wasn't about to rock it.

"Where's Mr. Johnson?" asked Manny as I squeezed in next to him. Everyone was huddled around a small console. Manny was wrapped in a thick blanket as Pippa and Chelsea sat nervously looking out at the city.

"You didn't see?"

He shook his head. I caught Pippa's eyes and she sent me silent messages. She didn't want Chelsea upset or stressed. The situation was scary enough.

"Didn't any of you see?" I asked.

Nobody answered me. I couldn't believe I was the only one who had seen Mr. Johnson die.

"He didn't make it. He jumped into the water, but we lost him. The building pulled him down," I lied.

The tall crewman who had been with Jonah earlier approached me. His blue eyes bored into mine and he pointed to a seat next to Pippa. "You should sit. We need to work." His tone was flat with a hint of frustration. I sensed he wasn't keen on having visitors on the boat. Thankfully, Jonah was in charge, not him.

I joined Pippa as the tall fair-haired man left us and went out onto the deck. The other two crewmen were looking at the console and appeared to be reading a chart. I had to admit my knowledge of sailing and the oceans was very limited. As much as I wanted to help I knew I would only be getting in the way. I still had some thinking to do about the creature I'd seen too.

"You'll be okay in here. Just sit tight and we'll get out of the city." The man who had helped me rescue Manny removed his wool hat and held out a hand. "The name's Gills."

"Luke," I replied, wondering what on earth kind of name Gills was. "This is my sister, Pippa, and her daughter, Chelsea."

Gills shook their hands in turn, offering a warm hello. He was instantly likeable, and appeared to have no problem with any of us being on board. In contrast to the tall fair-haired man, his manner was friendly, and I felt comforted that we weren't completely unwelcome.

"Don't mind Weir," said Gills, as if reading my mind. "He likes to think he's in charge."

Jonah grunted.

"He forgets this is Jonah's boat sometimes," said Gills. "He's been working the *Tukino* longer than any of us. He and Jonah go way back. This boat is his home, his entire life, and he's not that welcoming of strangers. He'll come around. He's fair if you give him a chance. For now I suggest you guys get down and find yourself a seat where you can stay out of the way and let us work the boat. These streets can be treacherous, as you know."

"Thank you Mr. Gills," said Pippa. "Thank you so much for coming for us and... well, just thank you."

"No need," he said, dismissing Pippa. "Truly. Jonah told us you were a good friend. In this world I think you need all the friends you can get."

Inside the wheelhouse it was beginning to get warm and I was conscious of Jonah trying to work. Away from the water and with the door shut, the air was heating up. The sun still shone and with the boat rocking from side to side I was beginning to feel a little queasy. I couldn't believe Gills wore a thick jumper, but I guessed he spent more time outside than in. I hadn't even thought about how we would cope on a boat or if any of us would get seasick.

"Come on Gills, let's get back to work. We need to check the winch wasn't damaged when we hit that truck. Besides, this city gives me the creeps."

The fourth crewman turned away from the console. I hadn't heard them speak yet and their face was hidden from me. He wore a dark green lifejacket over blue oilskins, and a crimson hat that had been pulled down snugly over their head. He walked straight to the door and held it open for Gills.

"That's Ava." Gills smiled. "Hey, Ava, don't be rude. Say good afternoon to our guests. And take your damn hat off." Gills winked at me. "She's just shy."

I couldn't hide the surprise on my face as Ava removed her hat. Blonde hair spooled out around her shoulders and the girl looked at us with a weary smile. I wasn't sure if she was shy or had the same attitude toward strangers as Weir did. Still, if it wasn't for her and the crew Manny would have drowned, and my family would be under a ton of rubble. Her blue eyes looked tired and there was a mole above her left eyebrow. Freckles adorned her cheeks but her skin seemed to shine. I don't know if it was because I'd been cooped up in the apartment for months on end or not, but she was just about the most beautiful thing I'd seen in as long as I could remember.

"Pleased to meet you, Ava," I said. I'm sure my voice cracked when I spoke and my cheeks blushed. I had to admit she was not what I was expecting. Jonah, Weir and Gills were old hands, well over fifty, and had clearly worked the *Tukino* together for years. Ava looked to be around my age and was stunning. Underneath the unattractive oilskins and crimson hat hid a woman who wouldn't have looked out of place on a catwalk.

Ava muttered a greeting as Pippa, Chelsea and Manny said hi.

"Okay, downstairs you lot," said Jonah. "Save the chit-chat for later."

"We'll leave you to it." Gills ushered Ava out and closed the door behind him.

I proceeded down the steps as my family followed me. At the bottom we hesitated, unsure of where to go. There was a narrow corridor with doors on either side. It was bare and gloomy, and nothing like I had imagined. There was a strong smell of fish too, not that I should've been surprised.

"How're you doing, Manny?" asked Chelsea. "You warm enough?"

"Me, I'm doing just fine. It was just a quick dip. It's Mr. Johnson I feel bad about. I tried to get him to follow me, but the stubborn old man was freaking out."

"I don't want to speak ill of the dead but that old man deserved—"

"Yeah, okay, mom, I've heard it before." Chelsea shifted to look at me. "Uncle Luke tried to get him to come and he's gone now, so let's just leave it. I don't feel the best and I can't be doing with you starting another argument."

I suppressed my laughter when I saw Pippa's face. Sometimes it was like she was the daughter being raised by Chelsea.

"Gills seems nice," said Manny. "I'm not sure about Weir, though. His frosty demeanor suggested he would rather we'd joined Mr. Johnson at the bottom of the ocean."

"We're strangers who just invited themselves into his home. I can understand why he's feeling threatened. Let's just give it time," I said. "Besides, they're not all bad. Jonah is a good friend and Ava seemed nice." Stuck on a boat with three men, I wondered how she coped. Perhaps she was a relative of one of them.

"*Nice* is not what I'm looking for, Luke," said Pippa. "A home. Food and water, and a roof over my head. Somewhere safe for Chelsea, for all of us. Please tell me you have a plan worked out?"

"One step at a time, Pippa." I had no idea what we were going to do. I had only agreed with Jonah that he would pick us up when the time came. Beyond that I had no plans. Would he want us to stay and work on the boat? Would he drop us off at the next building still standing? There was still dry land further inland, but access was awkward. The trawler wouldn't be able to get us there. And the more I thought about it, I wasn't so sure if that was where I wanted to go. We could find another home, set up playing happy families until the waters reached us again, but then what? We'd just end up back in the same situation as we'd found ourselves earlier, needing rescue and looking for help from others. I thought it was about time we took charge of our own destiny. I just hadn't worked out how to do it yet. The ocean was hardly much safer than land especially with that shark out there. I glanced upstairs. Jonah and his crew were working on the other side and I had absolutely no idea what they were saying about us, or what he thought we would do. Were we as welcome as Jonah had suggested? I looked at Pippa and put on my best nothing-to-worry-about smile. "We'll be fine," I said. "We'll be just fine."

CHAPTER 4

I trotted back up the steps, leaving Manny and my family below. I told them I wanted to talk to Jonah, but I just needed to see the city one last time. I said nothing when I was back in the wheelhouse, but let Jonah work. He gave me a disapproving look as I filed past him, but I figured he had enough on his plate without checking where I was every five seconds. The rest of the crew were outside, so I went on outside and found a quiet spot to myself. Watching New York disappear I almost felt guilty for leaving, as if I was abandoning a part of my own family. It had been our home for twenty years and the only place Chelsea had ever lived.

I had begun to feel claustrophobic tucked away down in the boat and the fresh air felt good. The air was amazing, so natural and clean that the first few gulps of it made me feel giddy. After breathing in so much stale air in our apartment it was wondrous to be out in the open. I heard the crew talking amongst themselves, but they paid me no attention and I had no interest in them. I just wanted the chance to see my home for one last time.

We sailed out into Upper New York Bay, past Governor's Island. Jonah had successfully navigated us back out into the East Hudson and I saw no more of the shark. We passed a few more buildings that had collapsed, more than I'd thought I'd see. Even the United Nations building had been badly damaged and the whole building was resting at a slant that suggested it would also fall soon. As we passed under Manhattan Bridge, more skyscrapers came into view. The upper floors appeared dark and quiet, despite the beaming sunshine illuminating their towers. The glass and steel structures stood like giants overseeing the city, the last remnants of civilization. We passed under Brooklyn Bridge and I looked for the Fulton Fish Market where I had worked and first met Jonah. There was no sign of it. The whole thing was underwater. I had no reason to expect anything else, but it was still a shock. The Staten

Island Ferry Terminal was gone too, now a submerged world reserved for fish and crustaceans.

"That must be Battery Park," said Chelsea, joining me out on the deck. "Sorry, I needed some fresh air too."

I quickly glanced back at Jonah but he and his crew seemed busy running the boat.

"I used to skate down the esplanade there," said Chelsea wistfully. She pointed at the top of a gray squat building, only its roof still exposed to the sun. "That's the Old Customs House, right?"

I nodded. "Remember when I took you there? You could only have been five or six. You loved the old films they used to play."

"I can remember you got me a mint-chocolate ice-cream and I got home and puked it all up. Mom reamed you out for that."

I laughed at the memory. "She sure did."

As I watched the city recede, we passed close by to Liberty Island. The Statue was still there but water lapped at her waist. It was hard to imagine what would become of her. Would the water continue rising? If we came back in a few years would there be anything left? The State Park was submerged, but I could see a few trees floating nearby. To the east, Brooklyn was completely submerged. I wondered how many people had stayed. How many had held onto the belief that things would change, go back to normal, or that the government would step in and do something? It felt like, as much as the world changed, it just stayed the same. Holding onto the past stopped us from moving forward. With Chelsea at my side I knew I couldn't make the same mistakes.

The trawler began to turn toward Brooklyn, and Chelsea slipped her hand over mine.

"Why are we turning?" she asked.

I looked at Jonah for clues but he remained at his console, his eyes downcast. Looking around the deck, I could see Weir and Gills pointing at something ahead. Ava was doing something at the rear of the boat where I couldn't see her.

"I'm not sure. Jonah knows what he's doing. I guess he has the best knowledge of the area."

The boat seemed to turn so far that I thought he was taking us back. For a moment I had visions of him returning us to our complex and throwing us in the water. But then the boat began to resume its course, and I saw what had caused Jonah to turn the boat so wildly. In the middle of the bay was an airplane. It sat on the surface of the ocean like a whale's carcass, its upturned belly glistening white in the diminishing sunlight. The wheels were still raised and I saw a flock of seagulls settle on it. The plane drifted past us silently. I stared at the black rectangular windows as it went past us, but the interior of the plane was dark. Nothing moved inside. I don't know what I was expecting to see, but it was still unsettling. Another plane followed it, its wings almost touching the first plane.

"They must have drifted down from JFK," said Chelsea.

The trawler soon got us past the planes and out of the city. New York shimmered in the settling light and a haze fell over what was left of it. The air got cooler and I knew the sun would go down soon. That meant we had a few things to figure out. I had no idea how many beds there were on the trawler, or even if we were expected to stay. I had to talk to Jonah. I still wanted to ask him if he'd seen the shark, or knew anything about it, but I didn't want to upset Chelsea and scare her. Now that we were out on the water there was no escape plan. There was no plan B. Whatever happened out here was out of my control and it was disturbing to think I had no way of protecting my extended family. I had to know what Jonah was thinking.

"Chelsea, why don't you go check on Manny?" I suggested.

"Mom's taking care of him. I think I'll go find Ava. No offence, but I've only talked to old people this last year. I could do with a change of conversation."

"Be careful," I said, as she made her way down the deck to the rear of the boat. Sometimes I forgot she was still a teenager. She was so mature that I had to remind myself she was only sixteen.

I quickly checked in on Manny and told Pippa where Chelsea was. They were content to stay in the warmth of the downstairs cabin, so I made my way back up to Jonah. The fair-haired man, Weir, was with him. I was feeling apprehensive even though I'd known him for years. I wasn't sure what he would say or what he would expect of me. I guess the whole thing had unsettled me and I was definitely out of my comfort zone now.

"Jonah? Everything okay?" I asked.

He smiled when he saw me and I relaxed instantly. I felt like I had been summoned to the principal's office to be scolded, yet from his reaction to me I knew it would be all right.

"Sure, Luke." Jonah rubbed his eyes. "Weir, I need to talk to my friend. You're in charge. I want to make Atlantic City before nightfall."

Weir grunted and looked at me. If looks could kill I would be six feet under. He almost looked Scandinavian with his fair hair and pale skin. I thanked him anyway, knowing it couldn't hurt to try and build a few bridges, and followed Jonah out onto the upper deck. We ended up on the port side of the *Tukino*, watching the city fade to nothing.

"I can just about remember sitting in a bar in New York City but my memory is a little fuzzy," said Jonah. "There was one place we used to go to regularly back when I was a young man with a full head of hair. It was one block away from where we rented this cheap apartment. The bar was, well, funky. They had red velvet everywhere. Like, on the chairs, the walls, even the ceiling. The barmaids were hot and the beer was ice cold, just how a good bar should be. They served up the best pizza slices in the city. You can take that to the bank."

Jonah often talked about the old days. He used to tell me about the gang he ran with and how he ended up on the trawler. The guy who used to own the *Tukino* had convinced him that a life on the ocean was better than a life running after skirt in New York somehow, and the rest, as they say, is history.

"It's a shame, Luke, but it is what it is. Things have changed massively. I'm sorry about your home. How are the girls holding up? I notice Chelsea's talking to Ava?"

"Sorry about that, we don't want to get in the way. I'll have a word with Chelsea."

"No, no, don't worry. It'll do her good. Poor girl's been cooped up with us old guys so long I'm surprised she didn't leave me long ago. No, it's good she has someone else to talk to; someone more her own type, you know?"

"What's her story?" I couldn't help myself. All the burning questions I had and yet as soon as he mentioned Ava I had to know. "She doesn't look like your usual fisherman. Or is that fisherperson?"

Jonah chuckled and rubbed the back of his head. "She sure ain't, but I'll tell you what. She's as good as anyone out here, and you can take that to the bank. Sure, she's got a few things to learn but she's a natural. Picked her up a year or so ago now. Her and her brother. Her parents had a catamaran down south so she picked up some skills from them before I got hold of her. There was a storm off the Keys and the catamaran got turned upside down. Her parents didn't make it. Lucky for her we were in the area."

"And her brother?"

Jonah leaned over the railing and spat in the ocean. His demeanor changed immediately and a darkness settled over his face. "He was with us for a while. I never took to him. Pain in the ass. Physically, you knew they were brother and sister: same cheekbones, same blue eyes and perfect skin. Man, they had some good genes. But he was nothing like Ava. Lance was a spoilt brat, a real creep. I was pleased when he took off after a couple of months with a different crew led by some Scottish guy. Nasty bunch. I haven't seen him since."

I couldn't resist having a look and turned to see Chelsea and Ava laughing over something. It was good to see Chelsea laugh. There hadn't been enough of it lately. After the Stamford came down there hadn't been any laughing. I noticed how Ava tried to cover her mouth with her hands when she laughed. It might be like a nervous tick or perhaps she was still shy around Chelsea. Still, it was damn good to look at her. I must've held my gaze a little too long because Jonah gave me a prod in the shoulder that felt like I'd been punched by a heavyweight.

"Don't even think about it," said Jonah earnestly. "She's like a daughter to me. We look out for one another out here. When you're on my boat you're part of my family. And that means no funny business. Got it?"

"Got it." I sheepishly turned back to watch the last high-rises in the city fade toward the horizon.

"I ain't saying you're going to get along with everyone in my crew, but they'll do their part and make sure you're safe."

"Yeah, Gills already helped us with Manny. He's a good man, I can tell."

"Damn right. Gills and Weir have worked with me longer than I care to remember."

"Weir. He doesn't like me. I get the sense that he would rather we weren't here."

"True, I won't deny it, he was against me picking you up. But don't take it personally. He's been out on the sea so long he doesn't know any different. He mistrusts anyone from the land. He'll be fine. It's not him you have to worry about."

"I guess not," although I wasn't sure what Jonah was getting at. Was he going to admit he'd seen the giant shark?

"Not everyone is as hospitable as me, Luke. As long as you're out here you're going to have to learn a few things. The *Tukino* is a well-run machine and I can find a few jobs for you to help me with. Truthfully, we don't really need any more hands. The fishing business is gone. There ain't no restaurants left anymore, so we fish now and again for ourselves. That's all. My main problem are the pirates. I could do with a spare pair of eyes. If we can spot them early, we can avoid them."

"Pirates? Out here?" I couldn't believe what Jonah was saying. "I thought they were history, the sort of kid's stuff they made films about."

"It's different now. Pirates have always existed, but this is the end of the 21st century. They don't wear eye patches or have parrots on their shoulders. Today's pirates won't make you walk the plank, they'll just shoot you on sight. Cutlasses are *so* yesterday. Today they're armed with guns and grenades. Marauders would probably be a better term for them. I've seen them in action. Merciless. They take whatever you have, kill your crew, and scupper your boat. Trust me, we do *not* want to run into any."

Pirates. Just when I thought our situation had improved he hit me with a bombshell like that. Quite how I was supposed to tell Pippa about them, I didn't know.

"I'll fill in Pippa and Manny," said Jonah. He pulled his oilskin up around his neck. "I'm going to head in. Getting cold out here."

"Um, Jonah, what about sleeping arrangements? If you've some spare blankets we can probably make do upon deck or in the wheelhouse. If that's okay? I've already asked too much of you. I don't want to put you out."

Jonah chuckled again. "Right little stress-head aren't we? There are quarters downstairs. My cabin is marked Captain, so keep your eyes off that one. Next to it you'll find two rooms with bunks for four people in each. They're pretty cozy but they're warm, and there's enough room to stretch out for a good night's sleep. I mean, there's always the fish hold but I wouldn't recommend it."

"Eight beds? Is the rest of the crew down there already?"

"No, what you see is what you get. The crew used to be a lot bigger back in the days when this was a working ship. I run a skeleton staff these days. Some of the crew left, some of them..." Jonah chewed his lip thoughtfully. "Well, like I said, the ocean is a dangerous place. You'll see one room plastered with photographs. That one is for Weir, Gills and Ava. They've settled in together and I don't want them upset. I figure Manny can take the fourth bed. The second room can be for you, Pippa and Chelsea. That'll do for tonight. If you want, we can talk about it again in the morning?"

"Sounds great. I wasn't sure we would have a bed at all."

Jonah shrugged. "No problem, Luke. I guess you have a lot to think about. Like how long do you want to keep your family out here? Life on the ocean has its ups and downs, that's for sure."

Literally, I thought, as a wave crashed against the boat and my stomach flipped.

"And if you don't like fish then you are shit out of luck. But it's a life and that's more than a lot of folk have these days."

Jonah yawned. The dim light hid the bags under his eyes.

"It's been a long day. We're almost there. Weir will get us to Atlantic Bay shortly and we'll drop anchor for the night."

"The city is still there?" I asked eagerly. Was it too much to ask? Jonah soon shot down my hopes.

"No. I guess we still use it as a point of reference. There's a sheltered area we found, out of sight of prying eyes. It's safe. Gills will cook us up a good feed and then we can get some shut eye. I suggest we all try to get some rest."

As Jonah turned to leave I caught his arm. "Jonah, just one more thing. Back in the city, when our apartment collapsed. Did you see... did you see anything... unusual?"

Jonah looked at me with tired eyes. "Apart from everything?"

"I mean in the water? Did you see what was beneath us, what came up and killed Mr. Johnson?"

Jonah frowned and the shadow on his face made it look like he wore a hood. "Luke, there are things out here in the ocean you don't ever want to meet. There are things that will snap you in half or devour you whole given half a chance. Most of them stay at the bottom of the ocean. I've seen creatures that will give you nightmares for weeks; giant squids and great whites that almost took the *Tukino* down. Weir believes he once saw a... well, never mind. But there was *nothing* in New York. The streets are too tight for them to navigate. Don't let your imagination get the better of you. What happened back there was traumatic for everybody. We got snagged on a truck and Manny was lucky you were there to help him. You should concentrate on Pippa and Chelsea. They need you, Luke. They need to know you're looking out for them, not sea-monsters and pirates. Don't worry about things you can't control."

I nodded, feeling suitably admonished. Maybe I had built it up in my memory. Maybe the shark was just that, a shark, and in all the drama of the building collapsing I had mistaken it for something it wasn't. I should be more concerned about the pirates Jonah had mentioned. Guns and grenades were not what I was expecting.

Jonah offered me a reassuring smile and looked up at the blue sky. It was starting to turn a rich, deep blue and the stars were beginning to appear. "Don't stay out here too long. Dinner will be served soon. Come down into the cabin when you're ready. We all eat together down in the galley. It's right next to the bunkrooms. Trust me, you can't get lost down there. It's..." Jonah searched for the right word. "It's—"

"Cozy, right?"

"Cozy." Jonah waved me goodbye as he departed for the warm cabin. "You can take that to the bank."

I looked up at the sky and exhaled slowly. The sun seemed to have set so quickly that I hadn't really noticed it. Jonah was right, it was getting cold. I leant over the railing and looked at the water churning beneath us. Could I really do this? Could I live out on the ocean? Would Pippa even want this for her and Chelsea? The warmth of the cabin was beckoning me and I heard Ava and Chelsea giggling their way past me. It was hard to believe what had happened. When I woke up that morning I hadn't reckoned our lives would become so complicated.

I knew that the mainland was out there somewhere, but as I scanned the horizon it was hard to find. Even the horizon was becoming a blur as the hazy blue sky met the ocean. We hadn't sailed far out since leaving New York and if we were heading for Atlantic City then we were probably following the coastline. But where there should've been scores of beachfront houses there was just water. Occasionally I saw some land, a rocky outcrop of something protruding above the water like a beacon. The moon and stars were beginning to take over from the sun and my stomach growled. It was time to eat. I still put off going into the cabin. I suppose I was nervous. I was nervous of what conversations might arise from our presence, and if the rest of the crew would really be as welcoming as Jonah. I was nervous about what Pippa would say to me and what Manny might ask. More than anything I was nervous about what answers I might have – or not.

Over the vast ocean, I looked west and scanned for signs of life. Finally I saw a light. It was just a twinkle, a faint dot too far away for me to possibly work out where it was coming from. It was motionless and had to be from a floodlight or perhaps a stadium. I'd heard they still had electricity in parts of the mainland, the parts far enough inland to have escaped the waters. Our apartment had consisted of several candles and wind-up torches. We relied on the natural light of the sun for light and warmth.

I heard a cough behind me and was surprised to find Ava stood on the deck.

"Evening, sailor," she said, holding out her hand. "Ava."

"Luke," I replied shaking her hand. Jonah was right. Her skin was perfect.

"I know, Chelsea told me. You're her Uncle, right? She told me a lot about you."

"Oh dear." I was beaming, but I couldn't help it. I felt slightly ridiculous and forced my eyes up to the sky. After all that the day had thrown at me, after all I had seen, the death of Mr. Johnson and the narrow escape from our building, I felt as nervous as I did on my prom night. It had been a long time since I'd spoken with a pretty girl. "The stars are amazing. And it looks like it will be a full moon tonight, right?"

"Yeah, looks like it," replied Ava. "When you've been out here as long as I have you don't notice things like that anymore. I guess we just take the stars for granted."

"There's a lot we used to take for granted. Still, we're here now. That's what matters, right?"

"Right."

I looked at Ava. She had removed her oilskins and replaced them with a light sweater and skinny jeans. I guessed it was knocking-off time. She still had her crimson beanie tugged down tightly over her head to keep the chill away, but I could see lockets of her hair poking out from underneath. In the dim light she looked stunning.

"Sorry, I actually came out here to say that supper will be ready. Gills is a good cook. You should come in."

"Let me guess. Steak?"

"How did you know?" Ava smiled.

"Mushroom sauce?"

"And a nice bottle of red to go with it." Ava laughed and raised her hands to her face, hiding her mouth.

"Sounds like we're missing out, Ava," I said, wishing she wouldn't hide her lips. I held out my arm. "Care to join me? I have reservations for two at La Maison Tukino. I hear the chef does the perfect steak."

Ava linked her arm through mine and I caught a faint smell of perfume as she stood next to me.

"As long as it comes with fries."

Laughing, I led Ava toward the cabin. Before we entered I caught sight of Weir. He was up ahead in the wheelhouse standing by the console. I smiled at him but he simply returned my smile with a glare. As I ushered Ava inside I had the feeling it was going to be a long night.

CHAPTER 5

The unsettling rocking motion of the boat left me feeling sick. Ava had been right about Gills. With a few simple herbs and spices he had turned what would have been an otherwise bland fish dish into something quite delicious. There hadn't been a scrap left after we'd eaten. I don't remember what type of fish it was, but after what we'd been living on, tins and stale food, it felt good to have a full belly. After eating our fish supper, Weir was true to his word and dropped anchor somewhere near Atlantic City. Jonah retired early and told us we'd best do the same as he intended to be up at dawn. I should've listened. Instead, we sat around talking, discussing our lives and getting to know one another. Weir was the only exception. He stayed quiet and when asked about his past retired to his bunk too. Gills told us that even he didn't know much about him, despite working together for years. Weir was a man of few words.

I tried to prise Gills' real name out of him, but he refused to spill it. He said he had spent so long on the ocean that he couldn't remember it anymore, but I could tell he was playing. He had been given his moniker on account of how he could hold his breath for so long. Only a week after joining the crew he had fallen overboard and they thought he was gone, only for him to turn up a couple of minutes later. This was all out in the middle of a freezing ocean. So, Gills had earnt himself an appropriate nickname and a place in Jonah's crew.

Ava opened up about her brother and parents. I guess it was healthy for her to talk about it. There weren't too many career choices left open for young people so she had decided to stick it out with Jonah. He'd looked after her and taught her how to fish, how to run the trawler. He'd taken her under his wing and I could tell how protective he was of her, and her him.

Eventually, Ava winked at Gills and then opened up a cupboard behind her. She pulled out a bottle of red wine and made us promise not to tell Jonah. They'd been saving it a while and finding alcohol was getting harder. After having to leave Manny's beers behind, we'd had little hesitation in polishing it off. Getting to relax and drink was a rare opportunity. Ava insisted we all share in it, and even Chelsea had a small glass. Soon, we all felt tired and with a full belly I crashed, sleep engulfing me quickly.

When I eventually woke I looked across the room. I had taken the upper bunk and Pippa the lower bunk beneath me. Chelsea had the bunk opposite us to herself, and was sleeping peacefully. The room was dark, and as I sat up I banged my head on the ceiling.

"Son of a—," I whispered, nursing my sore head. I'd forgotten just how cramped the bunks were. I swung my legs off the side and quietly dropped down to the floor. My bare feet hit the cold wood and I looked around for my shoes. Chelsea was still sleeping but Pippa was gone. I quickly dressed and slipped out of the room, leaving Chelsea to sleep. The other bunk-room was empty and I went upstairs to the wheelhouse. Jonah and Weir were studying something and greeted me with a smile and a grunt, in that order. I left them to it, not wanting to interrupt their work, and slipped out onto the deck. Ava and Manny were at the stern, and I saw Gills sipping on a cup of what I assumed was coffee. He was leaning back over one of the railings and waved me hello.

"Morning, sunshine," said Gills breezily, tipping his hat. "Coffee?"

"I'd love some."

"Wouldn't we all. This is just hot water. We're out of tea and coffee. Don't suppose you brought any with you?"

"Shoot." I was beginning to understand how difficult life could be out here. "Any breakfast?"

"We have cereal but no milk. There's fresh water down below if you feel like it?"

Out on deck the air was fresh and I inhaled, clearing my head. The events of yesterday felt like a dream.

"You ever get to Atlantic City when it was still a city?" asked Gills.

"No. This is my first trip." I looked out over the water and imagined what it must have been like. It was all under the ocean now. There was no evidence of a city ever having been there. The boardwalk and hotels were gone, the party atmosphere reduced to a stiff breeze drifting over the rim of the Atlantic. Water lapped gently at the side of the boat and my body was demanding coffee. We hadn't had any in months, the last of it running out after we'd cleared out the other apartments. Sometimes the body wanted what it just couldn't have, and I thought of Ava. Jonah was right, I had to get her out of my head.

"Pippa and Chelsea sleep okay?" Gills finished his hot water. "The Captain's keen to get going. Anchor's up in five."

"Right, I'll go round them up. Any idea what we're doing, or where we're heading?"

"I think you'd best talk to Jonah," said Gills. He patted me on the back. "Don't worry. It's all good."

Gills left me to my thoughts and the view over where the city used to be. Jonah was right that the place we had stayed the night was secluded. It wasn't a natural bay at all, but one forced out of the environment. Two skyscrapers loomed over us, the upper floors poking above the water like Meerkats in the desert. We were barely thirty feet from either one and I could hear them creaking. They appeared to have been gutted by fire at some point as all of the windows had blown out and I could see inside several rooms. Blackened blinds flapped uselessly from some of the rooms and the internal walls were charred. A seagull swooped past me and landed on the sill of one of the rooms. Its beady eyes looked at me and then it took off again. Between the two empty buildings the angle allowed me a view of the mainland. There wasn't much to see. There were a few other buildings still standing, their upper floors visible and their lower floors submerged, but there was no one living here anymore. It was evident that Atlantic City was now more like Atlantis. I tried to spot dry land, but all I could see was a hill in the distance and a road leading to nowhere. Apart from that, all I could see was water. This new world was going to take some getting used to. It was hard to accept that it was all gone. Even if we could find a way to get inland, what was the point? We had scavenged our own apartment block for food and there was no power. We had been surviving but we hadn't been living. We'd just been waiting to die, waiting for something to change instead of doing something about our own situation. Standing on deck it felt like that had changed, that somehow we were back in control of our own destiny. If we could help catch fish, find water, then perhaps Jonah would let us stay. I wondered if I should wake Pippa and Chelsea to discuss it with them. We hadn't thought any further than this. It felt like the *Tukino* offered a future though, more than any kind of future we could find on land.

"Luke, got a minute?"

Jonah touched my shoulder and I jumped.

"Sorry, guess I was lost in my thoughts."

"Time to leave. I thought now would be a good time to ask you what your plans were."

I watched Manny help Ava coiling a thick length of rope around some sort of stanchion at the base of the A-frame. I admit I felt a pang of jealousy but as the engine kicked in I looked at Jonah, bringing my mind back into the present.

"Weir and Gills are getting us underway."

"I should wake Pippa and Chelsea," I said, half of my mind watching Ava, the other half knowing I had to talk to Pippa.

"Leave them," replied Jonah. He drew his oilskins together and I noticed the chill in the air.

"So what's the plan?" I asked. "You want me to help, like, cast a net or something? I don't really know how this works but I want to chip in. We're not here for a free ride, Jonah."

"Appreciate that and I wouldn't expect it any other way. We have more mouths to feed, so you'll all have to help out. But baby steps, Luke, baby steps. First thing I need to know is how long you want to stay on my boat?"

Jonah looked at me intently and I felt like I was ten years old again explaining to my father how I'd scratched the side of his vintage corvette. If I didn't answer this right I could feel another beating coming on. "Well, I need to talk things over with Pippa, but I'm thinking it would be good if we could stay a while. We have nowhere to go and quite frankly I don't know where *to* go."

Jonah nodded but said nothing. I filled the silence with nervous energy.

"Like I said, we're happy to help and I think Pippa and Chelsea are grateful to have this chance. I can't say for sure if they're going to want to stay days, weeks or months, but we hadn't really thought what would happen next. The apartment was all about living day to day, rationing what we had and hoping you'd turn up before the building caved in. Now that I'm out here it feels different. I don't feel so trapped. I can see you've got something here, Jonah. It feels good to be a part of it. Maybe I should've pushed Pippa to leave earlier, but there's no point wondering about what if."

Chelsea came out onto the deck rubbing her eyes as the boat began to pull away from the two skyscrapers. Her eyes opened wide when she looked around and I smiled at her. She gave me a wave and crossed the deck to Manny and Ava.

"Here's the deal, Luke," said Jonah seriously. "I can take you on, all of you, but you'll have to help out. Like I said, this isn't a commercial operation anymore, but we get by. We catch enough fish and have a freezer to keep them on ice for when times get tough. I know a couple of places further down the coast who like to trade with us. Freshly caught fish gets us fresh water in return and a few extras, so we can try and have something resembling a balanced diet. There's a guy outside of Miami who gives us diesel and in return we give him what we can. I'd like to say that desperate times brought out the best in people, but not everyone is as welcoming. Still, we avoid those and keep our guard up against strangers, and do what we can.

"In a few minutes Ava is going to take us south and we'll follow the mainland fairly close to the coast until we get past North Carolina. You've probably noticed the weather changing. It's getting colder and we're heading south for warmer waters. Florida, to be precise."

"You got a condo down there, Jonah? Little place for your retirement? Maybe an old spinster to rub your feet?"

"You're a funny guy, Luke," said Jonah with a glint in his eye. "I remember now why I almost let Weir convince me to leave you behind."

I suppose I deserved that for the dig about Jonah's age.

"No, there's not much to see of Florida anymore. Parts of Miami are holding on. Besides, you really think I'd want to retire? I've got plenty of life left in me yet. I intend to captain this ship until the day I die, which is going to be a *long* time from today."

I admired Jonah's resilience. He had been working hard his whole life and even now, with all the difficulties of this changed world, he kept going. I hoped I would have his strength when I got to his age. "Awesome. Well, Florida sounds great to me. I'm sure that Pippa will be onboard with that idea, if you'll forgive the pun." I grinned. It felt like things were coming together. "Let's do it."

Jonah stepped closer and jammed a sharp finger into my chest. "Just remember, this ain't no holiday, Luke, and you can take *that* to the bank." Jonah looked me in the eye as he spoke. "There's gonna be some hard work involved, some cold nights and wet days. We don't take on new crew members lightly. Ava and Lance were an exception and I'm making one for you. I need to make sure you're going into this with both eyes open."

"You'll get no trouble from me. I get it. So, where do we start?"

Jonah removed his finger and softened immediately. "Get downstairs and get some food inside you. I don't want you passing out on me on your first day on the job. When you're ready I'll show you around the boat, what's what and who's who. Pippa and Chelsea too. I see Manny's already got stuck into it."

I looked back but Manny and Ava were gone, replaced by Weir. I saw Manny holding a mop and washing down the deck, while Ava and Chelsea were scurrying back into the cabin.

"Thanks, Jonah. For everything."

"All right, don't get all mushy on me, boy. Now get."

Jonah looked up at the gray sky as he approached Weir, and I felt my stomach rumble. Whatever food was on offer I would take it. I knew Jonah was right about getting a good feed in the morning, but it didn't take long to eat breakfast. Water and dry cereal gave my stomach little satisfaction. After that, the morning passed by in a bit of a blur. Jonah wasn't wrong when he said we would be working. He gave all of us a tour of the trawler. The *Tukino* was very much his boat. I could tell he was proud of it and kept things in good working order. Aside from fishing there was general maintenance too, to ensure the boat remained in good condition. None of us had any idea about engines but Gills needed a hand so I volunteered. It was a steep learning curve. I spent most of the time just watching and listening to him, getting dirt and oil all over me. When we broke for lunch I was pleased to be able to sit up on deck and get some fresh air.

"How's it going, grease monkey?" asked Ava as she sat down next to me.

"Great," I replied wiping my hands on the overall they had found for me. It was two sizes too big, but at least it kept my own clothes clean. I grabbed a plate full of fish and cold peas. "Think I'm ready to start running the place."

Ava smiled as she bit down into a fleshy piece of white meat. "Careful. Talk of mutiny will see you thrown overboard."

Chelsea and Pippa were close enough to hear our conversation, so I swallowed down the urge to flirt with Ava. I wanted to rip that red beanie off her head and look at her face but I simply smiled and continued eating my fish.

"Hey, Luke, you bring your cards?" Manny called out from the other side of the deck. "Gills said they haven't got any. I'm thinking poker night, you feel me?"

"Sorry, didn't think about it." I had only thought to pack essentials, boring stuff like the torch and matches.

"Oh well, maybe we can find some down in Florida."

Manny turned to Gills and began to talk about what card tricks he knew. If he was shaken up by his close call yesterday then he was doing well to hide it. Truthfully, I think he had brushed it off. He was an easy-going guy and had a naturally confident air about him. I could see that everyone had taken to him already.

"Don't waste it." Ava leant over and scooped up a piece of fish that I'd dropped on my lap.

"If you're not hungry, I'll eat it," said Chelsea. "I could eat this twice over. The fish is amazing."

"Ha! You say that now," said Ava, popping the scavenged food into her mouth. "Wait until it's all you eat, day in, day out. You'll be craving hot dogs and potato chips in no time."

"Pizza," suggested Manny. "With Parma ham and hot sauce."

"Oh no, you've all got it wrong. Pancakes," said Pippa, looking at her daughter. "With bacon and maple syrup, *obviously*."

"No, no, no," said Manny flashing us all a big smile. "T-bone steak." He paused for dramatic effect. "*Tender and bloody*."

"Oh God, stop it, my mouth is watering." Ava giggled and raised her hands to her face. "Everyone, just stop."

I couldn't resist it. "Warm apple pie with French vanilla ice-cream." I let out a satisfying sigh as if I had a bowl of it tucked under my arm. "Oh, yeah."

Ava gently punched me on the arm. "One more word out of you about ice-cream and I'll throw you overboard myself."

I looked into Ava's blue eyes. "Dare you. Try and take me on, and I'll take you with me."

"Oh, so it's a challenge, is it? Don't test me, Luke." Ava grinned and grabbed a piece of my shirt. "You want to go swimming, right now?"

"Only if you're coming with me." I looked into Ava's eyes and the world around her melted away. I heard voices but they were lost in a distant fog. Ava returned my gaze and for a moment we said nothing. It felt like years but it could only have been a second.

"Knock it off, all of you," said Jonah gruffly as his feet stomped past us. "Break's over. We need to get moving again. Ava, take over from Weir so he can eat. I'm going down below. I need to do some work on the charts and update them. The water's risen much higher than I figured in the last few weeks. Without decent radar equipment, we're almost flying blind."

Ava let go of me and jumped up quickly. She offered an apologetic smile but there was no need. I brushed myself down and stretched as Ava went to the wheelhouse and took over at the console. I don't know how she did it. Just looking at all the controls and dials made me dizzy.

The sky had changed from a light gray to a dark gray. The air remained cool and as I got to my feet I caught a glimpse of the mainland. It looked the same as hours ago, before we'd left Atlantic City. A distant hill, an empty road and barren land on the horizon; a few buildings stretching for air above the water's surface before they succumbed to the rising sea-levels, and a lone seagull breaking up the monotonous cloud cover. The sun was hidden behind a blanket of dirty gray and it didn't seem like it was going to break through anytime soon.

"Back to the engine?" I asked Gills.

"You got it, grease monkey," he replied.

"Enjoy yourself, *grease monkey*," said Chelsea cheerfully.

"This is a thing now, is it?" I asked. "I get a nick-name just like that?"

"Would you prefer plain old monkey?" Manny picked up the end of a length of rope that was spooled around his mop. "Either works for me."

"Me too." Pippa looked me up and down, and I felt like I was under mom's gaze, her eyes examining me and probing me for my innermost thoughts.

"Whatever," I sighed. "Enjoy your childish games. I've got work to do."

"Sorry," said Pippa. "We should let you get on, grease monkey."

With Chelsea laughing, I followed Gills to the wheelhouse. I didn't mind that much if it gave them some fun. Chelsea particularly needed to have some fun. She'd spent too long cooped up in the apartment with only me and her mother for company. It was good to see her beginning to relax and act more her age.

As Gills opened the cabin door the boat began to turn and there was a bump, as if something had hit the hull. I paused and grabbed Gills' arm.

"You feel that too?" he asked. "The boat's not going fast and there's nothing out here. We've sailed these waters for years. We know where the buildings are and where to avoid."

"Luke?"

I turned to see Pippa and Chelsea looking over the side of the boat. Manny was still coiling the rope together and looked at me.

"What was that?"

"Gills, let's check it out." Weir marched over to the doorway that led to the console. "Come on, leave the tourists. *Ava* hit something."

The way he said it inferred that she had made a mistake, but Gills had said there was nothing out here. I looked over at her and her face was full of confusion. It didn't appear there was anything to worry about, at least not yet.

Another bump and the boat lurched, almost knocking me off my feet.

"Throttle down, for fuck's sake, Ava." Weir marched back over to her and grabbed the wheel, pushing her out of the way.

"Hey, relax," I said, "we'll deal with it, Weir."

"Yeah? How about you do your job and leave me to do mine, *monkey*." Weir spat the words out and glared at me.

"Leave it." Gills took me by the arm and led me to the railings where Pippa and Chelsea were waiting.

"Anything?" he asked them.

"Can't see anything," replied Pippa.

"There's nothing here," said Chelsea.

"Felt like it was right underneath us," said Ava gently. She looked at me and then Gills. "I wasn't doing anything. I've handled the *Tukino* before, you know I have. You know I didn't do—"

"I know," said Gills. He lowered his voice so Weir couldn't hear him. "Don't let him get to you."

I sensed that Weir had issues with everyone on board, with the exception of Jonah. I could tell he was going to take some getting used to. I was mad at him for shoving Ava the way he had, but I let it go. Causing a scene wouldn't do anyone any favors and would probably only get Ava into more trouble. As long as that was all he did I was just going to have to accept it. For now.

"Manny, come with me," ordered Gills. "We'll check the fore and aft. Pippa, Chelsea, stay here and let me know if you see anything. Ava why don't you take monkey-boy and watch the stern. Holler if you see anything."

"Do we need to check below?" I asked. "What if we're taking on water?"

"Jonah's down there. We'd know by now if we were sinking."

As everyone went to their positions to scan the water for a sign of what we'd hit, I let Ava lead me to the other side of the boat. "Is he always like that?' I asked in a hushed tone. "Weir?"

Ava glanced over her shoulder, ensuring he couldn't hear her. "Yeah," she whispered. "He's not my favorite guy, but Jonah likes him. They go back years."

"Still, he shouldn't treat you like that. I'm surprised Jonah hasn't said anything."

Ava looked up at me. "He doesn't do it when Jonah's around. He respects the Captain but me... well, I'm just a girl."

"I think you're more than that and you know it. Surviving out here with these guys? You're incredible, especially with losing your family the way you did. And with Lance leaving you I'm kinda surprised you stuck around."

"Jonah told you? I guessed he would."

We reached the railings and leant over to peer at the ocean.

"I miss Lance, but my brother made his choice. I couldn't stop him." Ava shrugged. "I do what I can. I can put up with Weir's outbursts now and again."

"I'm not sure I can." I looked down at the water but could see nothing. It was dark and oozed around the boat like jelly. Clumps of seaweed floated by quietly, but the ocean appeared to be empty. I had no idea what we might have hit. I was hoping it was nothing serious but the two jolts we'd had didn't feel like nothing.

Ava nudged my arm. "Incredible, huh?"

I took my eyes off the water and looked at her blue eyes poking out from underneath her hat. I remembered what I'd just said and instantly blushed. "Well, yeah, sure. I mean... well, I think I was just meaning... you know."

"Smooth, Luke. Smooth," she replied, nudging my elbow again with hers.

I opened my mouth to try to come up with something witty but nothing came out. She giggled and covered her mouth. I wanted to stop her but I knew the others on deck would see me, so I forced myself to look back at the water.

"We really should... oh, shoot." I couldn't believe it. Down in the water, right next to the hull, something smooth and silvery was skimming the surface. It was moving silently right beside us and I recognized it immediately. It looked just like what had hit the boat right before Manny had fallen into the water. It looked like the same creature that had killed crazy old Mr. Johnson. It looked like the thing I had banished from my memory: it looked like a huge shark.

CHAPTER 6

"That's a twenty-footer for sure," said Gills. "Oh, boy—"

"Pippa, Chelsea, come look at this," said Manny excitedly. "You don't see this every day."

I felt a bolt of nervous energy hit my gut and for a moment could only see Mr. Johnson being devoured. But this was different. The shark was dead. The boat had hit its lifeless body, and Ava had called the others over to come see. As it floated harmlessly alongside us I felt relief take over. I'd thought the worst; that somehow it had followed us out of the city, yet this was a different animal entirely, nowhere near as big as the one I'd seen yesterday.

"I've never seen one this close," Ava said in awe. "Just look at the size of it."

As the shark's body shifted and exposed its rotting underbelly, the smell hit us. A rank odor of rotting meat and fish swept up to our nostrils. The shark's innards had been pulled apart and its guts washed out into the ocean turning the water a deep crimson. Fleshy entrails spooled out of its body spreading like tentacles as smaller fish picked at the juicy morsels that came free from the carcass.

"That... is... disgusting," muttered Pippa, walking away.

"That was all it was?" asked Jonah.

"Coulda been worse, right?" The shark looked as if it had been mauled, ravaged by something bigger and stronger; I didn't want to mention what I suspected whilst Chelsea was within earshot.

"Probably natural causes," said Ava. "The ocean did the rest. Another shark would eat anything."

"Okay, nothing to see here," said Jonah. "Back to work everyone. Ava, come below with me, will you? Weir and Gills can take care of things up here."

As the crowd dispersed I watched the shark drift away. It bobbed gently on the water and the air carried the stench away from the boat.

"Natural causes, my ass," I muttered.

"What you talking 'bout, Willis?"

Manny was right behind me and I jumped, startled. "Always the funny guy. I thought that you'd gone?"

Manny smiled. "You know, I could make a tasty sushi dish out of that bad boy," he said, looking at the disappearing shark. "Several dishes, actually. All that meat gone to waste. Such a shame."

"Yeah, right. Shark sushi."

Manny held a dirty rag in his hands and the smile on his face faded. "So, why don't you think it was natural causes? Nobody else seems bothered about it. It's dead, right?"

"Sure, but a shark that size? What are the chances of it just dying, for no good reason? Hell, I don't know how long sharks live for, but..." I glanced over at Chelsea. She had followed her mother to the wheelhouse where they were busy cleaning up after lunch. Weir and Gills were back at the console and I sighed. If I couldn't convince Manny of what I'd seen then maybe I should forget the whole thing. "I saw something. Yesterday, back in New York."

"When? You didn't say anything."

"Well, after you took a dunk everyone was busy, you know? I asked Pippa, but she said she didn't see it."

"See *what*, Luke?"

I knew it sounded crazy but I had to tell someone. "A shark. Bigger than the one you want to make sushi out of. Bigger than this boat, bigger than anything I've ever seen before."

Manny looked at me straight-faced and then burst out laughing. "Good one, Luke. You're trying to scare me. I get it. You should try Chelsea, maybe she'd be more gullible."

"I'm not kidding around here, Manny, it was huge. And it took Mr. Johnson."

Manny sniggered. "Sure it did. Jumped right out of the water and ate him whole, right?"

I sighed. I knew it wouldn't be easy but I hadn't expected this reaction. What was I really trying to achieve anyway? So what if Manny believed me or not? So what if any of them did? The shark was gone, back in New York. As long as we didn't meet again then did it matter what I said? The ocean covered most of the planet and the shark could disappear in the vastness of it all. I should let it go. I knew I should, and yet something irked me. I guess I just wanted someone to listen, for one person to believe me.

"Manny," I said, "just be careful, okay? There are things out there we don't understand, that we haven't seen before; this shark was big enough to take on anything. It was certainly ugly enough and big enough to kill a twenty-foot long Great White. And if it wanted to, it could take this boat down. So, don't believe me, I've no problem with that. But at least watch out for Pippa and Chelsea for me, okay?"

"Okay, man, okay. Chill." Manny looked at me as if I were insane. "I get it. I'm a little scared too. I never thought my future would be on a trawler and I'm not exactly keen on living out my days on the ocean. Yeah, there are things out there we don't understand. But I'm not going to worry about things I can't see. I'll look out for your family, *of course* I will." Manny took a step closer to me. "Just be careful yourself. They need you, man. Chelsea looks up to you, probably more than you realize. And Pippa needs you. She's a strong-willed woman, but she's also out here with a daughter in a place she doesn't know. She's going to need help getting through this, and talk of huge sharks eating people ain't gonna help her."

I nodded and bit my lip. "You're right."

"I know I am. So, maybe you saw a shark, maybe you saw something else. Whatever it was, it's far behind us. Let it go and concentrate on tomorrow."

"Tomorrow, huh? Any idea what that's going to be like?" I asked.

Manny looked at the dirty rag in his hands. "If Jonah's in it, I know it involves me cleaning his boat from top to bottom. And if I don't get started soon, you can bet I'll be hearing about it. Quite how I ended up being the janitor I don't know. Still, there are worse jobs I could've been lumbered with, right, grease-monkey?"

"Always the joker, Manny." I smiled and patted him on the back. "You enjoy your cleaning. I'm going to the engine room to do a *real* man's work."

"Oh no, you didn't just say that."

"Later, Manny." I laughed as I headed toward Gills. A dirty rag flew past my head and landed on the deck at my feet.

"You'll keep, Luke!"

I could hear Manny laughing behind me and I felt a little better. He was right. I had to forget about the shark and my fears. I had a job to do. We all had a place on the boat. I had to get on with it, focus on what I could do to make life easier for Pippa and Chelsea.

Gills took me to the engine room, leaving Weir up on deck, and we spent the next few hours going over things. If anything happened to Gills then they would be an engineer short, so I had to learn as much as I could. He dressed it up. Gills told me he needed help, an assistant, but I knew better than that. He didn't need any help. He knew his way around the boat and an engine like I knew the back catalogue of Springsteen. It wasn't a skill in much use anymore, but on quiet days back in the apartment I could sing most of his songs and it helped pass the time. With Gills, he was the same with engines and motors. Still, I was happy to learn what I could. I didn't know what the future held but there may come a day when I did need to know what to do, even if it was on a different boat, one of our own when Jonah got sick of us.

That night was quieter than the previous one. We were all tired. Manny helped Gills out with the cooking. I think he enjoyed it. He was a trained chef after all, and Gills seemed happy with the help. We all got on well. Even Jonah stayed up a little longer to chat to us. He told us about some of the contacts he had, people he would trade with and places that were still running. I began to feel better about things, and I didn't think about the shark anymore.

We stayed the night in a cove close to the Virginia border with North Carolina. It was quiet and sheltered, and Jonah seemed content. We saw nothing else all that day, no more boats, no more people, and no more sharks. Knott's Island was the closest land mass that we could see, the nearby State Parks now completely submerged. I didn't say anything to the others, but we used to have an Uncle who lived in Chesapeake. I hadn't spoken to him for years, and I couldn't help but wonder what had happened to him.

In bed that night I looked over at Pippa. Chelsea was asleep but Pippa was awake and staring at the ceiling. "You remember Uncle Herick?"

Pippa turned to face me. There was a small window above me and the dull stars gave me only a faint glimpse of her face. She looked tired. I hadn't noticed anything wrong, but when she spoke I felt her sadness. "Yeah, I remember. He'll be dead now."

Her words shocked me. It wasn't that she was so callous and cold about it, but that she was so real.

"Yeah, I guess so. You don't think anyone in Chesapeake is still there? There could be—"

"No. You know it's gone. Just like Norfolk and Hampton. All those places we used to visit as kids are gone, Luke."

"Right." I tried to see Pippa's eyes, but it was too dark. I couldn't read her properly and she turned away from me again, to face the ceiling. "You know, he might have evacuated before it got too bad," I suggested. "He might have headed inland, maybe to Raleigh or Charlotte. He always said he wanted to—"

"No." Pippa's voice was flat, lifeless. "He's gone, Luke. It's all gone."

I listened to the gentle waves lapping at the hull. My stomach had gotten used to the movement now and the nausea had passed. The way the cabin groaned was reassuring. It was cramped and uncomfortable, but it was home. At least for now. The *Tukino* was an odd place to live but it beat giving up.

"Jonah says we're headed for Florida. He wants to stop at some place near Jacksonville first, but—"

"I'm tired, Luke," said Pippa quietly. "We should get some sleep."

"How are you doing, Pippa?" I could tell it was more than tiredness. If she wanted to sleep she would've dropped off like Chelsea did. She wasn't snapping at me either. There was something on her mind. "What's wrong?"

"Luke, Uncle Herick is gone. Old Mr. Johnson is gone. Mom and dad are gone, Chesapeake is gone and half of the US is under water. I feel queasy all the time and have to bring my daughter up on a boat. That good enough for you?"

"They may be gone, Pippa, but we're not. *I'm* not. Things will get better."

"Better? I just want to go home. I wish we could go back to our apartment. I know it was cramped and smelly, and we had no food to speak of. But it was home. This isn't. What are we going to do? My head's hurting from thinking about it. That's all I've done the past couple of days. I'm trying to figure out what kind of future this is for Chelsea."

I looked across at Chelsea. She was perfectly still and breathing quietly. If only we could all sleep as well as her.

"And that shark we saw today? What if it hadn't been dead? What if we were attacked? I don't know the first thing about living on a boat."

"Jonah will teach us. He'll look after us as long as we want to be here."

"Do you?" Pippa asked. "Do you want to be here, Luke?"

I had to think about that one. I didn't think a simple yes or no would suffice. It wasn't really a choice I had contemplated. We were here and it was all we had. Going home was out of the question since it had fallen into the sea. Where else would we go? "We could cut and run, but I couldn't see any other option right now."

"I need to sleep," whispered Pippa. "We can talk more tomorrow. When Chelsea is awake. Let her sleep."

"Okay." I wanted to say something reassuring, to let her know that she shouldn't worry and we would be okay. But I didn't want to lie. "We'll talk more tomorrow."

Pippa remained silent and she turned her back to me. I hadn't considered that Pippa might have different ideas to me. I had assumed she was happy on the boat. The last two days had flown by. Chelsea seemed fine and so had my sister. Perhaps we were going to have to make some difficult decisions after all. But starting again, on the mainland? How would we find anywhere to live, anywhere with enough food and clean water to support us? I guess I had adapted to life on the boat quicker than Pippa. There was no prize for that, and I almost felt guilty about it. Pippa had never given me any indication she was unhappy. I knew she was scared, worried even, but the thought of returning home or finding dry land hadn't occurred to me. There was a lot to consider and if Pippa wanted off the boat then I was going to have a hard decision to make. I liked Ava and could imagine myself out on the ocean, catching fish and making something of myself. Yet I couldn't leave Chelsea. I had raised her like a daughter and to think of leaving her now troubled me. How could I leave Pippa on her own? I let troubled thoughts run through my mind as I tried to sleep. The cabin rocked gently and soon enough I felt sleep grabbing at my body, pulling at the frayed edge of my mind.

A drop of water splashed on my head and I felt it dribble down my cheek. Another followed it and then I heard the voices. They were muffled, disguised, but I knew it was the crew. They were up on deck. The cabin was pitch black and I called out to Pippa and Chelsea, but there was no answer. Another drop of cold water hit my face and I sat upright, banging my head once again on the low ceiling. Swinging my feet over the bunk I immediately felt water embrace my feet.

"Pippa? Chelsea?" I jumped into the water and felt in their beds, but they were empty. More muffled voices above me, sounding more and more like shouting. I rummaged beneath my pillow for the torch I stored there in case of an emergency and it wasn't there.

Feeling my way toward the door I felt something float past me in the water. Cold, slimy tentacles wrapped around my ankle and I fought the urge to scream. Reaching down I pulled at whatever had grabbed me and yanked the seaweed off me. I struggled forward and reached the door to the other bunkroom.

"Ava? Hello?"

No answer. I felt panic rising and the utter darkness wasn't helping. I lurched forward to the stairs and felt relief swamp me when my probing fingers found the handrail. The voices above me became clearer as I climbed the staircase. My vision began to become clearer too as I neared the bridge. The boat was illuminated by a bright moon and reaching the upper cabin I shivered. It was cold. It was the dead of night and I just knew that something terrible had happened. My legs were freezing from wading through the water and I was scared to turn and face the open deck. I knew it was bad.

Pulling open the cabin door, I came face to face with Jonah. He looked at me with wild eyes.

"Take care of her, Luke."

"Who?" I shouted. "What's happened?"

Jonah disappeared into the night and I heard footsteps marching toward the cabin. Weir strode past me, a harpoon in his hand and blood running down his face. I scanned the deck for the others. Dark shapes flitted across the boat urgently. I told my feet to move, to go find help, but they refused to budge. My hands gripped the cabin door and I was afraid. I was afraid we were sinking and I was already too late. I'd lost them.

"Pippa? Chelsea? Where are you?" I called to them, yelling as loud as I could, straining my voice. "Where *are* you?"

Suddenly the boat lurched and I felt myself twisting away from the cabin, my feet unable to support me. I crashed onto the deck, my hands taking the brunt of the impact. More feet ran around me and I reached up, grabbing hold of someone's leg.

"Please. What's happening?"

Ava looked down at me and raised her hands to her face. "You're going to drown." She laughed and laughed, looking at me with disgust in her eyes.

Shocked, I let go of her leg and she ran off into the night. I jumped up and saw Manny and Gills stood by the console. I had to find them. I ran to the stern, to the bridge, covering every inch of the boat, but they weren't there. "Chelsea!" I screamed. "Chelsea! Pippa, where are you?"

A hand grabbed my shoulder and I turned around to find Pippa staring at me.

"Take care of her, Luke."

Something slammed into the boat again and we both slipped toward the railing. Pippa was thrown hard against it and her head cracked against the wooden deck as she fell. I managed to wrap my hands around her as I was pulled toward the ocean.

"No!" I felt water splashing at my back and then a huge wave crashed over us. When the water had subsided, Pippa was gone.

"Pippa?" I clawed at the railing and got to my knees. The dark ocean was slamming into the boat and I saw Pippa's body floating face-down in the water. My heart raced as another wave slammed into us and the water pulled her body down out of sight.

As the second wave subsided I saw more bodies in the water. I recognized the oilskins of the crew. I saw Gills, Weir and Jonah and beside them my friend, Manny. They were all dead. Jonah's lifeless body bobbed to the surface next to them and then I saw it. A red hat. I felt fear pulling at my heart, tears stinging my eyes. The red hat sank beneath the water, the black water taking its victims down to the seabed. As a huge, third wave soaked me, I closed my eyes. I was too late. How could I have slept through this? Where was she?

With the boat leaning perilously close to tipping over I grabbed the railing and tried to hold on. We were at such an angle now that it was impossible to stand. Had we run into rocks? Was it a passing storm? Sea-spray stung my eyes and through gritted teeth I called out to Chelsea, but I still couldn't find her.

Another body. In the ocean, a few feet away, I saw a girl. Her bloated body floated free, her blonde hair flowing around her body. Her eyes were wide open, locked in a death stare, and seeing Ava like that made me terrified. They were all gone. Ava was gone. My sister was gone. The whole crew had been wiped out.

"Uncle?"

There she was. Chelsea suddenly appeared in the water right beneath me. She was gasping for air, her face scalded red with the effort of trying to swim. She reached an arm up to me and I held my hand out for her to take. She was too far away.

"Uncle? Please help me," she pleaded.

Beneath Chelsea, something stirred in the water. Its vastness was undeniable and for a moment I thought it was the shadow of the boat. Yet it moved and swam around her, circling her.

"Chelsea, take my hand!" I strained every muscle in my body to reach her, but it was just too far.

The shape beneath Chelsea began to take form. Even in the black water I could see. I saw its fin as it rose to the surface. I saw its big black eyes and its jaws open. I heard it roar as it broke the surface and its mouth opened wide. Hundreds of jagged teeth ringed Chelsea and she screamed, flailing as she fell into its jaws. The shark would swallow her whole and as it rose up out of the water I shrank back. It was inches away from the hull and I heard Chelsea scream as the huge shark closed its jaws around her.

"No. No, no, no!"

It couldn't come down to this.

"No!" I screamed again.

"Luke. Luke?"

A hand brushed my shoulder. Who was left? They were all dead.

"No!" The shark disappeared back into the ocean and I closed my eyes. I had been too slow.

"Luke!"

A hand slapped my face and I opened my eyes. Sweat drenched my face and I reached out to grab their wrist before they could slap me again.

"Luke, it's okay."

I could feel Ava's pulse as I held her and I felt confused.

"But... but you were—"

"You were dreaming," she whispered. "I heard you from the other room."

The cabin was pitch black and I called out to Pippa and Chelsea, but there was no answer. I sat upright, banging my head once again on the low ceiling. It felt all too familiar. Was it really nothing but a nightmare?

"Ava. Are you okay?"

Ava smiled. Her hair hung loose over her shoulders. "I will be when you give me my arm back."

"Sorry," I said, releasing her. I rubbed my eyes. "Sorry, I thought... it was just a dream, right?" I felt my head but it was dry, apart from a clammy sweat. There was no sea water. I looked down at the floor but there was no water there either.

"Go back to sleep." Ava looked at me and in the dark cabin I felt her hand rest on my chest. "Lance used to dream too. Just forget it. Go back to sleep."

"Sleep?" The thought seemed impossible now. It had been so vivid, so real, that the idea of sleeping was almost laughable.

"Well, I'm going back to bed. You should rest at least. Dawn is a few hours away yet. I'll see you in the morning."

As she removed her hand from my chest I grabbed her again.

"Thank you," I whispered.

Ava leant over me, her face so close to mine I could feel her warm breath on my cheek. "I didn't want you waking the others," she whispered. "I sleep lightly. Have done, ever since Lance left. I guess it can be hard to sleep sometimes. You'll be okay, Luke."

I wanted to kiss her so badly it hurt. I don't know if it was the relief of the dream being over or something else, but she had never looked more beautiful than she had right then.

"Good night," she said as she let go of me and slipped out of the room.

Ava left me and I tried to sleep. Dawn couldn't come soon enough.

CHAPTER 7

The voices were muffled, penetrating my sleep like lightning piercing thunderclouds. They sank into my thoughts, clouding my dreams before I realized they were real. As I opened my eyes I noticed our room was light. Beams of daylight came through the small window and I swung my feet off the bunk, half expecting to land in water. The cabin floor was hard and dry, and I rubbed my tired head. The dream had left me sleepless for a while until I'd finally drifted off again. Pippa and Chelsea weren't in their beds, and judging by the amount of light, I had overslept.

Dressing quickly, I knocked on Jonah's door. There was no answer. The galley and bunks were empty. It seemed like everyone was up on deck, so I made my way up to the wheelhouse where I found Gills and Ava. They were crouched over a cupboard by the back wall.

"What's going on?" I looked out of the cabin. The sun was up and there was no land in sight. We must have started heading south while I was asleep. I ran a hand through my hair wishing I could have a shower.

Ava stood up. She turned around and pointed a pistol at me.

"What the hell?"

"Morning, Luke. We've got company." Ava flashed me a quick smile and then left the cabin.

"Company?" I asked. I looked through the salt-smeared windows of the cabin but could see nothing but endless ocean. "Gills?"

He slammed the cupboard door shut, snapped the padlock shut, and shoved a key in his pocket. Then he turned to face me armed with three more guns.

"We don't have much but it's all we got. Can you shoot?" He held out a pistol grimly. "Don't know if it'll come to it, but we gotta be prepared."

I shook my head. "I've never shot anything in my life. I've never even held a gun."

Gills looked disappointed. "Figures."

He swept out of the cabin without another word, so I ventured out onto deck to find Pippa and Chelsea. The air was lifeless but fresh, and it helped wake me up. The nightmare still hung around my brain like an unwelcome visitor and I needed to think about something else, to get it out of my mind. Given the activity on the boat I didn't think I would have too much of a problem in that department. Weir and Jonah were in a heated discussion. Although they were keeping their voices down it was obvious they disagreed on something. Both of them had a gun held down at their hips. Gills and Ava had taken up positions at the bow and stern respectively, a gun in each hand pointed out at something on the ocean that I had yet to see. All of the *Tukino's* crew were armed which blew away the last cobwebs of sleep roaming my head, but offered me little by way of reassurance. Manny and Pippa were on the port of the ship, a pair of binoculars between them. Chelsea was on the starboard looking distinctly sick. Her head was bowed low and she looked pale. I decided it best to leave her alone for now, so I approached Manny and Pippa.

"What can you see?" I suspected it might be another shark, perhaps a Great White. What else would the crew need guns for? "Is there a..?"

"A boat," answered Manny. "There to the west. Pippa spotted it a few minutes ago."

Pippa looked at me. "I heard Jonah talking to Weir. He mentioned pirates. You don't think—?" Pippa looked anxiously at Chelsea. "Are we safe, Luke?"

"You should've woken me." I took the binoculars from Manny and held them to my eyes. I had to know what it was. Jonah had told me about the pirates, but truthfully, I didn't think we'd encounter any. I wasn't even sure I believed in them. "You should go to see Chelsea, Pippa. She doesn't look well."

"Yeah, I know, Sherlock. If you hadn't decided to sleep in you would know she's feeling seasick this morning."

With Pippa's words burning my ears, I looked for the boat. I couldn't afford to let her get to me, not today. After last night's discussion I was prepared to let it go. She was worried about her daughter and if we were going to run into pirates she had every reason to be concerned.

"A little to the left," Manny said. "You see it?"

I heard Pippa march away, her feet banging loudly on the deck. It was probably better that she left me with Manny. I needed to talk to him and I didn't want Pippa listening to what I had to say.

"Got it," I said as the binoculars finally picked out the boat on the horizon. I changed the focus slightly and found myself struggling to make it out. "It's hard to tell what it is. What did Jonah say?"

"Not much," replied Manny. "As soon as Pippa spotted it he got everyone riled up. I know Ava got their guns out. Jesus, they're all armed now. Is that really necessary? What is this Luke?"

I watched the black blob in the distance getting larger. Whatever it was, it was heading our way. "It could be a pirate, I don't know. It's too far too tell."

"Christ. You think it's trouble, don't you?"

I sighed. "Probably. Don't say anything to Pippa, but Jonah told me about the pirates. He said they're dangerous and to avoid them at all costs."

"He what?" Manny hissed. He grabbed the binoculars from my hands. "Why didn't you tell me?"

I licked my lips, thirsty and afraid. "Because I didn't know if anything he was telling me was true. He was sketchy with the details and what do I know about pirates? He said they managed to avoid them, mostly. Besides, you know how worried Pippa is. I didn't want to add to that with stories of pirates that might not even be relevant."

"Sure looks relevant now." Manny looked at the approaching boat. "Well, I guess we're going to find out soon enough."

We waited anxiously for the boat to get closer. It was only a few minutes before it became clearer. In the meantime, I heard Chelsea throwing up and saw Pippa holding her hair back. Pippa was rubbing her back and trying to soothe her. I guess the life I envisioned for us wasn't going to be as straight forward as I hoped. I wanted to do more to help. I was stood there watching the mystery boat headed toward us and had nothing to do. I felt useless.

"Manny, I'm going to see Jonah, see what we can do." The boat was idle, the engine alive, but we weren't moving. I wondered why Jonah hadn't taken us away, out to the ocean and far away from the boat. "I need to know what the plan is."

"I'll come with you. I feel like a sitting duck out here."

Weir and Jonah were huddled over the console and when we approached them, Weir glared at me. I sensed he would happily offer us to the pirates if it meant saving his own neck. Even after a few days onboard he had hardly spoken a word to any of us. He marched out of the cabin toward Ava as I greeted Jonah, and I was pleased to see him leave.

"Jonah, what's the deal?" I asked nervously. "How come we're not going in the other direction?" I tried to sound calm, but even to myself my voice sounded high and whiny. I cleared my throat. "It's a pirate ship, right?"

"You sound like Weir. I'll tell you what I told him. We're not wasting what precious little diesel we have left on trying to outrun something that could still catch us. We stay put and wait for them to come to us."

"Is that wise?" asked Manny. "I thought you said—"

"You want to skipper a ship, get your own. I'm the Captain of the *Tukino*, and I don't need you two questioning me. There are protocols we have to follow when we meet other vessels. They've kept us safe so far and nothing's changed today."

I hadn't seen this side of Jonah before. He was right though. "Sorry, we didn't mean to doubt you. I just... look, is there anything we can do? Given how fast that boat is approaching it won't be long before they're here."

"My crew are armed. The best thing you can do is get Pippa and Chelsea below deck. If there is any trouble I want them out of the way. Pippa did well to spot it and give us a chance to prepare. But right now she and Chelsea would do well to get out of sight."

"Would you take them?" I asked Manny. I needed to know they were safe but didn't think I could take hiding down below in the bunks if there was trouble coming. I wanted to be on deck where I could see, where I knew exactly what was happening.

"Sure." Manny handed me the binoculars and I watched him go and talk to Pippa. Within a few seconds they were all headed back to the cabin. They filed past me back to the bunks without a word. I felt relieved when Chelsea and Pippa were down below out of sight, and I raised the binoculars to my eyes. The approaching ship was clearer now and I began to make out what kind of craft it was.

"What do you see, Luke?" asked Jonah.

"A yacht. It's huge, like one of those things you see millionaire's showing off around Monaco. It's got a blue hull and I'm trying to make out the name but it's too far. I can see one person on deck, that's all."

"Male or female?"

"Not sure," I replied. "They're in shadow."

"Armed?"

I hesitated. The figure held something in their hands but it could be anything. Was it a gun or something harmless? I waited a moment hoping the figure would step out of the shadows, but they remained motionless. "Possibly. Can't say for sure."

"Then we wait."

I looked at Jonah. It was intolerable. How could he remain so patient and calm? "You've done this before?"

"A few times," he said gruffly.

Jonah said no more, leaving me to guess what had gone down on previous occasions. He kept his eyes locked on the approaching yacht evidently uninterested in making any more conversation. I wandered out of the cabin and scoured the deck for a weapon. If we were boarded then I would do everything I could, anything possible, to protect Pippa and Chelsea. My eyes fell upon a harpoon resting in a cradle above a length of rope. It was next to the winch, held in place by a rusty bracket. I took it and when my fingers wrapped around the cold steel handle, I have to admit I thought of Ava. I would protect her too. I barely knew her and yet she had already crept under my skin.

Gill's voice called out from the bow. "Contact!"

Jonah emerged from the wheelhouse with a grim face. He came and stood next to me and I prepared myself. All trace of sleep had gone now, driven out by the adrenalin surging through me. I watched the yacht approach and as it came closer I began to see more detail that I hadn't before. There was no sail, and it ran quietly, powered by an engine far superior to ours. A grinning cat had been crudely painted on one side of the hull with black paint. Down one side of the yacht were scratches, as if something had rammed it, and the windows of the upper cabin were all smashed. It was a large boat and probably could sleep all of us comfortably. There was a dining area on one of the verandahs and space on the back for a helicopter to land. It was like one of those superyachts, although it had been through the wars. I noticed the name of the yacht as I scanned it: *Bella*. I strained my eyes to see if the figure in the shadows was armed. I couldn't believe we were about to come face to face with pirates.

"Stay there," ordered Gills, as the boat came closer. He shouted to the shadowy figures. If they heard him, they showed no sign of it. The yacht came closer. "Pass on by," called Gills.

"Can't we just radio them?" I asked Jonah.

"No point. We tried that. They just lie. You can say anything over the radio. That's how they sucked in Lance. I'd rather talk to someone face to face. We need to see who they *really* are."

Ava and Weir suddenly brushed past me as they made their way up to the bow. Their guns were still raised.

"I said stop!" Gills raised his gun into the air and fired a shot.

The resultant bang made me jump. I'd never heard a gunshot before and it suddenly made everything seem so real. This wasn't like a TV show. This was real. It was happening. I looked at the boat expecting to see a dozen men run out of the cabin holding AK-47s, yet nothing happened. The boat slowed and came alongside us, barely ten feet away. Ava and Weir followed it, keeping themselves between us and them.

"That was a warning shot. Next one will go into your hull," announced Gills.

"Please. Please wait."

The mysterious figure on the *Bella* stepped out of the shadows with their arms raised above their head. It was a short man wearing nothing but a pair of board shorts. He was as old as Jonah, yet thin and tanned, and when he spoke I detected a clipped accent.

"We're not looking for trouble. My wife and I just want safe passage north. If you want to trade we have nothing of much use. We have information, something that can help you stay alive."

As the boat slowed, the man was joined by another figure. A woman appeared out of a nearby doorway.

"Step where we can see you, *both* of you. Keep your hands raised where we can see them," ordered Gills.

The man's wife stepped out to stand next to him. She was thin and tanned like him, and wore a loose white cotton top. A wide-brimmed sun hat hid much of her face. I detected a red stain on the woman's top and wondered if it was red wine or blood.

"Waste of time," muttered Weir. He looked at Jonah. "Let's get moving. Leave these tourists and get on with our work. We're supposed to rendezvous with Kath today, or have you forgotten? We need to get moving."

"I've got this, Weir. I don't need you to remind me about Kath. We'll make it. Let's hear what these two have got to say first."

Weir shook his head and marched toward the cabin. He slammed the door behind him.

"Kath? Who's that?" I asked.

"One of our trade partners," replied Jonah. "Lives at the top of a condo near Wilmington. We're low on diesel and she's low on everything else."

I watched Ava tuck her gun into her waistband. She was wearing her jeans again and I had to admit she looked better in them than her oilskins.

"Nothing happening here," she said, approaching Jonah.

"You've seen this before?" I asked her. "I thought they were pirates."

"Pirates?" Ava giggled. "I don't think so. Jonah been telling you how everyone is out to get you? Half the time the people we come across are just looking for food or a way home. When the waters rose, a million people jumped into the nearest boat and took to the oceans without any clue how to actually live out here. My guess is these two thought they would sail the Caribbean, seeing out the end of the world on a diet of fish and cocktails. Guess they figured wrong, huh?"

"Ava," said Jonah, "we'll get going to Kath's soon, but we can spare these two a bite to eat, can't we?"

"You're all heart, Jonah. Look at their skinny asses. I'll go get something."

Jonah turned the wheel and brought the two boats closer.

"Where have you come from?" asked Gills. He was obviously the conduit between strangers and the *Tukino*. "And why go north? It's getting colder. You should stay in the south."

The man lowered his hands and held onto a grab rail. He shook his head. "South is bad. It's too dangerous. We just came from there. You should head north too."

"Douglas, be quiet. We don't know these people." The man's wife removed her hat and fanned herself with it. "I told you we should avoid them. Look at their guns. They're probably part of it."

"Hold on, hold on." Jonah turned to me. "Stay there, Luke. I need to talk to them."

I watched Jonah go and stand by Gills. All sense of danger had gone. The threat had passed, and Ava and Weir seemed to think it was a big joke. Although I was relieved that the boat hadn't turned out to be pirates, I was still concerned. Their boat looked to be in bad shape and they had said something about heading north. Yet I knew we were heading south. I suspected Jonah was right to listen to them.

"Why didn't you avoid us if you've had trouble?" asked Jonah.

Douglas looked at his wife. "Honey, my wife, told me to go the other way. I saw you heading this way and I couldn't let you walk into a trap. I figured being a trawler it was unlikely you were with them."

"*Them?*" Jonah put his hands on his hips. "Who are you talking about?"

"The bastards who nearly killed us and tried to sink our yacht," said Honey. She began to sob. "The bastards who would've slit our throats if we hadn't managed to escape."

Douglas put an arm around his wife and looked at Jonah. "Don't go south. They've turned it into a war zone. They've taken control of everything. Follow us or go your own way. If you've got any sense, you'll head north."

I was glad Jonah had made Manny take the others down below deck. I didn't need Pippa and Chelsea listening to this.

"Douglas, who are they?" asked Jonah again. "Where are they? They can't have the whole coastline covered."

"Feels like it. They have outposts everywhere. We just came from Wilmington. We used to trade for a little diesel there."

The cabin door swung shut and I saw Ava emerge with something tucked in paper under her arm. She smiled when she saw me, then headed right over to Gills and passed him the parcel.

"So, you know Kath?" Gills tossed the food parcel over to Douglas. The boats were only a few feet apart. Douglas took it and held onto it tightly.

"Sure. Who doesn't around these parts?"

"Who *are* they, Douglas?" asked Jonah with growing animosity.

I sensed Jonah's impatience, but the more I saw of the thin couple on the *Bella*, the more I felt sorry for them. They appeared to have gone through some sort of ordeal. They didn't have much fat on their bones, and their yacht was in a bad way. Douglas and Honey obviously cared a lot for each other and had even risked coming to warn us off. Whatever awaited us down south was trouble.

"I don't know their names, just the leader. They're led by a man named Mckade. If you've been south of here you must have heard of him," said Douglas. "We've been around Grand Bahama the last few months and came to get more diesel. It's changed. Things have changed a lot. Mckade has taken over. You know him?"

"I do," confirmed Jonah. "He's trouble with a capital T, and you can take that to the bank."

Ava suddenly became animated. "Did you hear about a boy with him? Lance? Fair hair, about my height?"

Douglas shook his head. "No. He's got a lot of men, but I don't remember anyone by that name."

"What about Kath?" asked Gills once again.

Douglas and Honey looked at each other silently.

"We knew her," sniffed Honey. "But now… I'm not so sure… there was so much blood—"

As Honey broke down again, Ava staggered back repeating her brother's name over and over.

"Go," said Jonah. "Go north, Douglas, and take your wife some place quiet. Stay safe."

Gills raced down to the wheelhouse with Jonah at his side. I followed them, eager to know what the plan was.

"Are we following them?" I asked as Jonah started the engine up.

"No," he said firmly. "We're going south."

Facing the *Bella*, I saw the gap between the two of the boats grow. Douglas and Honey moved toward the grab rail, and Douglas signaled me over. I left and made my way over to the side of the hull.

"There's something else, something you need to know," said Douglas.

Ava ran past me toward the cabin and as the engine strained, the gap between me and Douglas suddenly widened. I wanted to go with Ava, to make sure she was all right, but I had to know what waited for us. I had to hear Douglas and I raced to the edge of the boat.

"Have you seen them?" he asked. "You can't have or you'd know. You'd know not to go south."

Our boat pulled away and Douglas looked downcast.

"Seen who? Mckade?" I shook my head, confused.

Douglas headed toward his own cabin, where Honey stood in the doorway waiting for him.

"No, I meant the monsters. The ones that eat the sharks. The Megalodons."

CHAPTER 8

"Didn't you hear them? They said we should head north." I couldn't understand what Jonah was thinking. Why sail into a storm when you had the option of bypassing it? "Look at them. You can see that they're not lying."

Douglas and Honey had retreated into their yacht. I stood in the open doorway of the wheelhouse. The *Tukino* was moving now, gaining speed and causing the swell to splash over the side of the boat. Droplets of salt water hit my face. I had no idea what a Megalodon was, but I figured it wasn't good. If they were south of here along with this Mckade, then it made no sense to me to go in that direction.

"I know," replied Jonah. "They're telling the truth. There are a *few* decent people left in this world, Luke, and those two deserve a chance. So does Kath. We're going south."

I looked across at the *Bella*. It was already far away from us. The smiling cat painted on the hull had probably looked cute once, but now its salacious grin just reminded me of how dangerous the ocean was. It seemed that pirates were real after all. We had been lucky that Douglas and Honey had turned out to be friendly. This Mckade sounded anything but, and despite Jonah's affections or responsibility toward Kath, I couldn't see why we would willingly head into danger.

"There must be a better way," I said. "Perhaps we can send a scout ahead or gather some more information about this Mckade? You're not really going to—"

"Back off," said Weir as he put a hand on my chest, shoving me back. "We've got work to do. Run along, grease-monkey."

"Watch it, Weir, I was talking to Jonah." I met Weir's fierce gaze, refusing to back down. He might have superiority over me in terms of being a crew member, but we were all in this together. I had pussy-footed around him long enough. He was a bully, plain and simple. We didn't have to like each other, but we did have to get on and ensure the safety of everyone onboard.

Weir curled up the corner of his mouth and narrowed his eyes. "You don't like it, go for a swim."

Ignoring Weir's veiled threat, I knew I had to try and make Jonah understand. "Douglas said something else. He told me about monsters that—"

"You've got five seconds, then you're going down Jacob's Ladder. I think you'll find it's a long swim to the mainland from here."

Exasperated, I looked at Gills for support but the look in his eyes told me otherwise. Jonah said nothing, concentrating on navigating the boat. I could see that continuing to argue with Weir would get me nowhere. He wasn't going to back down or entertain having a serious discussion with me. This was a fight I was going to have to save for another day.

"Later. I'm going to check on my family."

I heard Weir chuckle as I turned my back on him. He was stubborn and his voice carried a lot of weight with Jonah. I could see they had made their minds up. How far were we going to get? How far could we get? Jonah had told me they were running low on diesel. Perhaps we had no choice but to try and trade. Jonah wouldn't knowingly put us all in jeopardy, I was sure of that. Weir, on the other hand, had his own agenda. And seeing me thrown off the boat seemed to be part of it.

With the cool morning breeze behind me, I headed for the steps leading down to the bunks. I bumped into Manny on his way out and we squeezed past each other on the narrow staircase.

"Hey, man, Pippa and Chelsea are down there. Chelsea's pretty sick. What's the deal? We heading south?"

"Something like that. I need to talk to Pippa. There could be trouble ahead."

Manny looked at me and nodded his head as if he knew everything. "Okay. I'll go help. You take care of yours. We'll be okay."

Manny departed upstairs and I heard him offering Jonah his assistance as I continued down. He was a good friend, always positive and ready to help. I was grateful he was around. It was nice to have someone on my side. It was beginning to feel like we were in the way, and after Weir's threats I needed to know I wasn't on my own.

Before I headed on down to the bunk rooms I noticed that Ava was sat in the galley with a gun on her lap. She faced the wall, seemingly staring into space, and gave me the merest glance as I approached her. I wanted to go into the sleeping quarters and check on Pippa and Chelsea, but first I needed to know that Ava was all right. Something had upset her and none of the others seemed unduly concerned. I sat down quietly beside her, keeping one eye on the gun in her hands.

"Are you okay, Ava? What was that about?"

She didn't answer so I reached across and opened the blind, the roller springing up to reveal the ocean beyond the window. Spray lashed against the glass as the wind hurled the ocean's waves against our trawler. The weather seemed to be deteriorating along with my mood. Ava tugged her red hat down over her ears.

"Lance is with Mckade. He left me a while back and I haven't seen or heard from him since. I wasn't sure I would ever get the chance to talk to him again."

"You know much about this Mckade character?" I asked. "Why did Lance leave you to join him?"

Ava shook her head and looked down at the gun in her lap. I wished I could see her eyes, look her in the face, but she kept her back to me.

"I asked myself the same question every night for months after he left. We used to be close. We were close until the accident. After mom and dad passed, he kind of freaked out a bit. He didn't take to being told what to do very well, and Jonah was more patient with him than I was. But when Mckade came along I guess he saw an opportunity to break free."

"How did you come across Mckade? From what Douglas and Honey told me they had a narrow escape. You saw the state of their yacht. Did Mckade try anything with you?"

"Yeah." Ava sighed. "It feels like a long time ago now. Jonah knew of a good spot to fish where Brunswick used to be, down in Georgia. Mckade was fishing there too when we arrived. He had one of those superyachts. We caught him with his guard down, which is the only reason we managed to get away. Lance was impressed by Mckade. He had a way with words. I mean, his operation was small-scale back then but he knew what he was doing, what he was building. It sounds like he's moving up in the world. If he's taken control of Kath's diesel trading post then we've got problems."

"He's not the sort of man who gives you a fair deal, I suspect."

"No way. When we met him we thought we might be able to trade information at least, but he just wanted our gear. He bragged about how he had destroyed a marina only a few weeks previously and taken everything. He's a small man with big ideas. Lance fell for it hook, line and sinker. Jonah refused of course, wouldn't give him anything, but when it came down to it, he had the upper hand. That was the first time we had to get our guns out and since then we haven't greeted anyone without them. I hate him for that. I hate him for stealing Lance away from me. If I'd had more time, if only I'd said or done something… Mckade is trouble but I want to find Lance. I want to know that he's okay." Ava's head dropped further. "There was blood on Honey's shirt."

I remembered the stain. Honey had said something about blood too when Gills had asked her about Kath. I put my hand on Ava's back and rubbed it gently. She sniffed and when she turned to face me I saw tears forming in her eyes.

"Talk to Jonah. He's fair. I've known him a few years and I've never known him to be unreasonable," I said. "He must understand."

"True, he is, but he's also got Weir in his ear. That guy has it in for me."

"You too? He didn't warm to you over time? Jonah told me you were part of the crew."

"Not in Weir's eyes. You haven't heard him snipe at me. He thinks he runs this boat. He hated Lance, too. My brother was difficult to get along with, I'll be the first to admit it, but Weir didn't help. When Mckade offered him the chance to leave he took it gladly. I think he wanted to get away from Weir as much as anything else." Ava lowered her head and rested it on my shoulder. "Sometimes I think I should've stayed with him, gone with Mckade so I could at least keep an eye on my brother. I don't know. It wasn't easy after we lost our parents. If Jonah hadn't come along when he did, then… everything's just so hard. I wish things could go back to how they were."

A lock of Ava's hair brushed my face and I put my arm around her. She had been shaken hearing about her brother, and after the way Weir had reacted with me I could understand her worry. If we did find her brother then would he want to come back? How would we convince him to rejoin the *Tukino* and his sister with Weir still around? I felt my shoulder getting wet and knew Ava was crying. She was trying not to show it so I just held her and said nothing. There was little I could do to help and offering up platitudes and reassurances about how everything would be fine would only ring hollow. I hated lying and wasn't about to start with Ava.

The boat felt like it was going at full speed. More waves kept crashing against the hull and I wondered how long it would take us to reach Kath and the trading post she had set up. A few days ago, I had been safely cocooned in my apartment with Pippa and Chelsea, completely unaware of how the world was. I was oblivious to what was happening outside of our own four walls. In a way I was glad things had changed. We couldn't have survived much longer living like that. Out here on the open water at least I felt like we had options, a possibility of something different than just surviving.

Ava stirred and looked up at me. She sat upright and wiped her face. The soft tears had gone and she offered me a half-smile.

"Sorry, I don't normally get all melancholy like that."

I shrugged, looking at her blue eyes. Against a backdrop of gray sky littered with dark clouds they sparkled like diamonds.

"No drama. We'll work it out. Jonah is set on finding Kath so at least you'll know soon enough what's happened."

I heard footsteps descending the stairs behind me, and Gills marched in, bringing with him a blast of cold air. He looked at us and I was all too aware that I had my arm around Ava. To his credit, Gills said nothing.

"Ava, you good? Jonah wants you out on deck to help."

"Sure, of course."

Gills frowned. "Why don't you take a moment? It'll be a while before we get to Kath."

I think he could see she was upset and I was grateful that Jonah had sent Gills to fetch her rather than Weir. "Hey, Gills, can I ask you something?"

"What's up?" Gills scratched at the stubble on his chin.

"Douglas said something to me before we parted. Something about a mega... a Megalodon. You know what he was talking about?"

Gills looked shocked and then laughed. "I think he and Honey have a vivid imagination. There's no such thing."

"That's not strictly true," said Ava. "There used to be, right? Didn't Weir say..?"

Gills put one foot on the lowest step and sighed. "Ava, forget what Weir said. The Megalodons were wiped out. They're a myth. Get yourself together and get out on deck. And put the gun away. You won't need that, not yet anyways. I'll tell Jonah you need a minute."

As Gills left us alone I looked at Ava. "You know what they are?"

"I know what I've been told. They're like a prehistoric shark. They don't exist anymore, which is good news for us."

"Why?" I asked, intrigued. "Douglas warned me about them. He said they were monsters. I didn't get a chance to ask him anymore."

"Well they're way bigger than a regular shark. That dead twenty-footer that we ran into earlier? A Megalodon is three or four times the size. They'll eat other sharks, boats, pretty much anything. An animal like that is not something you want to come across. Can you imagine if the *Tukino* hit one of those? It could be bigger than this boat. The mouth on that thing could swallow us whole."

"That's a lot of teeth," I said quietly. Old Mr. Johnson reappeared in my head, disappearing into the jaws of a huge shark. Had that been a Megalodon? Could they have somehow resurfaced now that the land was succumbing to the oceans? Had they not really been extinct but just dormant, hidden in the icy depths of the deep trenches that covered the darkest places of the ocean's floor?

Ava nodded. "Sure is, Luke." She got up and put the gun back in a cupboard. Then she took it back out and tucked it under her jersey, sitting back down beside me a little closer than before. "Just in case." She continued to look at me and I felt like there was a question coming, as if she was plucking up the courage to ask me something important.

"What was New York like? Before all this." Ava opened her arms, indicating the ocean outside. "Forget about ancient sharks. Tell me what the *real* world was like."

I smiled. "You would've liked it. It was so full of life. You could do anything there, anything you wanted to."

"And I bet you took full advantage, right?" Ava dropped her arms and one of her hands came to rest on my leg. "Chelsea told me you helped bring her up but you never married. I can imagine you running around the bars and clubs. I wish I'd had a chance to visit them, but I never got far from home. New York was always a dream to me. Now it's just a creepy place, like so many cities I see. Clogged with dead bodies and completely lifeless."

I couldn't take my eyes off Ava. The blonde hair enveloping her face looked so soft, and her damp eyes sparkled when I looked into them. "It feels like a dream to me now. I can remember what it was like but it doesn't feel real. Everything now is submerged. I mean, you can still see the tops of buildings and a few landmarks are still visible. But the city, the streets and the bars, the cabs and malls, the people who made it what it was are all gone."

Ava's smile faded and I realized we were both sinking into melancholy. I needed to snap us out of it and try to make the atmosphere more positive. I wanted to see Ava smile again. I racked my brains and then it came to me.

"Want to hear a joke?" I asked.

Ava looked at me and raised an eyebrow. "A joke?" She raised her hands defensively. "That's a lot of pressure. If it's not funny you're going to look like an ass."

I cleared my throat. "What did the Pacific Ocean say to the Atlantic Ocean?"

Ava looked at me with a curious expression on her face, but at least I could see her smile returning. "I give up."

"Nothing," I said, "it just waved."

I was relieved when Ava chuckled. She raised one hand to her face and hid her mouth but I definitely heard her laugh. Even over the barrage of waves hitting the boat I could hear her.

"Okay, I know, not the best joke in the world. But if nothing else I like to be topical."

"Topical? You can get *that* from Christmas crackers?"

"Wow. Here I am trying to crack jokes and you just insult me." I rolled my eyes mockingly. "And just when I was starting to like you too."

"Oh yeah? Got any more dad jokes, Uncle Luke?"

"Prepare yourself." I desperately thought and then it popped into my head. "Ready? Why did the crab cross the road?"

Ava looked at me expectantly and pursed her lips. "To find the chicken? No... oh, I don't know."

"To get to the other tide."

Ava began to laugh again and raised her hands to her face.

"No more, please," she muttered through her laughter.

I reached out and grabbed one of her arms. I lowered it so I could see her face. "You know you do that every time you laugh, right?"

Ava said nothing. Her eyes locked on mine and she twisted her arm free from me. Then, to my surprise, she leant toward me and gently kissed me. Her lips locked with mine for only a brief moment but her soft lips were even more amazing than I had thought. I wanted that first kiss to never end. I wanted to talk to her all day, but she pulled away.

"Thanks, Luke. For trying to cheer me up. For listening. For—"

"*Luke*?"

Startled, I turned to see Pippa in the doorway to the galley. "When you can find the time, perhaps you can grace us with your presence? Chelsea isn't feeling well and I'm guessing from the speed we're going that we're heading somewhere with an intent?"

"Sorry, I was just coming to see you when—"

"I can see."

Pippa turned and headed back to the bunkroom we shared. The look on her face told me that I was in serious trouble.

Ava jumped up. "I should be out there helping." She raced out of the galley and up the steps.

"Ava?" I went to follow her and then stopped. I couldn't go, not with Pippa like that. Looking up at the daylight behind Ava, I wanted to go too, but I knew I couldn't. "Wait," I said, "Pippa is just worried about—"

"It's fine, Luke. I have to work."

Ava hurried away and out of the cabin quickly, turning away so I couldn't see her face. I had no idea if she was hurt or angry or just plain embarrassed. I went back to the galley, gathering my thoughts before I went to see my sister. She couldn't have come in at a worse time. I faced the window and looked out at the ocean. Sometimes Pippa acted as if she was my mother. I knew I had a responsibility to her and Chelsea, but why should I feel as if I had done something wrong? What right did she have to make me feel guilty? And besides, what could I do? There was nothing to organize, nothing to do except wait. The ocean was a vast expanse ahead of us, the clouds looming over the horizon like empty threats. We had nothing to do but wait.

CHAPTER 9

"I don't want to hear anymore," hissed Pippa. "I thought this might be a fresh start for all of us, Luke. I don't want to hear about pirates and sharks, and God knows what else is out here."

"Would you rather I lie to you? Isn't it best that you know what we're facing?"

After Ava left me, I ventured into our bunkroom to face the music. I found Chelsea lying on her bunk, her face pale and drawn. Before I could even ask how she was doing Pippa dragged me back into the galley so we could talk without disturbing Chelsea.

"And now we're off to this Kath woman who we don't even know, despite the warning from the other boat. Why, Luke?"

"Look, Jonah knows her and wants to know if she's okay. It's his boat. I can't tell him to turn around. Well, I could but he wouldn't listen. I tried to warn him away but he wasn't interested. Lance is also there, apparently."

"Lance?"

"Ava's brother. She wants to see him."

Pippa shook her head and gave me a glare that was usually reserved for times when I was in Trouble with a capital T. "So, that's what this is about. Ava. I should've guessed."

"No, she's got nothing to do with this." If it wasn't for the fact we were confined to a small boat with nowhere to go I would've left. At least back in the apartment when we argued we each had our own rooms to retreat to. Even other rooms that had no one occupying them could be used. Here, there was no escape. Pippa's wrath would follow me around everywhere.

Pippa pointed to the corridor we had just left. "Luke, your niece is across the hall in there sick, half-scared to death. In case you hadn't noticed half the country is under water and we have no home. Do you really think I intend to live on this boat for the rest of my life? That I would bring Chelsea up on this *trawler*?"

She spat out the last word as if it was a prison cell. Pippa sighed and slumped down on a seat. When she said Chelsea was scared to death she was only partially correct. Pippa was too, not that she would ever admit it. I could see that the situation was getting to her. It was stressful living like this and I had fooled myself into thinking we would be okay. We weren't fishermen. We'd lived in a city all our lives. What did we know about living on a boat? I thought things would just work themselves out, but Pippa had other ideas. She was angry, yet hurt too. I opened my mouth to apologize, to try and explain, but she instantly shut me down dismissively.

"I don't want to hear it anymore, Luke. Why don't you run along to Jonah and Ava? You fit right in. You've got it all worked out, haven't you? Didn't take long for you to move on. I guess I should've known you wanted out of the apartment. Well, you got your way. Well done. You can drop me and Chelsea off at the first port we come to."

I slammed my hand down on the table and the cutlery left aside clattered together. I tried to keep my voice down, but it was impossible to think clearly. "You have *no* right, Pippa. I've stuck by you since you got yourself knocked up with Chelsea. You don't have bragging rights just because she's your child. You think this is easy for me? You think I want things to be this way? All I've ever done is try and do what is best for you and her. I'm not looking for a thank you, but the least you can do is give me the fucking respect I deserve. I haven't abandoned you. I'm right here. I'm trying to figure out what is best for *all* of us."

Pippa raised her face and smirked. "And kissing Ava helps us how?"

"Oh my God, I can't do this. Are you serious?" I reeled away from her sighing. The galley offered no way out. The room rocked from side to side and anything not locked down rattled and banged together. My head was buzzing with anger at my sister. I felt like I just couldn't get through to her. "You've always been like mom," I said, "but you're not *actually* her, you know? Ava has nothing to do with you, or what's going on here. You're not losing me, Pippa, and neither is Chelsea. We're a family. Bitch at me all you want, but that will never change. Jesus, I can't believe you. Just because you fucked up your life you seem to think I can't have one either."

Pippa got up and walked across the room to me slowly. Her brown eyes looked at me with sadness and then suddenly she slapped me across the face. The sting on my cheek was a justifiable rebuke. I knew I had said too much.

"Chelsea *is* my life," said Pippa quietly. "You didn't have to stick around. You want to blame me for being trapped in New York, try again. You were so scared of living you took the easy option. Sure, Uncle Luke was nice to have around. But it was all a bit pathetic. You hung around like a bad smell until it was too late. You missed out on doing anything for yourself or making a life of your own. I have a daughter. What do you have?"

As Pippa's eyes welled up with tears I stumbled back. She had never spoken to me like this. We had spent so much time together, living in the same apartment, and she had never mentioned how she'd felt once. Did she really resent what I'd done, staying to help her? I wanted to shout and scream at her, to tell her she was wrong, that she was only saying this in the heat of the moment, but deep down I knew that she was right. Maybe I had been scared to go out there on my own.

"So, that's that." Pippa sat back down and looked at me. "Anything to add, *Uncle Luke*?"

I was burning with rage, yet I couldn't walk away. We had said too much. It was just the situation we had found ourselves in, the small confines of the galley forcing us to confront everything that had been bottled up for so many years. I'd had enough of arguing. I'd had enough of everything.

"You win," I said calmly, rubbing my sore cheek. "You win." I exhaled loudly. "Whatever you want, Pippa. You want off this boat, we'll do it as soon as we reach land. You want me to stay or go, that's up to you. You have to do what's best for Chelsea. I can't do this anymore. We're like an old married couple. What are we doing, here? I love you, but I can't do *this* anymore."

I broke eye contact from Pippa and walked to the door. I needed some fresh air. The swaying of the boat was making me feel sick. I had to be up on deck where I could see the sky. I couldn't look at Pippa anymore.

"I know you don't like this, Pippa, but the truth is we have to deal with reality. You and Chelsea are on this trawler until we find something better. There's a good chance we're sailing right toward danger. Mckade is a pirate and if we find him we could be in trouble. I can't stop Jonah and I'm not going to try. There could be other trouble too. I know you don't want to hear about the sharks or the Megalodons, but you can't bury your head in the sand."

"Megalodon. What a weird name," said Chelsea from behind me.

I jumped and Chelsea brushed past me to sit by her mother.

"Where did that even come from?" Chelsea caught her mother's withering gaze. "Sorry, I couldn't help but hear you." Chelsea yawned. "If you're going to argue on this boat then you've got to expect someone's going to overhear you. Privacy is about as easy to find on this boat as Wi-fi."

"How are you?" asked Pippa. Instantly she was back in maternal mode, fussing over Chelsea and feeling her forehead. I was pleased to see that she looked a little better. She was at least up on her feet again. I wasn't used to seeing Chelsea knocked down like that.

"I'm fine," said Chelsea, trying to bat away Pippa's advances. "I just had to lie down. My head was beginning to spin and trust me, fish does not taste any better on the way up than it does on the way down."

"Pizza tonight?" I joked.

"I'll pay if you fetch it," replied Chelsea.

"I think you should go lie back down," said Pippa ignoring me. "Your skin feels kinda clammy, and you shouldn't be up and about on an empty stomach. Let me fix you something and I'll bring it in. I'm sure we can find something here to eat that isn't fish." Pippa reached for the tins stacked above her, held in place by a length of bungee cord.

"Tuna. Figures." Pippa put it back as Chelsea broke out laughing.

"Forget it, mom, I'm not hungry anyway. And quit stalling. I asked you a question."

Pippa glared at me and I felt myself shrinking under her stare. It was hardly my fault that Chelsea had overheard us arguing. Well, it was at least a shared effort. Pippa couldn't lay everything on me, as much as she wanted to.

"And don't blame Uncle Luke. If he hadn't agreed to the deal with Jonah we'd be dead, at the bottom of the ocean like our apartment."

I stifled a grin and waited for Pippa to answer.

"What do you want to know, Chelsea?" asked Pippa reluctantly. "I forgot. Does it really matter?"

Chelsea rolled her eyes. "*The Megalodons*? What gives? I heard you talking about sharks. What are they?"

I looked at Pippa who glanced back at me nervously.

"A shark," I explained. "The Megalodon is an ancient beast that eats other sharks. It's—"

"It's a legend," muttered Pippa. "People with over-active imaginations spreading rumors."

It was my turn to glare. Chelsea was mature enough to handle the truth. "Just because you haven't seen it, doesn't mean it isn't real."

"Does it matter?" huffed Pippa. "We avoid sharks no matter how big they are, right? Megalodons or Great Whites or any kind of shark. It is what it is. If it's even real, then there's no point dwelling on it. It's just another creature trying to live in this world like—"

"Like us?" I scoffed. "I don't think so. It's nothing like any other creature on this planet. I saw it, Pippa. I swear, I saw it."

A barrage of noise hit us from above and then I heard the staircase creaking. Footsteps pounded the wooden steps quickly and I looked into the corridor.

"Up top, come on," said Manny breathlessly. "You're not going to believe it."

Before I could question him, he turned and ran back upstairs. "Maybe you should wait here," I said, looking at Chelsea.

"Get real. I'm not staying cooped up in here while all the action takes place elsewhere."

Pippa shrugged. "I guess it doesn't make much difference. But if you feel sick again you tell me, Chelsea."

I suspected Pippa wasn't done with me, but I was pleased Manny had interrupted us. Arguing with my sister wasn't how I wanted to spend the day and I'm sure Chelsea didn't want to listen to us. As I carefully made my way up to the cabin I wondered what had got Manny so excited. Perhaps we had found land or reached Jonah's friend Kath. If there was somewhere dry and safe to live, it might be good for Pippa. I think she needed to know there was more to life than this.

The waves were still crashing into the hull when I made it out onto deck, and the sky was as murky as old dishwater. Jonah had throttled down the engine to a respectable speed and stayed in the wheelhouse while the rest of the crew were stood with Manny on the starboard side of the boat. Ava was sandwiched between Weir and Gills so I decided it was best to leave things alone for now. I approached Manny.

"See it? Over there?" Manny extended an arm and pointed toward shore. There was land, although there was nothing to get excited about. A small rise out of the ocean that stretched for a few miles before sinking back beneath the water. The land looked barren, just patchy soil with a few thin trees. The buildings were sparse and empty. Even from this distance I could see there was nothing there, nobody to talk to, nothing that would draw the attention of the crew.

"What is it?" I asked.

Manny sidestepped me and put a protective arm around Chelsea. "You feeling better?"

Chelsea nodded. "Sure. But what's got you worked up? I can't see anything. Unless there's an invisible movie theatre on that sorry excuse for land."

"I see it," said Pippa. "I see *them*."

Manny handed me the binoculars. "Exactly. It's not the land. Apparently, that's the start of a cove. We can't get much closer or we risk grounding ourselves. Jonah told me he saw a yacht get too close once and they hit some rocks. It's pretty treacherous around here."

"So, if we're not stopping, then why are we here?" I raised the binoculars to my eyes. "What do you see, Pippa?"

I felt hands tenderly turn my head and I swiveled to where I was being directed.

"Look in the water," said a soft voice in my ear. "Forget the land. About twenty feet offshore."

I knew it was Ava. I said nothing but followed her directions. Soon I found what had everyone captivated.

"What are they?" I asked.

"Orcas," replied Ava. "A large pod if I'm not mistaken. I counted at least seven different ones, but it's hard to tell precisely how many there are. They're close to shore and it looks like there's a calf with them."

Gripping the binoculars, I found myself drawn in, amazed at what I was seeing. Several of the whale's fins broke the surface and I could spot their black and white skin slipping through the water. They were swimming slowly, lazily, as if unsure of where to go.

"Do they usually swim so close to shore?" I heard Chelsea ask.

I handed the binoculars back to Manny.

"Not too sure about that," replied Ava. "We figure either they're lost or they're looking for shelter for the little one. Jonah thinks the weather is going to get worse before it gets better. I just think it's pretty cool to see them at all. I've never seen one before."

"Orcas are killers, aren't they? Killer whales?" Pippa leant over the grab-rail and stared at them despondently. "Is it wise to be so close? Won't they resent our presence? What if they attack us or—"

"They won't, not with the calf. As long as we keep our distance they'll be fine and so will we." I looked at Ava. Her eyes were sparkling with wonder, looking out at the pod of whales. I wondered if she felt as awkward about our kiss as I did, but now was not the time to bring it up.

"Resident whale expert, are we?" Pippa looked over her shoulder at Ava. "What were you before joining the crew? Marine biologist?"

I thought I detected sarcasm in Pippa's tone but if Ava did then she hid it well.

"Hardly. I wanted to be a song-writer. I'm not much of a singer but I liked writing music. Not much call for that these days."

Pippa looked back at the ocean. "So, you don't actually know anything about these creatures? I think we should spend less time whale-watching and day-dreaming, and more time actually finding—"

The pod of whales suddenly seemed to turn into a flurry of activity. The ocean around the orcas began to turn white as they thrashed and splashed around. I felt nervous energy punch me in the gut as I watched. It was surreal. They had been calmly swimming along the coast and then suddenly they were panicked.

"What's all the commotion?" asked Chelsea. "What's..?"

Right beside the pod a huge plume of water suddenly gushed into the air like a geyser. It was as if the ocean had exploded and I saw a shape in the water that made me cower in terror. The monster attacked silently. There was no roar, no cry or bellow of rage. The shark flew out of the water, its snout smacking one of the orcas clean out of the sea. The orca was large, almost as large as the *Tukino*, but the shark was bigger. *Much* bigger.

"Oh no!" yelled Ava, grabbing my forearm.

"It's real," muttered Chelsea.

I said nothing but watched in awe as the Megalodon tossed the orca into the air and then rose up out of the sea to devour it. The monster's jaws clamped around the poor orca and I saw red rivers of blood run down its body before it was dragged down under the water. The foamy waves turned a crimson red and I saw the rest of the pod scatter. They were trying to escape but the shallows had them confused. I didn't know whether the shark had forced them into it or if they were just unlucky, but what followed next made me feel sick.

The Megalodon exploded out of the water again, this time smacking two orcas into each other. The shark ripped its teeth into the first one, biting a huge chunk out of its body. The other floated motionless on the surface, either stunned or dead. The shark circled around and then took a massive bite out of the floating orca. By now the ocean had turned red. There was so much blood it was hard to believe it was real.

"I can't watch this," whispered Chelsea.

Pippa took Chelsea's hand and led her away, probably relieved to have an excuse to leave. The carnage was incredible.

Ava kept a firm grip on my arm. I had no words. The pod was decimated as the shark circled around and around them, keeping them contained as it picked them off one by one. It didn't even eat them all. It was as if it was satisfied with just the killing. Perhaps the act of murdering them was all it needed.

"What kind of shark is that?" asked Manny. "Jesus, what... what *is* it?"

I glanced at Ava who met my eyes with a look of fear.

"Megalodon," said Weir plainly. He looked at Ava and his icy stare forced her to remove her arm from mine. "It's nothing. Just another big fucking fish that wants to eat us. Get back to work."

"What the hell is a Megalodon?" asked Manny.

As Ava reluctantly sidled away from me to follow Weir, Manny looked at me. "You know about this?"

"Back in New York. I thought... I don't know. It's—" I had no idea how to explain it. The shark was bigger than I had imagined, bigger than I remembered; the way it was killing the orcas was impressive and yet sobering. If it could do that to powerful beasts like that, to killer whales, then what would it do to our little trawler?

Another plume of water blasted out of the ocean and I saw the massive shark pick out the calf. Whilst I had no knowledge of whales, its size suggested it was still very young, perhaps only a few weeks or months. The orca was thrown into the air and the shark followed it. The orca was swallowed whole.

I felt weak, numb, and unable to accept what I was seeing; yet it was so vividly and undeniably real. The ocean current was bringing the blood toward us and I heard Weir urging Jonah to turn away.

"This changes nothing," I heard Jonah say. "I need to check on Kath. We keep going south."

CHAPTER 10

"Has it gone?"

It had been almost an hour since we'd left behind the decimated pod of orcas. I'd spent much of that time watching the ocean for the tell-tale fin of the Megalodon, in case it was following us. Nothing broke the surface of the water apart from clumpy seaweed and debris that I assumed had floated out from the mainland. There were a lot of plastic bags and bottles, rubbish and flotsam that the ocean had swallowed only to spit back up. There was precious little visibility that mankind used to rule the planet, but our mark was everywhere.

"I think so. I think it's long gone." I looked at Chelsea and Pippa. They had been shaken by the events we'd witnessed and I had to admit I was too.

Pippa shivered and wrapped her arms around Chelsea.

"Why don't you go back down?" I suggested. "There's nothing you can do up here."

"No way. We're staying where we can see what's coming." Pippa gripped Chelsea tighter.

"So that was one of those things? A Megalodon?" asked Chelsea.

I looked out at the ocean. The wake we left dispersed quickly and there was no sign of the huge shark. It had stayed to feed on the whales and apparently not noticed us. "Yes. That was one."

Pippa sighed. "Where are we even going, Luke? We don't know this Kath. We should ask Jonah where he can drop us. He must know a safe place where we can get back on the mainland. There has to be somewhere we can live. One of his traders, perhaps? We can find a new home. All of us, I mean. We shouldn't be out here. This isn't us, Luke. This isn't our home and it never will be."

I looked at Chelsea to see if she agreed with her mother, but there was no indication either way. Chelsea just looked sad, lost in her thoughts. It was obvious Pippa wasn't going to adjust to a life out on the ocean. Chelsea could, but she was too young to go it alone. She needed her mother and as much as Pippa would hate to admit it, she needed me too. We were going to have to get back to the mainland and make a fresh start there. I have to admit I felt like it was the wrong decision. I wasn't convinced that it was any safer on land than it was on the water.

"I'll talk to him."

Pippa ran her hands over Chelsea's head and kissed her forehead.

A laughing seagull flew close to the boat and I watched as its white wings propelled it through the air without even moving. It rose higher against the gray sky, floating on a current, and I felt jealous of its freedom. I had no desire to fly but I would've traded places with the bird right then. Its yellow eyes seemed to look at me for a split-second and then it was gone, darting back from where it had come without a sound.

"Almost there," said Gills, walking past me.

"Almost where?" I asked. "Does this Kath live on a boat like you or does she have a place?" It occurred to me that if she had a home on dry land then she might be open to taking us in, just temporarily.

"She has a condo. Didn't Jonah tell you? She controls the oil refinery out there."

I had no interest in the oil, but the fact she lived in a condo was good news. Perhaps there was a chance for us. There may even be an empty apartment close to her. If we could help with the refinery perhaps it was an opportunity to strike up trading again, to find a new home for Chelsea.

As Gills took Manny into the cabin I went to the side of the boat and looked out across the water. Leaving the *Tukino* so quickly was at odds with what I had begun to expect. I thought we might make a go of it out here under Jonah's command, but I could see Pippa wasn't going to come around. I would convince myself that this was the right thing to do. I could tell myself that I was doing the right thing getting Pippa and Chelsea off the boat. Yet I knew deep down in my heart that it wasn't what *I* wanted. And I had to realize that part of the reason, hell a big part of the reason that I wanted to stay, was Ava.

Gills and Manny emerged from the cabin carrying guns with them.

"You think that's necessary?" I asked, as they made their way to Weir.

"Jonah thinks so," replied Manny. "You saw how messed up that other boat was. They said there was trouble so we have to be prepared, right?"

Weir took a gun as Gills tucked one for himself under his arm.

"Manny, you take one," said Weir. "I want you down below deck. You're the last line of defense. Just in case."

"Right. Okay, well if you want." Manny took the gun. "It's been a while since I handled one, but—"

Weir grunted. "If you can't handle it, then—"

"No, it's fine. I'll be fine." Manny looked at me almost apologetically and headed toward the wheelhouse as Jonah came out. He took a gun and waved Manny inside.

"Jonah, what gives?" Ava wiped the sea-spray from her face and approached him. "I can handle a weapon, you know I can. Four guns, four crew members. I'm sure Manny can take care of himself. How come..?"

"I think it best you stay up here and help me," replied Jonah. "I want you by my side, Ava. Back at the bridge, now."

"Why?" Ava pouted and put her hands on her hips. "Don't give me any shit about me being a girl again. I thought we were past that."

"It's not that," said Weir, smiling. "If Lance is there we can't have you running off on your own with dreams of rescuing that fool. I think it's really a matter of trust."

"So, we're going to Wilmington and that's it? I get no say in this? My brother is in as much danger as Kath if Mckade has them, so why not let me help? Jonah, why you insist on listening to Weir, I will never understand."

"Enough, Ava. Weir's right. I can't risk you compromising us. There's too much at stake."

"Right, and I'm to stay by your side like a poodle. And do what? Wait for Weir to find my brother? He doesn't give a damn. I may as well be waiting for the return of the Messiah."

I couldn't help but chuckle. Ava had a point. Whatever had happened with Kath meant Mckade and Lance were involved. Ava wasn't about to stay on the boat and wait to hear.

Jonah glared at me. "Luke, get yourself to the bow. Yell out if you see anything. Gills is monitoring the deck so he'll be around if you need anything."

I wanted to stay and argue for Ava. I knew Jonah was just sending me away to get rid of me. "Don't you think Ava has a right to..?"

"When the Captain gives an order, grease-monkey, you follow it," said Weir gruffly. He fingered the gun in his hands idly. "Disobedience is taken seriously so I suggest you get gone, *boy*."

I offered Weir my best smile and raised my middle finger to him. It was Ava's turn to chuckle.

"I'm going with Luke, Jonah," said Ava. "And when we finally get to Wilmington I'll be sure to trot back here and keep you company while Weir fucks everything up as usual."

It was a delight to see Weir's face fall and I took hold of the grab rail to make my way up to the bow. Ava followed me and when we reached the front of the ship I asked her what she meant when she'd said Weir would mess things up.

"He's just always interfering. We used to have a good deal with a guy in Virginia but Weir took offense to something he said and so that was that. The only reason Kath tolerates him is because she's sweet on Jonah."

"I guess we just have to put up with him, right?"

"Nothing else we can do."

I leant over the railing. The boat was ploughing through the ocean and spraying us with icy salt-water. In the distance, a rainbow was forming close to the mainland. A gentle green slope cowered beneath a black cloud resembling a giant umbrella. I tried to identify where we were, but the landscape gave me little to go on. Across from the green slope was higher ground. Atop it sat a rundown farmhouse flanked by two barns. Long grass grew up the wooden boards of the building and ivy ran along the roof, dripping from the guttering like green rain. A blue car sat silently outside, parked up for eternity until the ocean or the rust claimed it first. Further away I saw more buildings, the facades a light-gray and speckled with holes as if they had been used for target practice. I saw what looked like the first towns leading to Wilmington but there was nobody alive. The coastline was deserted. We began to pass boats, mostly smaller ones, yachts and skiffs, some anchored, some drifting free. It was beginning to feel like there were very few people left. How many had managed to get inland before the waters rose so dramatically? How many had stayed in their homes like we had and not been able to escape when their apartments and houses were submerged? The boat veered toward the coast and I noticed we were slowing. We passed next to some power lines that were protruding above the surface and then carried on past more buildings. I saw rooftops barely three feet above the waterline, some of which looked as if they had been home to several people.

One building rose up taller than the others and as we passed by I spotted words on the eastern wall that had been scrawled in black paint: **GO BAcK**

A skull and bones had been painted next to the words though whoever had done it must have long ago left. The building was empty despite still being almost ten floors clear of the water. We continued on and we came close to another building, an apartment complex not dissimilar to the one we had left behind in New York. Drapes flapped uselessly from the broken windows and smashed pieces of furniture drifted aimlessly around its base, as if seeking a way back in. There was more painting on the building, this time in bright red letters: **MCKADE COUntRY**

I felt Ava tense up. "Babylon, this ain't," she muttered.

"You've been here before?" I asked.

Ava looked miserable. "A couple of times to see Kath and get diesel. We usually come in from the south though. This is weird. I haven't been through this area before. We must be over the old coastline."

"You see the signs?" I wanted to know it wasn't just me that was feeling nervous about going in any further.

"Mckade is full of hot air. Probably just trying to steer people away if he's taken over the refinery. He was always full of himself. That's how he convinced Lance to go with him."

As the boat slowed further, more buildings appeared in the water, tall erect structures that hadn't yet succumbed to the ocean.

I spotted one with balconies beneath every window. Years ago it would have been a modern complex of luxury apartments with ocean-views. Now it was a derelict monolith, no more luxurious than the bunk I slept on in the *Tukino*. Staring at the upper floors untouched by the ocean I thought I saw movement behind the glass of one apartment. With the movement of the boat it was impossible to get a clear look at it. There were clothes hung out across the balcony, but I wasn't sure if they were fresh or just remnants of an old life. I stared intently at the glass but saw no movement again. On the balcony beneath it a sheet had been draped over the balustrade and more warnings painted on it: **tURN ARoUND NOW**

I looked down at the sea below us, my hands gripping the rail. I had to admit I didn't know what to expect. Had Mckade put up those signs or were they warnings from others who had been here before? The weather was unsettled and now that the boat had slowed down, I was beginning to feel a little on edge. I looked back over my shoulder to check on Pippa and Chelsea. They were talking to Gills but seemed fine, or at least as fine as they could be. Pippa looked sad with her arms hugging Chelsea, and in that moment, I would have done anything to be able to go back and change things. We should have left New York when we had the chance. Maybe then we could be living on the land, living in a real home, growing fruit and vegetables instead of barely surviving and relying on strangers. Pippa thought I had chosen the easy way out by sticking with her, but in truth I just felt responsible for her. How could I leave her and Chelsea alone? Pippa had already seen one man in her life leave and I wasn't about to be the next.

"Luke, about before." Ava put her hand over mine. "I should apologize for running out like that."

I looked at her. I'd only known her for a few days and yet staring into those blue eyes I felt like I had known her my whole life. The feeling was unnerving. I had never had that with anyone before. It felt like she was a part of me, the piece of my life I had been missing all my adult life.

"I want to… I just want to explain."

Ava tugged on her red beanie, pulling it lower to cover her ears. The cold wind made me shiver too, but I knew Pippa was still watching me. If I made any kind of move toward Ava I could expect another lecture, so I waited to hear what Ava had to say.

Suddenly, the boat jolted and Ava's hand slipped off mine. It felt like something had hit the bottom of the hull.

"That's not good. We've hit something," said Ava. She stood up straight and looked around at Gills. "High ground?"

Gills looked confused and turned to face the wheelhouse. "Jonah?"

"No, we're clear," replied Jonah confidently.

Weir marched to the stern and looked around. We waited impatiently and after a minute he returned with a perplexed look on his face. "Nothing."

I followed Ava as she made her way across deck to Gills. "That wasn't nothing, Gills."

"No, it wasn't."

"Could be a boat or vehicle that's washed out?" suggested Ava. She itched her nose and then lowered her voice. "Gills, we shouldn't be doing this. It isn't safe. We don't usually come this way. What if..?"

Another bump caused us all to jump. There was an audible banging sound as something hit the hull again. I almost lost my footing but Ava grabbed my arm and I managed to stay upright. Pippa and Chelsea came to us, and we all converged by the winch for the beams.

"Still getting your sea-legs, huh?" Gills took in a deep lungful of fresh air. "I think I'd better check on Manny down below. Just in case."

"Mom, maybe we should go too," said Chelsea timidly.

"You feeling sick again?" asked Pippa. She looked at me, but not before noticing Ava still holding onto me. "You know, it's probably nothing. Jonah knows what he's doing, right?"

"Of course. The boat's fine." Pippa was looking at me with distaste. She was polite enough to not say anything in front of Ava, but I could tell she was bursting to. As much as I respected my sister she had no reason to be jealous of Ava. "It's probably just debris. You've seen how much is littering the water around here. We're close to land. It's probably—"

The next jolt knocked me clean off my feet. There was a huge crashing noise and I suddenly found myself flat on my back. The hard deck knocked the breath out of me and I felt sea-spray splatter my face. A hand reached for me, grabbing my arm and I turned to see Pippa reaching for me. Terror was etched over her face and I took her hand as the boat began to tilt alarmingly to one side.

"Uncle Luke!" screamed Chelsea.

She wrapped her arms around the grab rail and as I struggled to get up I heard Jonah shouting orders, something about having to go back. I coughed and gasped for breath as I got to my knees. Pippa held onto me for her life and together we crawled over to Chelsea. The boat was tilting to port, so we had to climb up to reach the safety railings. Once I knew that Pippa and Chelsea were safe I looked around to find Ava. She had slid across the deck and was hanging onto the cabin door that had blown open. The A-frame loomed overhead menacingly. There were a lot of things on the boat that could hurt us. Even though everything was anchored down it was still unnerving.

"Ava? Are you okay?"

She nodded, but the look on her face suggested otherwise. She looked across at Jonah and I could see he was struggling in the wheelhouse. Even Weir was helping him. Both men were by the console. I couldn't see what they were doing, but I understood they were trying to control the trawler. I could hear the whine of the engine as the boat struggled against whatever was beneath it.

"Christ, Jonah, what the hell is going on?" shouted Ava. "What should I do? Gills is—"

Just then whatever was beneath the boat seemed to let go and we lurched back down to the ocean, the boat rocking violently as we hit the water. I twisted to grab Pippa and Chelsea knowing the starboard side of the boat might even go under the water, and we hit the ocean with such force that it took my breath away again. The impact of the boat hitting the water sent shudders through my body. I heard Pippa and Chelsea scream as the surface rushed up to meet us and then suddenly we were in the ocean. I felt the cold water pull at me and I tried to wrap my arms around Chelsea. She slipped from my grasp and I frantically reached for her. Letting go of the grab rail was a mistake. Instantly I was sucked out into the ocean. I tried to keep my eyes open, but the saltiness stung my eyes and it quickly became dark. The clouded sky offered little light and once I was submerged the weak sunlight only penetrated the water a couple of feet. I caught glimpses of the boat righting itself and Pippa hanging onto the rail. I caught a glimpse of Ava on deck falling toward the railing, and then I saw the underside of the hull. The water became darker quickly and I kicked hard, trying to propel myself upwards. The coldness of the ocean was hardly unexpected but it was still a shock. My clothes felt like lead weights and my lungs were burning. I couldn't believe I had fallen in. Trying not to panic I stopped kicking for a moment and let the ocean take me. My body was being tossed around like a rag in a washing machine and I had to hope that Chelsea had managed to hang on. If I was the only one who had fallen in I was going to feel beyond stupid. As the water calmed around me, I opened my eyes. I wasn't even sure which way was up and I had to get my bearings so I could swim back up. When I opened my eyes, my heart exploded with fear and my blood ran cold.

A shark was swimming around the boat. And not just any shark, but *the* shark. It appeared to be the one that had killed the orca pod as it was at least as big. The massive creature seemed to move lazily as if it had all the time in the world. I caught sight of the monster slowly moving away from the hull as the saltwater pinched at my eyes. Its sleek body moved silently through the water, but I had no doubt that it was longer than the *Tukino* and about twice the size. The shark's gray body disappeared quickly into the murky ocean and I knew I was lucky it was swimming away from me. If it had been going the other way I had no doubt I would've been on the menu. But how long did I have before it returned?

CHAPTER 11

I pushed myself upward, straining with every muscle I had to reach the surface. I was struggling to hold my breath and every kick of my legs felt like it was taking too long. The ocean wanted me to stay, to join Davey Jones and the half of the world it had already claimed.

"Luke? Luke!"

I heard the shouts as I burst free and sucked in a mouthful of air. Spluttering, I tried not to think about what was potentially swimming beneath me. I needed oxygen first and foremost. My body ached for it and I shook my head as I gratefully breathed in a mouthful of clean air.

"Where are they?"

The boat listed before me and although I tried to see who was up there calling out, I couldn't see. Waves kept crashing around me and it was hard to stay afloat. Kicking and using my arms was testing my strength, and with the weight of my clothes threatening to suck me back under, it took everything I had not to panic.

"Luke, grab the life saver."

I heard something splash in the water close by and spotted the ring which had saved Manny just a few days ago. I began to swim toward it, all too aware of how exposed I was, and what was lurking in the ocean depths somewhere close by.

"Chelsea?"

Pippa's voice sounded frantic. I grabbed the ring and wiped my face. For the first time since being plunged into the cold water I could see the boat. It was intact at least. I'd feared the shark may have ripped a hole in the hull. Perhaps it was just being inquisitive and had figured out the trawler wasn't as tasty as whale meat. Pippa, Manny and Gills were lined up by the safety rail, their eyes fixed on me. Gills had his hands wrapped around the rope that was attached to the life saver, and began to pull me in.

"Luke, have you seen her?" asked Pippa. "Where is she?"

Dread filled me as I realized Chelsea must have slipped into the water as well. I looked around me and tried to find her.

Nothing had changed. The buildings were still and silent, the ocean dark and menacing, and there was no sign of life anywhere. I couldn't let them pull me back on board without her, so I let go of the life saver and plunged my head under the water. I heard cries of frustration from the others, but there was no way I could return knowing she was still out there.

My eyes stung again and I blinked rapidly, trying to see her. She couldn't have gone far from me. The water was just as difficult to swim through underneath and I barely got six feet when I saw something. Beneath the hull a shape gradually began to form. It was like a shadow, forming slowly in front of me. It was large, larger than the hull, and I suspected the Megalodon had returned. If it was coming back we had little time to avoid it. I had to find Chelsea and get back on the boat quickly.

"I can't see her," I shouted, as my head broke the surface.

"What about Jonah?" Gills asked.

I was stunned. If he was in the water too we were going to run out of time. I didn't even know if the others had seen what I had, or if they knew what had hit the boat.

"Luke, you have to… you have to—"

I saw Pippa breakdown, her hands clinging onto the railing as tears fell down her face. My heart ached to see her like that. I felt terrible knowing Chelsea was in the ocean. She might not be my daughter, but she had always been my priority, even over Pippa. Suddenly, something brushed against my leg and I pulled away fearing the worst, terrified that something with big teeth was about to grab me.

"There!" yelled Manny. "Right there"!

I took a deep breath and sank under the water again. Floating right beneath me was Chelsea's lifeless body. Her sandy hair waved at me slowly and her closed eyes suggested she was in a deep sleep. Her spread-eagled arms made her look content, but I had precious little time to marvel at how peaceful she looked. I kicked furiously and managed to reach her, wrapping one arm around her waist. I spun around and as I dragged her to the surface I caught sight of the shark once more, swimming dangerously close to the bottom of the hull.

"Take her!" I yelled as we broke free of the water that kept trying to pull us back under. I grabbed the life saver again and put it over Chelsea's head. Hearing Pippa scream sent shivers down my spine. I was already on edge knowing the shark was beneath us, and Chelsea didn't appear to be breathing. I tried to think things through logically. Get Chelsea on the boat and then get the hell away from here. One of the crew had to know CPR. Just get Chelsea back on the boat.

As Gills and Manny pulled at the heavy rope, I pushed the ring toward the boat. It felt like hours, yet in reality it took no time at all before we were at the side of the *Tukino*. I pushed Chelsea upward as the others reached down and pulled her up. Once more I was sent under the surface. Bubbles erupted around me as the trawler's engine kicked into life.

"Wait!" ordered Gills from above me. "Weir, just fucking *wait*!"

I couldn't see what was going on up there, and as I reached up for help I felt arms grab me. Finally, I was pulled up onto the deck and I collapsed in a soggy heap.

"Is she..?"

"She'll be okay," said Ava leaning over me.

She swept the wet hair from my face and I rolled over to my side to see Gills and Pippa nursing Chelsea back to life.

Ava rubbed my back. "Gills brought her round. Thank God. Are you okay, Luke?"

I felt exhausted. My arms and legs hurt, throbbing and aching, and my back was sending sharp jolts of pain to my brain. As I lay there on the boat I just stared at Chelsea. We had come so close to losing her. It could have ended up so horribly different. What was I thinking? Bringing her and Pippa onto the boat had been a stupid idea, *my* idea, and the sooner we found somewhere safe to live again the better.

I coughed as another shiver ran down my cold back. "I'm fine," I lied. "Is everyone okay?" I turned to look at Ava, but she avoided my eyes. I was freezing cold, but when Ava turned away from me I felt like I was atop Everest, breathless and turned to stone. "Who?"

Ava bit her lip. "It's Jonah. We can't find him. Weir wants to leave."

I sat up and coughed again. It felt like the entire ocean had gone down my throat and I spat the foul-tasting saliva in my mouth onto the deck. "Fucking idiot."

"Don't," said Ava, as I stood.

She knew instinctively what I was thinking. Weir had taken control of the boat. It was just what he wanted. Even as we stood there, Chelsea still crying and me still recovering, I could see him turning the wheel. I could hear the engine powering up as he prepared to leave.

"Hey, man." Manny was still stood by the railing, peering over the side into the murky water. "You good?"

I nodded. "Any sign of him?"

Manny shook his head despondently and shrugged. "Nothing."

I looked at Ava. "I owe Jonah. He came to help me and my family when we needed him. I can't let him go like this. I owe him more than just leaving him out there."

Ava made an attempt to grab my shoulder, but I shook her off and marched towards Weir. "Keep looking," I told Manny. "Ava, help him. We're not leaving without him."

Weir smiled as I approached the wheelhouse, looking as if he had won a battle instead of starting a war.

"You need to wait, Weir. Jonah is down there. Give us two minutes more and we can find him. You saw what happened to Chelsea. We found her, we can find him. It isn't over for Jonah, not yet. He deserves more respect than this."

Weir pulled harder on the wheel and I felt the boat turn around.

"I'm not asking again. *Wait.*"

Weir looked at me with utter disdain and sniffed. "*Too bad.* I liked Jonah but he wasn't a friend, he was a colleague. The Captain's gone, and that means I'm in charge of this boat and crew. The safest course of action is to retreat until we know what hit us. We could be taking on water. Jonah would do exactly the same if it were me. We're leaving until—"

"Until you find a fucking backbone? That's going to be a long wait." I lunged for the console but Weir pulled a gun out from under his oilskins, pointing it right at my chest.

"Touch that again, grease-monkey, and you'll be joining our dear departed Captain."

"Weir, do you even know what is going on? You know what hit us don't you?"

Weir shrugged. "Probably struck a tanker or truck. Doesn't matter now. We're free of it."

It gave me no satisfaction to tell him he was wrong. "That wasn't a truck. That was a shark. Not just a shark, but a Megalodon."

For one moment Weir looked at me differently. He believed me. I know he did. But then the old Weir took over. "You lubbers are all the same. You don't know anything about what's out here. You're full of bull, just like Lance. I feel bad for Jonah, but I know he would get us moving. I've seen—"

"There, in the water!" Ava's voice caused me to turn away from Weir. She was pointing into the water as Gills and Manny raced next to her. "I see him."

Forgetting Weir, I ran to Ava. I saw Jonah too. He was alive, swimming toward us. "Christ, get that life saver to him, quickly," I shouted before I realized Gills had already grabbed it.

Watching Jonah struggle against the rough seas I wondered if I should jump in to help. I was freezing cold and soaked through already, so what did it matter if I got wetter? I kicked off my shoes and grabbed the rail.

"Luke, you can't go back in there," said Ava, studying my face. Her blue eyes sank into mine and I hesitated. "You need to get warm. Pippa's taking Chelsea down to her bunk. You should go too. Let me deal with this."

Manny kicked off his shoes next to me. "I'll go."

Watching Manny prepare to jump into the ocean I had to admit I felt relieved that he had offered to go. It wasn't the cold or the water that put me off going back in, but the knowledge of what was down there. I hadn't imagined the shark. I hadn't ballooned it up in my head to a size bigger than it actually was; the Megalodon was real and it was down there somewhere.

"No," I said, "you can't go, Manny. There's something down there."

I saw Jonah struggling to reach the life saver and I felt awful for him. But was it worth more of us risking our lives to save him? Ava and Manny waited for me to explain, looking at me as if I was mad.

"The Megalodon," I revealed. "I saw it. That's what hit us. It's down there right now." I waited for the inevitable questions, or for them to tell me that I had probably imagined it. But Manny simply nodded as if it was the most obvious explanation for it all, whilst Ava simply turned to the ocean and screamed at Jonah.

"Hurry, Jonah. Hurry!"

Jonah was weak. He was old and fully clothed, and the waves were pushing him back, propelling him further away from the boat. Weir, to his credit, had stopped the boat, but it wasn't doing Jonah any good. His energy had been sapped and he wasn't going to make the life saver. Every time he took a breath I could see him fighting back the water that threatened to engulf him.

"Fuck it," I said, and I climbed up over the safety rail.

"Luke, don't."

I should've listened to Ava's words, but I ignored them and dived into the ocean. Even though I was cold the icy water still shocked me when I hit it. I held my breath and went under, aiming to come up as close to Jonah as I could. When I was submerged I opened my eyes and nearly died of shock. The Megalodon was right beneath us, coming up at the boat. I saw its huge gaping jaws lined with tremendous teeth, sharp enough to rip open anything, including the metal underbelly of a small trawler. Its sleek body barreled through the water at surprising speed and I knew the boat was done for. At that speed it would tear a hole right through the hull and sink us for sure. Somehow, it diverted itself away at the last moment. I don't know if it was because I had jumped in and distracted it, but something caught its attention and instead of crashing right through the boat it merely glanced off it. The shark's fin struck the underside of the *Tukino*. I heard the impact and felt the pressure wave hit me the moment it struck. Then the shark turned and swam right past me. Maybe I was too small for it, maybe it was just playing with us, but whatever the reason, it ignored me. It was barely fifteen feet away and as it swept by me I felt its powerful strength. Its body was long and graceful, fins as tall as the apartment complex I had grown up in. The motion of the beast flying by me disturbed the water and it felt as if a hurricane had hit us. I was tossed back and forth with no control over where I ended up. The most terrifying aspect of the monster were the eyes, deep black orbs that seemed to penetrate into my soul; they showed no remorse or intelligence, just a belligerent creature with an appetite for destruction and death.

As the giant shark's tail whipped past me I broke the surface and gasped. The fin was receding into the distance now. Was it leaving? Had the shark had enough of toying with us, or was it just steeling itself to come back for more? I saw the life saver within reach and Jonah just a few more feet away. A rain had begun to fall now making it difficult to see and I wiped my face, afraid that if I took my eyes off him we would lose him again. Voices behind me were calling and crying out, but their words were drowned out by the falling rain that splattered against the surface of the sea like icy bullets.

"Jonah, come to me," I yelled. "Hurry, Jonah."

The ocean water around me felt different, thicker. I realized it was turning bright red, washing around me like dye. I mentally checked myself over but felt no pain.

"Jonah?"

He didn't answer me. I heard a faint gurgle and swam toward him. The red water splashed my face and stung my eyes. I knew what it was, what it *had* to be, but I couldn't think about that. I splashed through it, drenching myself in cold water and warm blood, the sinking feeling in my stomach propelling me onwards. I had to get Jonah out of there before the shark came back.

"Jonah, hold on," I said urgently. His face was pale and drawn, and his eyes labored to focus on me. I grabbed the life saver and pushed it down over his head just as I had done with Chelsea. He wrapped his arms around it and I signaled for the others to pull him up. I swam with him as far as I could, unaware of exactly what his injuries were. It was only when we reached the trawler, and Gills and Manny pulled him up, that I saw both of his legs were gone. As Jonah dangled above me, fleshy entrails and intestines fell from his waist. The shark had severed him in two, slicing off his legs and leaving only the upper half of his body. More blood rained down on me as they pulled him into the boat, and the smell of death soaked my head.

Ava and Manny helped me up and then the horrible reality of what had happened sunk in. Jonah lay on the deck, or at least what was left of him. Gills knelt beside him as blood pooled around them, spilling over the deck as the boat began to turn. Jonah mumbled something as Gills took his hands.

Ava whispered something in my ear as she hugged me.

"I know," I replied quietly. "It'll be over soon."

Jonah was splayed out on the deck of his boat gutted like one of the fish he used to catch. His innards were exposed for all to see, and the life was literally draining out of him before my eyes. His eyes rolled back and Gills leant over him, whispering something in his ear that was only audible between the two of them. I hoped it was a prayer or some words of consolation. There was nothing we could do for him. We all knew it, not that it made it any easier to accept. Jonah had been like a father to me, and I expected Ava felt similarly. The crew had known him for years. Jonah wasn't supposed to die like this, not cut in half gasping for breath on his own boat.

Manny put a hand on my shoulder and said nothing. His eyes were threatening to spill more salty water. I knew if we spoke he would only set me off. Manny nodded at me, acknowledging that I had done the right thing in bringing him back, even if it was so we could simply read him his last rights. Manny turned away and I felt Ava's head against my neck, her tears soaking into my collar once more. Gills lifted his head and looked at me.

"He's gone. He's gone."

Jonah was dead.

CHAPTER 12

"Shape up, I need you," shouted Weir. "This boat won't sail itself."

Dumbstruck, I looked at him. Had he not seen what had just happened? Did he not realize we were all in shock? I couldn't even say I was grieving for Jonah yet, it was too soon; the man had been talking to us, looking after us for the past few days, and to be suddenly without him felt surreal. With Jonah laid out on the deck like that, I felt awful. Thankfully, Manny appeared a moment later and placed a blanket over Jonah. Not having to look at the body didn't change anything, but it gave him a little decency at least.

"Save your whining," said Weir, without any prompting, as if he could read my mind. "In case you hadn't noticed we have company. That bitch hasn't had her fill yet."

The *Tukino* was picking up speed, charging through the water and I realized we were facing the open ocean. The land was behind us now, and Weir nodded his head in the direction of the tall apartments we had seen earlier. There, in the distance, was the shark's fin, cutting through the water like an eagle soars through the air. The fin was huge, masterful, and I knew the shark meant business. It was heading for us at full pelt. Weir had to get us moving, and fast. As much as I hated the man, he was right. We had to lose it before that thing came back and took us all down.

"What do we do?" asked Gills, wiping his eyes with the back of his arm. Blood had soaked into his chest and sleeves, and Jonah's death would hit him hard, probably harder than any of us, but I knew it would take more than that to stop him.

"Jesus, it's coming back," said Ava, her fingers gripping me, her nails pinching my skin even through my shirt. "It's coming. It's really real."

I didn't know what the hell we could do. "Manny, you still have your gun?" I asked.

"You bet. It's not leaving my side, not now."

"Be ready. You too, Gills. That thing gets close enough, you shoot it. Maybe we can scare it off. I doubt we can kill it with what we have, but we might be able to injure it. Let's make it think twice about attacking us again."

"I need to help Weir plot a course to Kath," said Ava, her voice breaking. "Maybe she can take us in. Maybe she can help if we can outrun it."

Manny and Gills took up a position to the boat's starboard. I was grateful that Pippa had taken Chelsea down below. If she had seen Jonah, she would have freaked out. As it was, I was still going to have to explain what had occurred here; that was assuming the Megalodon didn't capsize the boat and kill us all first.

"Weir," I said, approaching him with hidden trepidation and loathing. I hadn't forgotten how he had pulled a gun on me, or how callous he had been when confronted with Jonah's grisly death. We had to have him on side for now and he *was* the Captain of the ship. "Ava can help you get to Kath's. If Kath is okay then maybe she can shelter us until it's gone. You think we can get the *Tukino* going fast enough to outpace this monster?"

Weir yanked the wheel sharply as he navigated us past a floating container. Its rusty doors were shut tight and whatever cargo it held would remain a secret. The container flashed past us as we sped by and I hoped our increasing speed was enough.

"If I can get us past that barge and beyond the freighter up ahead, then maybe. And that's a *big* if," said Weir, looking over his shoulder.

I knew he was looking at the fin, judging how far back it was. I didn't want or need to know. It would do no good to see how close it was, so I focused my energies on helping Weir.

I looked ahead at the barge he had mentioned and the huge cargo ship just beyond that. The derelict ships were motionless, either abandoned or anchored waiting for help that never came. I figured if Weir could take us in and around them, there was a chance the shark might lose us, perhaps even tackle one of the bigger boats. It didn't know what was on board and it seemed like as good an idea as any.

"Weir," Ava said breathlessly, "we need to go due southwest or we're going to miss Kath's. She's our best bet. Other than

Mckade, and God knows where he is, there's no one else around here. She might have weapons or know what to do."

Weir looked at Ava and raised one eyebrow. "I know, girly. I don't need a map to tell me that. We're not going to Kath's."

Confusion spread over Ava's face and I had to admit I was concerned. Whilst I didn't know Kath, it made sense to seek help. We had a lot to deal with and a friendly face was just what we needed. She had an apartment which meant sanctuary, away from the water, away from the boat, and away from the shark chasing us.

"We can't just keep going out into the ocean and hope it loses interest." Ava rolled her eyes at me, the tears on her cheeks dry and her confusion turning to frustration. "Come on, Weir, just let me help."

"Help? Throw Jonah back in the Goddamn ocean. He's no good to us like that. The rest of his body might just give that shark something else to think about other than us. You're damn right it's not going to lose interest. It's had a taste of blood now, got the scent for us. The Megalodon is a cruel monster, worse than anything else you might encounter in any ocean. I thought I'd seen it all but this... this is nothing but a fifty–foot mouth with the instinct to kill. It won't lose interest, so *we* have to lose it. Our only way is to get to shallower water where it can't follow us. Soon as we get around that barge we're going to a place where that shark can't get at us, the Frying Pan Shoals. Kath will have to wait."

"The shoals," said Ava incredulously. "Are you *insane*? You'll ground us and lose the *Tukino* if we don't drown first. You might as well let the shark take us now."

Weir grunted. I noticed the gun tucked under his oilskin poking out of his belt loop. I thought of grabbing it, of forcing him to take us to Kath's or wherever Ava thought we were safest, but something told me to wait. A wrestling match would do none of us any good. And the truth was, some of what Weir said actually made a horrible sense. If we could get to shallow water then presumably the giant shark wouldn't be able to follow us.

"Weir, you must have flare guns or something else we can use. If it gets close to us we can try and ward it off."

Weir looked at me skeptically.

"Look, I understand you're the captain now, I can deal with that. And if you say heading to these shoals is our best option then I'm all for it. But my sister and niece are under our feet right now and their lives are depending on us getting this right. So let me help. Give me a weapon so Jonah didn't die needlessly and we can fight back."

Weir seemed to consider it and as he opened his mouth I waited for the inevitable criticism or order to get off his boat.

"Galley. Look under the seat. Flare guns are there."

"Jesus." Ava suddenly turned on me. "You're taking his side?"

"I'm doing what I can to protect my family, what I can to protect you. Maybe Weir is right about shallower water."

"And maybe you're just another asshole out for himself." Ava stormed away.

"One job, before you go, grease-monkey" said Weir. "Toss Jonah's remains overboard. I wasn't kidding about giving that shark a diversion."

"I'll think about it," I replied, leaving Weir to navigate us to the shoals.

I had no intention of throwing Jonah overboard. Weir just wanted him off the ship, to remove all trace of the former captain so he could assume command without a constant reminder of how he had got it. Did he really think the shark would stop to munch on Jonah? Even if I did throw him into the sea, the Megalodon would swallow him whole without even pausing. As I marched to the cabin, trying to ignore the twists and turns of the boat that threatened to trip me up, I wondered if I should go down and explain to Pippa what was going on. I wanted to, but time wasn't something we had much of. She was just going to have to wait. If I saw her when I was retrieving the flare guns I would tell her, but otherwise she was just going to have to figure it out herself and concentrate on looking after Chelsea.

I went through the wheelhouse and made my way down to the galley. It wasn't long before I had two flare guns in my hands. As I left the galley, Pippa poked her head out of the room where

Chelsea was lying down. I could see in the darkness that she was lying on her side, her eyes closed.

"Sleeping?" I asked quietly.

Pippa nodded. She looked tired, like all the anger and fight had been sucked right out of her. When she saw me she looked scared and confused.

"Should I be worried? What the hell happened to you?"

How did I answer that? Telling her that we were likely to be killed by a giant shark in the next few minutes hardly seemed like a conversation opener. She could see the flare guns in my hands, and my shirt covered in blood. "Stay and watch her," I said. "We'll take care of it. The blood's not mine so don't worry about me. I have to go."

Pippa reached an arm out and gently brushed my hand with hers. "Thanks, Luke. You know, for—"

"I'm just glad she's okay."

I was so proud of my sister in that moment, for who she was and the daughter she had raised. I played my part in that, but ultimately it was on Pippa. She was the one who had shaped Chelsea and made her who she was. Losing her would have devastated both of us, but Pippa would have been inconsolable. I put a foot on the first step back up to the cabin and looked back at Pippa.

"Jonah. He didn't make it." It felt like I was lying to her if I didn't at least give her that. "It's his blood. Weir's in charge now. We're trying to get to somewhere safe."

Pippa nodded, understanding and accepting what I told her without saying a word. She would have plenty of time to digest the information whilst looking over Chelsea.

I returned upstairs and went back out onto deck. Immediately, the cold wind confronted me with a slap in the face and I regretted not changing. My clothes were still cold and wet, soaked through with water and blood. I felt sick seeing the blanket covering Jonah as I stepped around him. Some of his blood had soaked through it and dyed it a startling maroon. I took a look around and tried to figure out where I was best placed. Gills and Manny were at the stern, Weir was manning the helm and Ava was at the boat's starboard. I made my way over to the portside, crossing underneath the winch.

I had no intention of speaking to Ava right now. The way she had accused me of not caring and picking sides was out of order. I thought we had a connection, but maybe I was wrong. I could handle Weir's barbs but Ava's words stung. It wasn't a case of siding with Weir but simply choosing the best option to keep us all alive. She had to understand that.

I shoved one of the flare guns into my pocket and kept the other out, ready to use. I looked out at the ocean. How many more were there? How many Megalodons were out there? The one chasing us had gotten closer, much closer. Its fin was still visible above the surface of the ocean and I could just make out some of its body as it sped toward us. I closed my eyes for a moment, wishing I was a world away. The light rain on my face washed away some of Jonah's blood and I wished it would turn into a downpour. I felt dirty. We had lost our captain and almost lost Chelsea too. We were heading to an area with a huge shark chasing us that Ava said could leave us grounded. We had little food or water left, and I knew the *Tukino* was low on diesel. The area where we could replenish all of those things was apparently controlled by a pirate. How much worse could it get?

The boat began to turn and I saw we were approaching the barge. Weir had done it. We'd beaten the shark and gained ourselves a small advantage. Weir brought us around the abandoned barge and the shark disappeared from view. The barge was derelict, nothing but a heap of rust waiting to die. Nobody came out to greet us or wave for help. The whole thing was strangely silent and eerie. We passed close to it and then by the large cargo ship Weir had pointed out. This was much larger, even larger than the Megalodon, around sixty meters long. It was on a slightly uneven keel and I noticed several containers on the deck had come loose. There were a few bobbing in the water close by and I guessed the one we had seen earlier must have come from this ship. Yet again, nobody came out on deck and there was no indication that it was still in use. As we charged past it I hoped Weir was right. Would the shark show any interest in these ships? Could we throw it off? The sky grew darker and the rain continued to fall, and passing between the barge and the cargo ship it felt like for a moment we were safe, like nothing could get us in this little valley. That feeling of safety was fleeting, yet I held onto it for as long as I could. With Jonah gone I wasn't sure how long Weir would trust me, and my feelings of security rapidly faded to be replaced with anxiety once we left the two ships behind. There was a lot of debris in the water, and I spotted an upturned boat, its occupants a long time dead but its name still visible: *The Mangahoe*. I hoped it wasn't portentous and turned to Weir.

"Anyone got sight of it?" I yelled, hoping he might have seen the shark turn away.

I scanned the ocean. The fin was gone. I studied the water for any clue it was still following us, for a mysterious shape beneath the surface of an unusual ripple that suggested an unnatural disturbance below the waves. Nothing.

"No sign of it, Captain," yelled Gills.

I turned to look at Ava. She had her back to me and didn't turn around when she called out.

"Nothing here."

It was gone. At least we now seemed to have a little more time. Even if it was still out there somewhere, we might manage to get ourselves more time to find a decent place to stay. Surely even Weir would understand that it was no longer safe out here on the trawler. His fishing days were over. Now that I had a moment to think and the soft raindrops pelting my face had cleared my mind, I knew I needed to know more about the shoals. But approaching Ava wasn't something I was keen on yet, so I made my way carefully over to Gills and Manny. The boat was still going at full speed and I was pleased Weir wasn't letting up. We couldn't assume we had lost the shark for good, so it made sense to plough ahead.

"How're you doing, Manny?" I asked.

"Ready to chuck up everything I've eaten in the last twenty-four hours but I'm still alive. That's something."

Stood side by side they appeared almost like father and son. Gills had to have thirty years on Manny and there was a faint resemblance. I could imagine Manny growing older, maybe losing some hair, putting on a little weight, and turning into Gills before he knew it.

"You should get out of those clothes before you get sick." Gills kept glancing nervously at the ocean. "You can take some of my clothes. They might be a little big for you but they're dry."

"Will do. Soon."

"And Chelsea?" asked Manny with concern. "Did you talk to Pippa?"

"Yeah, I spoke with her briefly. I think they'll be okay. Chelsea should be all right. Thank God we found her."

"Amen," replied Manny, looking up at the gloomy sky. The rainclouds showed no sign of dispersing. If anything, they were growing blacker.

"Gills, you know much about where we're going? Weir wants to take us to some shoals nearby. What was it? The... the fire pan shoals or something?"

"Frying Pan Shoals, you mean. Yeah, I know them. There's some good fishing to be had around there. They got a Light Tower and a cool little bed and breakfast place. Well, they *did* have, before things changed. It's underwater now. The shoals are notorious though. You gotta be *real* careful around there."

"Careful? More than usual?" asked Manny. He stole a glance at Jonah's body. "Why?"

Gills sighed and looked out at the ocean. There was still no sign of the shark. "Well, the clue's in the name. It gets shallow for one. Out of the fire and all that. A lot of shipwrecks in that area. Like I said, it's good fishing, but it's claimed a lot of ships and a lot of people. It ain't some place I'd want to be, but if Weir reckons it's our best shot, then I'll run with it."

The three of us let Gills' comments sink in as we kept our eyes peeled for any sign of the shark's fin. If it was following us then it had gone deeper underwater. I knew there was a chance it could hit us unexpectedly from underneath, but somehow I didn't think that was its style. As every minute crawled by I felt better about our chances. The longer that it didn't reappear, then the further away we got from it. Maybe it had found something better, a larger food source like the orca pod from earlier.

The rain continued unabated, growing stronger every second we were out there on that miserable deck, but it didn't matter. We weren't there for a pleasure cruise and I was already soaked anyway. The ocean remained silent. Waves crashed against the hull and the roar of the engine was the only other noise. I began to feel slightly silly with the flare gun in my hand. What could I really do against a creature of that size? And yet putting it back felt wrong too. At least with something in my hands I wasn't completely defenseless.

"Guys, tell me I'm not seeing things." Manny raised his arm and pointed. "Is that someone waving at us?"

I thought he was going to tell us he had spotted the shark's fin, so was surprised to see him pointing to the starboard of the boat. Up ahead on the horizon, there was a small boat. We were aiming right for it, and as it became clearer it became apparent that it wasn't even a boat. There was a man waving at us from what appeared to be nothing more than a dinghy.

"You're kidding me," said Gills, as he ran across the deck to Weir.

"What the hell are they doing out here?" I asked.

"You think he'll stop for them?"

I didn't need to know who Manny was referring to. Gills would stop to help anyone, but Weir? I doubted it.

"No. He wants to get to shallow water in case the shark's following us. Can't say I blame him."

"But we haven't seen it for a few minutes now. It might have gone. The Atlantic Ocean is a big place."

"Yeah, and that means there are a lot of places for it to hide. Look at how it came up on us back there. It hit us from underneath without us even knowing it was there. How do we know it's not there now?"

Manny wiped the raindrops from his face. The patter of rain as it fell on the deck was soothing, like nature's music, but I was on edge. I hadn't meant to snap at Manny and thankfully he didn't react.

"Hey, brother, we don't know shit. Let's be honest. But we can't let Weir go right past that guy. You said yourself that we don't know if the shark is still with us. A guy in a rubber dinghy is easy pickings for that monster. We have to help him. Hell, we're going right past him. It would be rude not to pick him up."

I really didn't want another fight with Weir, especially not when it seemed as if I had just got him onside. Manny was right. I knew what Gills and Ava would do, and what Jonah would do too. We had to stop, no matter what the consequences.

I was about to go when Manny grabbed my arm. "Oh damn, look."

Shielding my eyes from the rain I leant over the rail. Manny was pointing at something and it took a second for my eyes to find it. About a hundred feet away was the unmistakable outline of the shark's fin. The large triangle sped through the water and it wasn't coming for our boat, but for the dinghy up ahead.

"Shoot, we'll never make it," I whispered. I felt Manny's hand tighten around my elbow.

As the shark neared the dinghy, the fin quickly disappeared. I wanted to believe that meant the shark had gone, perhaps changing its mind and coming for us, but I suspected the worst. The man in the dinghy kept waving and his voice began to drift over the waves to us. I heard him call for help. There was nothing more, at least nothing I could hear. I prepared myself to look away, not wanting to see the inevitable carnage, but before I did, a second figure emerged from the dinghy: a woman.

The Megalodon blasted out of the sea sending a huge plume of water into the air fifty feet high. The magnificent creature erupted like a geyser that had been pent up for a thousand years, its ferocity and power obvious to all of us. I assumed it would simply come up beneath the little boat and devour the whole thing in one gulp, yet it came up beside it, showering the man and woman with salt and fear. The creature jumped above them in an arc and drenched their dinghy in shadow. We were too far away to see the shock and terror on their faces, but I could imagine the fear they felt when that monster emerged from the ocean. Even from this far away, I knew it meant death for them. The shark's glistening white and gray body slammed down on top of the dinghy with such force that it must have been obliterated. The resulting crash as the shark reentered the ocean sent a huge wave toward us, and I steadied myself on the safety rail. I scoured the ocean for the two inhabitants of the wrecked craft, but all I could see was the tumultuous water raging and roiling as if it were on fire.

"We're too late," said Manny. "We couldn't have done anything for them. Jesus."

The shark's fin reappeared and little bits of the dinghy began to float to the surface. The sea had been whipped up into a frenzy and the shark seemed even more animated than before. Was it not satiated by the couple it had just eaten? Had the whales not satisfied its urge to kill? The fin disappeared once more and the disturbed water began to settle. I guessed it was returning to the depths, perhaps preparing to come after us again.

"Let's go," I said. I turned to Manny, unable to watch the thing anymore. "Weir needs to make that shallow water. Those two people are gone. They're dead. Let's make sure that—"

Manny's eyes wandered from me to the ocean and suddenly widened. "Luke, wait. I think… I think one of them is still alive."

CHAPTER 13

Peering through the rain I couldn't believe that anyone could have survived the attack, and yet Manny was right. In the distance there was a figure in the sea, one arm above their head waving at us. The *Tukino* was rapidly approaching the area where the dinghy had been destroyed, which meant the shark was close. But if we attempted to rescue them it would put us at risk of an encounter with the shark ourselves. As soon as I considered leaving them to save ourselves, I knew that I couldn't do it. Leaving them behind was certain death. If the shark didn't take them then they would drown. There were no other boats around here and land was a long way off.

"We have to get them," said Manny, reading my mind. "I'm going to talk to Weir."

As it turned out we weren't the only ones. When we reached the wheelhouse we found Gills and Ava already there, pestering him to stop.

"You *cannot* leave them, Weir," said Ava firmly. "What if it was one of us out there?"

"Look, we can do it quickly." Gills already held the life saver in his hands. "It doesn't even take us off course. We only have to stop for a second and—"

"And then what?" Weir showed no sign that he was going to slow down and help them. "Then we're a sitting duck. You saw that monster? You want to die too? No. We carry on."

"Weir, for Christ's sake, stop the boat," pleaded Ava.

"You can't do this, Weir," said Manny. "Come on, man, we're all in this together. Let's—"

"No. This isn't a democracy. You can't accept that? Then get the fuck off my boat." Weir still held a gun in one hand. "We're seconds away from the shoals and safety. I'm not about to jeopardize that for some idiots out here in a dinghy. They're stupid enough to get themselves killed, that's their problem."

It seemed that Weir's recent diplomacy had vanished and he was back to his usual blustery self.

"Weir, look around. There's no sign of the shark." I nervously glanced at the ocean. It was true there was no sign of it, but I knew it was still out there somewhere. "It would've used up a ton of energy in smashing that boat up. I'll bet we have a few minutes before it resurfaces for another go. Enough time to rescue that person."

"You willing to bet your life on that?"

I gritted my teeth. Weir's smirk had returned and I was beginning to remember everything I hated about the man.

"You want to rescue that fool, grease-monkey, go ahead. Jump in. Gills will toss you the life saver. We'll shelter at the shoals a while and come back for you in a few hours. Good luck."

It was almost too late. The person in the water was clearly visible now, surrounded by the remnants of their boat. I could see now it was a woman. She was so close that I could hear her pleas for help. However dangerous it was, we had to help. I couldn't just let her go like that.

I slowly and reluctantly raised the flare gun, pointing it at Weir. I assumed it would still work in the rain, although I had no intention of shooting him. I just wanted to shock him, to let him know that he couldn't play God with people's lives like that.

Weir laughed. There was no fear on his face as I held the gun up.

"You'd better be sure about what you're thinking. That gun looks dangerously like it's pointed at me. You know what we do with mutineers, *boy*?"

"Weir, just stop this," said Ava.

She put her hand on my extended arm. I didn't know if she was trying to reassure me that I was doing the right thing, or that I should lower the gun. I kept my arm steady and could feel her trembling. I was sure she could feel me trembling too. I kept my eyes on Weir though. He could just as easily shoot me and turn the deck into a bloodbath. Slowly, Weir's eyes turned to settle on all of us. He looked finally at Gills and then turned us toward the woman.

"Fine. You get one chance at this. And if I see anything of that shark we're gone, whether she's aboard or not."

Weir throttled down the engine and I lowered the flare gun. I exhaled quietly, not wanting to let him know that I was scared. That was the first time I'd pointed a gun at anyone and I hoped it would be the last. I stepped back, not taking my eyes off Weir. I didn't trust him one bit. He had relinquished this time, but it had been a close call. It was really only because every one of us had gone against him. He was like a cornered animal, ready to lash out, and I knew it would be best to keep clear of him for a while. If Jonah trusted him, then there had to be a good man inside him somewhere. I was struggling to find him though.

As I monitored Weir, the others ran to help the woman. Ava grabbed a dry blanket as Manny and Gills raced across the slippery deck. Gills shouted out instructions to Weir so that we got as close as possible to the woman, and then Manny threw the life saver into the water. The rainwater trickled down my cold body and I was beginning to feel jealous of Pippa and Chelsea who were still down in their bunks.

"Go!" shouted Gills.

The woman they'd hauled up onto the boat collapsed onto the deck and Weir instantly throttled the engine up. The whole rescue only seemed to take a minute. Manny and Gills helped the crying woman up as Ava draped the thick blanket around her shoulders. I looked around the boat, scanning every direction, but saw nothing of the shark. Perhaps it had realized where we were going and knew it couldn't follow. The woman was distraught. She was shaking and crying, and uttering something in Spanish. She had long brown hair that was tangled around her shoulders and wore cut-off jeans and a red vest that clung to her skin. She was far too young to be out in these treacherous waters. Ava tried to calm her down and get her warm, but the woman was getting more and more animated.

"She okay?" I asked Manny, as our boat roared back to life.

"Physically, she's okay, just a few cuts and bruises. But I have no idea what she's going on about. Sounds like Spanish or Portuguese to me."

As the boat took us away from the remains of her dinghy, she raced to the safety rail, throwing off her blanket and pointing out to sea.

"No, no, stay. Por favor? El padre... no. Socorro!"

I felt bad for the poor girl. She looked like she was barely out of her teens and probably had no idea what was going on. Her wide brown eyes looked from the crew to me.

"Can somebody *please* shut her up?" asked Weir. "And can I get a little help, Gills. If that's not too much to ask?"

Resisting the temptation to plant my fist into Weir's face, I crossed to the girl as Gills went to help Weir. As I approached I began to think she wasn't even out of her teens. She had that natural slender frame that adorned so many girls around their mid-teens, and an innocence etched across her face that I recognized from Chelsea.

"Hey, hey, it's okay," I said. I kept my voice low and non-threatening. She looked scared out of her mind. "Luke. I'm Luke," I said, patting my chest. "You?"

"Estelle. Por favor—"

I could see her struggling for the right words.

"Your boat?" I pointed out to the sea behind us. "Your boat is gone, Estelle. I'm sorry for your friend. You're safe with us. Safe on this boat. Safe, understand?"

"Luke. Luke, por favor, el padre. Hay que volver. Hay que encontrarlo. Mi padre no sabe nadar."

The girl turned and looked at the water. Her shoulders slumped and I felt a familiar hand on my shoulder.

"She said something about her father. She wants to go back for him." Ava tugged down her red beanie and glanced at me. "I learnt a little Spanish once. I can't understand everything she says but... enough."

I understood too. Estelle and her father had been on the dinghy together for some reason. Now that he was gone she felt alone, surrounded by strangers. There was little I could do to calm her down. The harsh fact was that her father was dead.

"Estelle," began Ava, "you are... salvo. Salvo, okay? Your padre is... he is... muerto."

Estelle said something so quiet I could barely hear it. "No lo puedo creer. Muerto. Ay no!"

"I think she understands." Ava sighed and draped the blanket around the young girl's shoulders. There was no reaction from her.

Estelle simply kept staring at the spot where her dinghy had gone down. "But processing it may take a little longer."

"She'll be okay now. Thanks, Ava."

Ava shrugged and rubbed Estelle's back.

"You know, I think—"

"Save it," said Ava. She refused to meet my gaze. "You should check on Pippa and Chelsea. Make sure they're okay down there. I'll stay here with Estelle."

I could tell from her voice that Ava was blocking me out. I didn't detect any anger in her tone, but the inference was clear. She wanted me to leave her alone. I trudged solemnly back to the cabin, trying not to look at Jonah's body. How were we going to explain that to Estelle? Manny met me at the cabin door. The rain still fell and he was sheltering inside.

"Hey, man, how is she?" asked Manny, as I entered the wheelhouse trying not to look at Weir.

"She's in shock, I think. She's cold and I left Ava looking after her. The girl's just lost her father. Estelle. Her name's Estelle. She doesn't seem to know much English. I guess we'll look after her as best we can until she figures out what she wants to do." I felt exhausted and slumped down on a seat. I grabbed an oily rag and wiped my face. It was already coated with blood and rain, so it made no difference. I just wanted to feel dry again. "I have no idea what they were doing out there like that. Her father must have had good reason to take his daughter out to sea on a dinghy, but I can't imagine what."

Manny smiled and nodded. "Right. Estelle, huh? You know, Luke, I actually meant Ava when I asked how she was."

"Ava?" I threw the dirty rag away and stood up. I had to check on my family. "She's fine, I guess. I should go talk to Pippa, let her know what's going on."

I went down the steps, eager to get away from Weir and to talk to Pippa. Manny followed me down, and when we reached the bottom of the stairs he stopped me by the galley.

"Luke, you can't fool me. What's going on with you and her?"

I tried to get to the bunkroom, but Manny stood in my way, refusing to move. I ran my hands over my head, through my hair, and wiped my damp palms on my pants. "Sheesh, that's a million dollar question." I smiled at Manny. It was good to have a friend with me. I hadn't spent enough time with him since we'd gotten onto the *Tukino*. I truthfully had no idea where me and Ava were, or what I could tell Manny. Jonah had warned me from getting involved and it was obvious that Pippa resented her. But Jonah was dead and Pippa was right when she said I had to live my own life. Was Ava even still interested? After everything that had gone on, I could understand if she wanted to back off before things became too much. How on earth would you even have a relationship with someone whilst living with six other people on a trawler? "Manny, it's… it's complicated."

Manny chuckled. "When isn't it?"

I looked into the galley where the ocean lashed against the solitary window. Upstairs I knew that Ava was comforting Estelle, Gills and Weir were navigating us to the shoals, and the dark sky was only getting darker. The rain was pelting the trawler and the deck, soaking the blanket that covered Jonah's body. Life was complicated. I thought this boat would be the answer to everything, that with Pippa and Chelsea we would be able to make a fresh start. I hadn't counted on giant man-eating sharks. At least that was one thing going in our favor. The shark hadn't reappeared after destroying the dinghy. I hadn't seen the fin, or any sign of it out there, although admittedly it was so gloomy that it was getting hard to see far at all.

"Go," said Manny. "Talk to her. She's into you. I can tell."

I shook my head and kept my voice quiet. "No, I have to talk to Pippa. She's been stuck down here looking after Chelsea, while we've been dealing with this. I should—"

"*I'll* go." Manny pushed me back toward the steps. "Talk to Ava and then get some dry clothes on. For the love of God, Luke, you look like a drowned rat."

I feebly protested but Manny kept pushing me up the stairs. "Okay, okay, I'm going. Just don't say anything to Pippa about Ava, please? She's got enough on her plate without me making things any harder for her."

"Yeah, yeah, whatever, just go and—"

The boat lurched wildly and it felt like we had slammed into another boat.

"What the hell was that?" asked Manny.

I turned and charged up the stairs, Manny bounding after me. I rushed past Weir and Gills, racing out onto the deck.

"Luke, hold on," said Manny.

I looked at him stood in the open doorway of the wheelhouse and then turned to find Ava. The deck was awash with water and I couldn't see her or Estelle. I began to panic.

"Ava? What's..?"

The booming noise hit my ears and I hit the deck as our boat suddenly slowed. The trawler started to lean to the starboard and blood-soaked rainwater that had pooled on the deck around Jonah's body splashed my face, cascading over me in a torrent. I slid helplessly toward the edge of the boat and grabbed onto a discarded piece of netting. I slid my fingers into it and held on tight as the boat veered off course.

"Weir, what the fuck?" I yelled.

I heard glass breaking and then wood stretching in ways it wasn't meant to. It sounded like the boat was being torn apart and I instantly knew what it was. The shark was back.

"Luke!"

It was Ava. I clawed my way to a standing position next to the A-frame. Some of the metal holding it in place had buckled, bolts and screws becoming loose as the pressure on the boat twisted it beyond its natural means. Ava and Estelle were clinging to a safety rail. They were safe for now, but the boat was on such an angle that I was concerned we would tip over. Weir was still in the wheelhouse whilst Gills was next to him on his knees, trying to get back to his feet. The door swung wildly as Manny tried to hold onto it.

"Weir, what's going on? Get us righted!" I shouted to him, and then suddenly the boat tipped back toward the horizon, correcting itself. We hit the water with such force that I was knocked off my feet again and a huge wave washed over the deck. I saw Jonah's body slide past me but I was powerless to stop it. The blanket caught on something and revealed his decimated body which continued sliding down the deck. Jonah was out of my reach and the last I saw of him disappeared into the rough water.

"Hold on!"

Weir yelled out as the boat was tossed around on the rough water and I desperately fought to hold onto the netting. I dug my hands into it, knowing it was all that would keep me aboard the boat. Another wave crashed over us, swamping the deck and forcing me to hold my breath. The foamy white water receded from the deck removing any trace of the blood from Jonah, and I looked for what we had crashed into. I saw no rocks in the ocean, no other boats, nothing that we might have crashed into; a little way off in the distance I noticed the water churning and then a dark shape appeared above the surface. It rose up out of the water silently, a huge fin, swimming toward the boat. I instantly thought of Pippa and Chelsea trapped below deck. If the shark took a giant bite out of the hull they would inevitably be in the most danger. If the lower compartments flooded they would be drowned instantly.

"Weir, get us moving." I had no option but to let go of the net. I extricated myself from it quickly so that I could make my way to him. The boat was rocking back and forth, but the engine was still turning over. We were moving slowly, too slowly to escape the shark. If we didn't get moving, it would take us down like it had the dinghy. "The shark – over there!" I yelled.

With both hands on a safety rail I began to pull myself along the boat toward Weir. I reached a rusted bollard and managed to get a few feet closer to Ava and Estelle before the shark hit us. I don't know if Weir heard me or saw it, but we turned too late. The shark rammed into the side of the boat and sent a shuddering jolt through the whole of the trawler. Its massive head struck us on the port, near the stern, and the boat was propelled forward through the crashing waves. I kept my hands on the rail as the *Tukino* was hurtled through the water and I prayed that the shark hadn't just torn a hole in us. Ava and Estelle screamed, and I reached for them. They were beyond my reach. I stretched a hand out desperately for Ava but she was too far away. If I let go of the rail I knew I would lose my footing and end up in the ocean. We had no choice but to ride it out.

With the rain and rising wind whipping my face I turned to see the shark circling around for another go. Its huge body defied belief. It reminded me of a whale, sliding silently just beneath the surface, preparing for another strike. Even if our boat was still intact I didn't think we would be able to cope with another blow. The giant monster was going to take us down. It glided like an eel, obviously completely at ease in the water. It had plenty of enemies, but none that could match it. It was the king of this world now. There was no doubt in my mind that the Megalodon was the new master of the seas.

"Luke?"

I felt cold fingers grope for mine and turned away from the terrifying beast to find Ava had crept forward to me. Her eyes searched mine for answers, but I had none to give. We were stranded, bereft of hope and destined for a horrible death. What could I say?

"Ava." I had nothing else to offer. There was no point in lying, in telling her that it would be okay. It wouldn't. We were going down, as simple as that. The shark was going to win. When I opened my mouth, the rain swept in and I felt the urge to scream. I could see the shark out of the corner of my eye. It was charging back toward us now, slicing a deadly path through the ocean to its target: us.

"Ava." I smiled and looked into her beautiful eyes. She said nothing in return. I don't know if it was tears or rain falling down her face. I wished we had met long ago, long before this horrible situation. I squeezed her hand and waited for the impact that would kill us all. The cold rain soaked through to my skin and goosebumps rippled my flesh. I had no doubt it would be the last thing I felt, and took solace from the fact that when I died the last thing I would see was Ava's face.

CHAPTER 14

With a grinding, screeching noise, the *Tukino* came to a sudden halt. We lurched forward and I lost my grip on Ava. The railing slipped away from me and with it almost my sanity. A tremendous wave broke the bow of the ship cascading us all with bracing water.

"Land," yelled Weir. "Land!"

I lay breathlessly on the deck, reassuringly solid, waiting for the shark to rise up and swallow us, but it never came. The rain pelted my face and my bare feet struggled for purchase on the deck, but eventually I pulled myself up. I scrambled forward and helped Ava up, with Estelle still clinging to her.

"We're taking on water," yelled Gills, running past me. "Get off the boat. Get everyone off."

I could feel the boat tilting forward, wanting us to follow the deck to the bow. Through the rain I saw it. Land was hardly a fitting description for the slim slice of sand ahead of us. It looked more like a sandbank. There were no trees or plants, no other ships or buildings, and no shelter from the growing tempest that seemed determined to drown us.

"Luke, come on." Ava tugged on my hand. "Follow Weir."

My eyes drifted to the wheelhouse and I saw Weir running away, to the front of the ship. He tossed a rope ladder over the side and looked back. His eyes caught mine and for the first time I saw doubt in them; more than that, I saw fear. Something had finally gotten to him. Waving the gun above his head he beckoned us over.

"Go." I let go of Ava reluctantly and took a step back. "Get yourself and Estelle to that sandbank."

"No, come with us. Don't leave me," pleaded Ava. "We have to get off the ship."

The *Tukino* began to list and I wondered how shallow the water was. It had saved us from the shark, but to what end? I had no time to think about it.

"Go. I have to make sure Pippa and Chelsea are okay."

Turning my back on Ava, I charged up the sloping deck, the whine of the boat's engine fading as it ceased struggling. I saw Gills yank open the cabin door and I raced to join him.

"Pippa? Chelsea!" As I reached Gills I had a terrible feeling I was too late. I could hear the water below and something splashing around in it.

"We'll get them." Gills held the door open for me, and together we ventured down the stairs to the bunks. It was dark down there and as we reached the galley I realized my feet were wet. The water had already come up to my ankles and was rising quickly. I could hear it gushing in, but in the gloom it was impossible to see where.

"The engine's gone and the fish hold will be flooded by now," said Gills, as he checked the galley. "Empty."

"Pippa?" I yelled, frantically kicking my way through the water to the bunks. I left Gills behind me, charging forward to where I had last seen my family. "Chelsea?"

"Luke, in here."

I heard Pippa's voice and knew it was bad. It was hard to walk with the boat listing as it was, and I used the walls to pull myself forward. Wading through the now knee-deep water, I found Pippa and Chelsea. They were in the bunkroom where I'd left them, only Pippa was on her knees. It looked as if the room had been turned upside down. Books and bottles floated in the water, the small window had cracked and was leaking water into the room, and worst of all one of the bunks had been ripped from the wall. It lay asunder, stretched across the tiny room like a barricade.

"Luke, I can't get her out. I can't—"

It was then that I noticed Chelsea. Her head was poking above the water that was already up to her shoulders.

"What the hell happened?" asked Pippa, as I sank to my knees.

"We've beached," grunted Gills behind me.

"Chelsea," I said, "help me push this off you." I wrapped my hands around the metal bunkbed and pulled. Nothing budged. Pippa was right next to me and pulling, but it was stuck fast.

"I can't do it," said Chelsea. "My leg is stuck underneath. I can't get it out."

The rising water was freezing cold and my hands were already beginning to turn numb. I could only imagine how Chelsea felt. Taking a huge gulp of air, I dunked my head under the water to look at Chelsea's leg. I ducked under the bunk to see what the problem was. The metal had buckled and was twisted around her ankle. I tried to pull the bed away, and although it moved an inch I couldn't get her leg free. I gave it one last tug and then, running out of air, I reluctantly resurfaced.

"Damn thing's stuck fast."

"Luke, I can't... I can't—"

The water reached Chelsea's chin and she was panicking. Her wide brown eyes stared at me and I could see a lot of her mother in them. There was no way I was leaving her.

"Fucking thing!" Pippa began to cry as she pulled at the metal, heaving on it with all her might before she lost her grip and fell.

Gills got down on his knees next to me and looked me in the eye. "On three we all pull *together*. Ready?"

I nodded. "Chelsea, I think we can do it. When you feel it move, you kick your leg out. As hard as you can, okay?"

She was trembling and the water was threatening to submerge her completely, but I knew she would do it. Pippa wrapped her fingers around mine and together we gripped the bunkbed that had Chelsea trapped.

"I love you, Chelsea," said Pippa through her tears. "Just a second longer, honey."

"One... two... three!"

The crash was tremendous and for a moment I thought we had pulled the whole wall down. One moment it was there and the next the ocean was all around us. The metal flew from my hands and the room simply blew apart as the Megalodon ripped open the hull of the boat. The snout of the giant shark crashed through the hull and I felt myself being pulled from the boat as the water rapidly flowed in. I heard Pippa scream and then chaos exploded all around me.

The shark's huge jaws crunched through the hull of the *Tukino*, its sharp teeth mangling the wreckage, twisting and tearing metal, turning it into jagged confetti. Bracing water rushed in and everything turned upside down. The shark pulled away as the walls caved in, but before the ocean claimed us I noticed a scar above the shark's left eye. We were swept out of the boat along with the contents of the bunkroom, toward the shark. I felt Pippa grabbing for me, her hand clutching my leg. I saw the bunkbed twist free and Chelsea was freed, only to be pulled out into the ocean too.

A horrible wrenching noise surrounded me as more of our boat was ripped apart. As the saltwater stung my eyes I tried to reach for Pippa but she was pulled away from me. A thick clump of seaweed floated past and I recognized Gills' green hat tangled up in it. I was upside down, bubbles drifting upward past me, as I was helplessly pulled by the current out into deeper water. My arms and hands groped for the others, but found nothing. It was cold and dark, and as I strained against the forces trying to drag me from safety, I caught a glimpse of the boat. Its front half had hit the sandbank and the whole thing was now taking on water. I saw the shark too, its elongated body gracefully gliding away from the boat only to circle back around. I suddenly realized I was running out of air. The swirling water had calmed a little, but I needed to get to the surface. I managed to force my body upright and looked for Pippa and Chelsea. They were nowhere near me. I couldn't go without them, but I couldn't look for them any longer. I needed to breathe.

As I kicked my legs furiously, I saw the shark again. It was swimming right for me, silently and swiftly moving through the icy cold water before it got too shallow for it. Its eyes rolled back as its jaws opened and then it abruptly turned. There was something else in the water, something that had drawn its attention away from me. When I saw the shape of someone in its sight I couldn't stop myself from calling out to warn them. Pippa or Chelsea were right in its sights. But as the shark clamped its jaws around the person's flailing arms I realized it was neither of them. It was Gills.

The shark could have devoured him whole but opted to turn him into an appetizer, severing his arm before taking a leg. The Megalodon's huge serrated teeth scythed through Gills' bones and snapped him almost in two, the way a lumberjack would split a log with a clean strike from his axe. I kicked my legs faster, desperate for air, desperate to get away from the monster, and desperate to live. I could only imagine the power held within the shark's muscles and knew I only had seconds before it came for me too. I felt terrible for Gills, but there was nothing I could do. The seawater in my throat made me want to vomit and the fear in my stomach turned my insides into knots. I had no idea where Pippa and Chelsea were. Had it already taken them?

Blood spurted ferociously from Gills' limbs. He appeared to be trying to swim away even as his life oozed out of him, but the shark was done playing with its food. I saw the shark roll its head around and swallow him whole. Gills was dead. There was nothing left of him, just a dark patch of blood in the ocean that would soon dissipate into nothing. I clawed my way to the surface, barely able to contain my fear. How long would it be before I felt the shark snap its jaws around my legs or just bite me in half? How long would it take to die inside that foul monster? If it swallowed me whole would I die instantly, or suffocate inside its belly full of body parts and dead sea-creatures?

As my head broke free I spewed out the water burning my throat and sucked in fresh air. I coughed and coughed, feeling as though I was drowning, all too aware that the shark was somewhere behind me.

"This way!"

With the incessant rain blinding me I swam toward the voice. I swam away from the shark, putting my faith in the hope that Gills was enough to satiate the beast.

"Hurry, Luke. Hurry!"

It was Pippa's voice. I couldn't see her, but I could hear the urgency in her voice. Whilst I was pleased to know she was safe, the fact that she was telling me to hurry told me I wasn't out of danger yet. Stupidly, I glanced behind me. The shark's towering fin was right behind me and I could practically feel its teeth nipping at my heels. My arms felt like lead weights but I pushed on, not daring to look back, not daring to think or hope or pray. I focused on Pippa's voice, swimming as hard as I could against the ocean that kept trying to suck me back.

Suddenly my fingers struck something solid and I felt a piece of metal beneath me. My knees hit it next and then my hands dug into sand. I felt hands pulling at me, grasping my body and hauling me out of the water. The sand beneath me sucked at my weary body and I collapsed onto my back once I was free of the ocean. The raindrops hit my face, but I didn't care. The gray sky was beautiful. After the gloom of the ocean I was grateful I was still alive. I wiggled my toes, counting every one, scarcely able to believe I had made it.

"Chelsea," I whispered. "Is she..?"

"I'm here. I'm fine."

Faces crowded above me, looking down at me with concern. I saw Pippa and Chelsea, both crying. I saw Weir look at me with what appeared to be concern. I saw Manny, Estelle and then Ava. I rolled onto my side and heaved up, more water erupting from my throat. I spluttered once more, spitting the last of the ocean from my lungs.

"Don't try to speak, Luke. Catch your breath."

I felt Ava's hand on my back, gently rubbing concentric circles that were both harsh and soft simultaneously. Gritty sand stained my face and biting salt-water snatched at my shivering flesh. I heard a crashing sound, as if something had hit the remains of our boat, but had no energy left to turn. Ava said something about resting, and I was sure I heard Manny murmuring over something. Ava's hand on my back felt good. It felt real and warm, and nothing like the ocean. The ocean was a cold, dark bitter place where a man could get lost. The ocean was a place for monsters and dead men.

"No, leave him be, leave him—"

Ava's words faded in the rain as Weir's thick calloused hands grabbed my shoulders. He hauled me over and forced me to stand. My legs were like jelly and offered no resistance. His fair complexion was soured by fear, disguised as hatred and anger. His brutish manner had no effect on me, which probably only irritated him more.

"Where the hell is he?" asked Weir. "Where the hell is Gills?"

The *Tukino* was stuck fast, half submerged in the sea and half of it stuck on the sandbank. The gray sky whirled around us, the wind galloping like horses sending larger and larger waves into the boat's hull. It wouldn't be long before our temporary home would be destroyed completely. The sandbank we stood on seemed to be no more than fifty feet long. Where was Gills? He was where we would all be soon.

"Out there." I raised an arm and pointed out at the vast, endless ocean. "It got him, Weir. I'm sorry. It ate him up."

Weir grabbed me by the shoulders and drew me up to him. His blue eyes sparkled in the grayness and when he spoke, little spits of phlegm landed on my face.

"That's your fault, grease-monkey. This is all your fault. I should've—"

A tremendous splash caught my attention and a shape seemed to fly from the ocean up into the air, not far from the final resting place of our boat. A dark shape like a zig-zag coursed through the air, a flash of white and red catching my eye.

"Oh my God," exclaimed Pippa.

Manny yanked Weir off me. "Christ, Weir, look at it. It's... it's—"

The Megalodon jumped clean out of the water and when it returned to its natural home the resultant splash sent a wave over the *Tukino* that would have dragged us all into the ocean. The shark's tail suddenly reappeared above the water and slapped down hard on the surface. It was as if the shark wanted us to know who was responsible for our situation, who really was the king of the seas. It might have been frustration at not being able to finish us off, but it felt more like a victory dance, a salute to our naivety and impending doom.

"That's where Gills is," I said calmly to Weir. "Decomposing in the belly of that fucking beast. And that's *your* fault."

CHAPTER 15

I didn't even see it coming. One moment I was watching the world's largest predator show off its aquatic skills, and the next I was lying on my back nursing a bruised jaw.

"You're dead meat, *monkey*. Stand up. Get up, right now." Weir stood over me like a hungry grizzly bear, his fists balled up ready to go again.

"Weir for Christ's sake, leave it alone," demanded Manny.

I saw Manny attempt to drag Weir away from me, but Weir simply pushed him back.

"Stop it. This isn't helping." Pippa tried next, as I slowly got to my feet. "You're supposed to be our captain, Weir, so try figuring out how we're going to get out of this mess."

As soon as I was on my feet Weir hit me again, and once more I found myself on my ass with stars circling my vision. I had no problem fighting Weir, but the condition I was in hardly made it a fair fight.

"Stop it!" yelled Chelsea.

I saw Manny wrap his arms around her and hold her back as Pippa prepared to intervene.

"Stay there," I said, as I dropped to my knees. I was utterly drained and taking on Weir was the last thing I wanted to do, but I didn't want anyone else getting involved. I wasn't about to back down despite my sluggish body defying orders from my brain.

"Weir, you need to listen to me. I know you're scared, but we can work this out," I said, getting to my feet. Weir's face danced in front of mine and I tried to focus on his piercing blue eyes. I felt dizzy and sick. "You have the knowledge of this area and without you, we—"

Weir sent a hard punch to my gut and I was too slow to react. I tried to dodge it, but he still landed a decent blow and I reeled back, doubling over.

"We were doing just fine. You and your pathetic excuse of a family don't deserve my help."

I looked up to see Weir advancing on me.

"I'm going to show you what it takes to survive, *monkey*. You have no idea."

"Weir, stop this."

Ava reached for him, putting a hand across his chest, but he pushed her back. He sent her tumbling over the wet sand and I heard her cry out in pain as she landed. As I regained my breath, I realized he wasn't going to stop. He was seeing red and nothing we said was going to stop him.

Weir reached me and grinned. "You've destroyed my crew, my boat, and—"

I'd had enough of his garbage. If this went on he was liable to kill me or hurt one of the others. I lunged at him, catching him off guard, and with my arms wrapped around his waist pushed him back until we lost our footing and collapsed on the sandbank together. With Weir underneath me I had to move quickly and take advantage of my position. I grabbed his hands and pinned him down beneath me.

"Get the hell off me," he yelled.

"Quit it, Weir, just stop it." I found my strength again and though my arms ached, I had enough energy left to hold him. He was built like an ox and I wasn't entirely sure how long I would be able to control him. "Listen to me, nobody cares about blame. Nobody here wants to be in this situation, but we have to deal with it. We have to figure out how to get out of here."

Weir pursed his lips and looked at me. Freckles ringed his lips and I noticed the creased lines around his eyes. I remembered how old Jonah was and suddenly I felt pity for Weir. He had spent his life on the ocean, on the *Tukino*, and suddenly it was all gone. Jonah and Gills were dead, and the boat was sinking. He had nothing left to lose. I relaxed my grip on him slightly. "Weir, just calm yourself. You're still the captain, right? So take charge and help us." As he looked at me I thought I was getting through to him. The rain was soaking through the both of us and I was aware of how close we were to the water's edge. I wanted to stop wasting what precious little energy I had left, and focus on what to do next. "There's no need to fight. We can—"

Weir slammed his forehead into my nose, whipping his head up with such force that I felt my brain rattle around my skull. I yelped in pain and let go of him, putting one hand over my bleeding nose. Suddenly Weir was slipping out from under me, pushing me onto my back.

"Fucking city boy."

I felt Weir's boot smash into my ribs and I doubled over, wincing and coughing with pain. It was all so quick that I didn't know what to do.

"You want to tell *me* what to do?"

Another boot landed in between my shoulder blades and another around my kidneys. Another boot came toward my face and I tried to curl into a ball, too late. I held my hands over my face and I heard the crack of my nose break before the pain surrounded me. My failing vision became full of stars and I tried to crawl away from him. My fingers sank into the wet sand as I felt another boot land on my back. Pain shot through my whole body and my head felt like a balloon full of helium trying to escape my body. I opened my eyes and saw blood dripping from my face onto the sand. I kept crawling away, unable to summon up any more energy. I got a couple of feet before I collapsed, devoid of energy and still conscious only by the grace of God. No more kicks came my way. I expected Weir was about to haul me to my feet and throw me in the ocean. Yet as I lay there panting and trying to stem the bleeding from my nose, nothing happened. There were no more blows or boots in my face. I waited for the inevitable. Still, nothing.

A hand finally touched the back of my neck and I wondered if he would just snap my neck and end it right there. The hand wound around me and another draped across my torso. The groping hands turned me over and I felt the cold rain hit my face again. It felt deliciously refreshing and I almost laughed. My nose was still bleeding and my back felt like it had been twisted into a corkscrew, yet that fresh rain felt so good on my face that I even smiled.

"Luke?"

I opened my eyes and through the falling rain saw Ava and Pippa kneeling over me.

"Luke."

As Ava sobbed she put her face against mine, her warm breath brushing over my face like soft linen. She felt good. She felt alive.

"Can you stand?" asked Pippa.

My heart broke to see Pippa looking at me with such pity. Mom used to look at us the same way when we were sick. It was usually followed by a glass of milk, but I knew there would be no comforting warm milk this time. Pippa wiped away a tear and helped me up. Ava clung on to me as if she thought that by letting go I would collapse. It was probably true. When I was finally upright I looked around me. My fight with Weir had churned the sand up and the boat was still there, grounded and taking on water. I took slight solace in that there was no sign of the shark.

"Luke, is it true?" asked Ava. "About Gills?"

Blonde curls poked out from beneath her red beanie, and as I looked into her blue eyes I almost lost myself. Without her arms around me I had no doubt that I would crumple to the ground. It was as if she was transferring her strength to me. I had to remind myself that the others were still around. As much as I could've stared into her eyes all day, there was a lot to sort out.

"Yeah. Sorry. The shark… it was so fast there was nothing we could do."

"Here." Pippa handed me a damp cloth and pressed it against my nose. "Hold it there until the bleeding stops."

I took it and tried to ignore the pain streaking through my head when I touched my nose. "What about Weir? What happened?"

We began to trudge back toward the others. I moved slowly as every step was difficult. Manny and Estelle were watching me carefully, as if I might turn into a zombie any second. I finally saw Weir on his knees with his hands clasped around his head. He was fuming and it was clear why. Chelsea was in front of him holding a flare gun. She had it pointed right at him.

"Chelsea? What the hell?"

She glanced at me quickly but resumed her watch over Weir. "I couldn't just stand by and watch. He wasn't going to stop, Uncle Luke."

As I looked at Pippa she just shrugged. "He's lucky she didn't shoot him."

"Where'd you get the gun?" I asked. "I thought we'd lost everything."

"It's probably wet and won't even work," muttered Weir.

"You want to test that theory?" said Chelsea menacingly.

"Washed up," replied Pippa. "A few things came ashore, but nothing else of use. Jesus, Luke, what are we going to do?"

I felt woozy, but there was no time for feeling sorry for myself. Gills had suffered far worse than me. I heard a splashing sound coming from close by, and as I looked at the ocean I thought maybe I saw something, just a flash of something dunking under the water. It was out there. Somewhere, it was still there, perhaps biding its time or waiting for the tide to rise and swamp our tiny sandbank. It knew these waters. It knew we were heading for shallow water and had chosen to attack when it did. It had miscalculated how much time it had, and that was the only thing that had saved us. Out there it was in charge. While my feet were on solid ground though, we had a chance.

"Weir, how close are we to land?" I shielded my eyes from the rain and the wind buffeting us, but saw no land close by. The ocean appeared to be all around us. We were stranded on an island, and with the boat half submerged we had no way off. "What are the tides like? If the water recedes and this storm doesn't get any worse perhaps we can walk to the mainland. Any chance more of this sandbank will reveal itself to us?"

Weir glared at me and said nothing. Rain poured over his head, turning his golden hair into a soggy mess of spaghetti. Raindrops and sweat dripped from his nose. I wanted no apology nor did I expect one. Our captain had only one goal: self-preservation.

"You know, Weir, if you help us, maybe we can help you?" I breathed heavily. Every breath I took made my body ache and my lungs burn. My nose was shattered and it felt like there was an invisible weight on my chest that I couldn't shake. "You brought us here, so you must have an idea of where we are, where we can go?"

Weir rolled his eyes and kept his mouth firmly closed.

"Why don't we just shoot him? Here, give me that." Manny took the flare gun from Chelsea. "He got us into this mess. I vote we get a new captain."

"Back off," said Weir. "You can't do that."

I sensed that Weir suspected Manny might just kill him, even though Manny would never do something like that. I knew Manny well enough. He would go out of his way to avoid squashing a spider, and certainly wouldn't kill a man.

"Why not? What good are you to us now?" asked Manny.

"Sounds like a fair question to me." Ava stood by my side and slipped her fingers in mine. "No great loss if you ask me. Do it, Manny. Shoot him and I'll throw his body to that shark myself."

"Woah, hold on, have you forgotten who you're speaking to?" Weir threw his hands up defensively. "I'm in charge here. Maybe I was out of order earlier. Fine. But you're taking things too far now."

"Shall we vote on it, Weir?" asked Manny, stepping closer to him and aiming the gun at his head. "What do you think the outcome will be? You think you've got anyone on your side? Estelle has only known you for five minutes and even she hates your guts. Give me one reason why I don't blow your head off?"

"Okay, okay, Jesus Christ."

Weir seemed to visibly shrink as he spoke to Manny. It was suddenly a different story when his own life was in threat. It was amusing to see him change, to see how he turned from the aggressor to a victim so quickly. I felt no pity for him anymore. He had brought it on himself. He had forgotten that without Jonah and Gills around he had lost all of his friends. There was no one left who would stand up for him now. He was on his own.

"The truth is, there is no way off this sandbank. The whole area is littered with shipwrecks and we've just chalked another one up. The mainland is miles away. There's no way of reaching it. The only way out of here is if we get lucky, someone passes by and spots us."

"That can't be true," whispered Pippa.

Her lips trembled as she spoke and I could see she was shivering with cold. We were all drenched and the never-ending rain didn't look like it was going to stop soon. The biting wind ran through our bones and the thought of waiting out here for someone to spot us was depressing. I didn't want to put all my hopes on luck. I wanted to do something, to find a way to the mainland.

"What about the shallow water?" I asked. "Do you know what direction we were headed in before we crashed? Maybe we can wade or swim to the next sandbank, make it to the mainland? If we avoid the open water we could—"

"No. It's too far. There's no way of knowing what direction to go either. You take one foot off this tiny stretch of land and you're liable to end up in deep water as much as you are shallow. Forget swimming anywhere. That shark will pick us off one by one."

"I want to go home," said Chelsea quietly.

She let Pippa run her hands through Chelsea's fine, sandy hair, wiping it from her eyes. It stuck to her wet forehead and when she revealed her brown eyes I saw a despair and bleakness there that I didn't want to see again. She was still young. There was still a chance for her to make a life, if only we could figure this mess out.

"Me too, honey," said Pippa, as she kissed Chelsea's head. "Me too."

Had I done the wrong thing? The *Tukino* hadn't been the answer, just a temporary home when our old one crumbled. There was no way they were going to live on a boat for the rest of their lives. I had to find a new home for us all, a dry one on solid ground. But first we had to find a way off this sandbank.

"If you're telling me that we're finished, that there is literally nothing we can do, then I guess I may as well just shoot you after all." Manny pinched the bridge of his nose. "This is ridiculous, Weir. You can't tell me you came here with no plan. What did you think would happen?"

Weir shrugged his shoulders and looked at the trawler. "The plan was to sail right through. The plan was to get away from that shark." Weir turned away from the decimated boat and looked at Estelle. "We might have made it too if we hadn't stopped and wasted our time picking up that Goddamn *puta*."

Just when I thought Weir was starting to accept us and take on a more conciliatory tone, he reverted back to his old ways. Manny raised the flare gun and smashed it against Weir's temple. Weir groaned in pain, but stayed on his knees.

"You deserved that," I said. "You forget that *you* were the captain of our ship. You were in charge. If you want to blame anyone for our predicament, I suggest you take a look at yourself."

Blood oozed from the cut on the side of Weir's face. If he expected sympathy he was going to be sorely out of luck.

"Shoot me. Better a quick death than dying out here, waiting for that bitch to eat us. Once the water's high enough she'll be back. She knows we're here. She's got the taste of blood now and I can guarantee you she wants more. That shark is what you should be worried about, not me. So, go ahead, shoot me." Weir pushed himself up and lowered his arms. He took a step toward Manny. "Do it."

For a second I thought Manny was going to do it.

"Why waste it on you?" Manny wasn't scared of Weir. He stayed toe to toe with him. "Let that shark eat your sorry ass."

Suddenly, Manny raised the flare gun to the sky and pulled the trigger. There was a popping noise and then the flare shot up into the sky leaving a trail of smoke behind it. A few seconds later and the sky was lit up by a red light that arced away from us.

"Like you said, we have to hope someone might spot us," said Manny. "So, sit tight, Weir and hold on to your hat. Because trust me, if nobody comes for us, I'm going to make damn sure that shark gets you first."

Weir gritted his teeth and stepped back. "Whatever."

"You think anyone will see it?" asked Ava.

"Well, it worked, so that's one piece of good luck we've had. I didn't think it would do anything. I guess we have to wait and see now."

"You okay, brother?" Manny approached me and tossed the flare gun aside.

"Sure," I lied. I could still see the shark, how it had devoured Gills and then circled back for me. I still remembered how it had felt, knowing it was beneath me as I swam to shore. "I just hope that flare works. If not—"

"I know," replied Manny. He looked at the ocean and sighed. "If it doesn't work we may as well have stayed in New York and gone down with our apartment."

Cold rain pricked my face and I looked at the ocean. With Ava's hand in mine I felt optimistic. I had to get Pippa and Chelsea home, wherever that was, and take care of Estelle too. All we could do now was wait, and pray.

CHAPTER 16

Manny had done the right thing using the flare. Remaining optimistic was difficult, but the alternative was giving up and I wasn't ready for that. Somebody just *had* to see our flare. I refused to believe that this was it. We huddled together as the tempest thundered around us. Every time a huge wave splashed us I thought the sandbank would be submerged. We stayed close, using each other for warmth and comfort. The exception, of course, was Weir. We tried to coax him in, tried to offer him support even after what he'd done, but he stubbornly refused any help. He stayed away from us, muttering to himself and staring out at the ocean. I don't think he felt any remorse or guilt for our situation. He just didn't want to be part of the group. I guess losing his old friends, Jonah and Gill, affected him more than us. He felt like an outsider.

Ava and Chelsea talked to Estelle, and got a little more information out of her. She was a sweet girl, looking for somewhere safe to go like all of us. She and her father had come from Florida, a place I knew had been decimated by the rising sea levels. The swamps had disappeared and the alligators had spread. That southern piece of paradise had become a watery grave for a lot of people. Her father had tried to get them north, unable to find any way inland. They had hung on until the end, until there was nothing left. They'd been adrift for two days and if we hadn't come along when we had, then there probably wouldn't have been a good ending for either of them.

Pippa fussed over me, worried I would have concussion or something, but I managed to assure her I was fine. Sure, I felt beat up, but I would be okay. I was more concerned at the lack of response to our flare. Time was hard to judge, but it felt like hours. With the cold rain battering all of us and nothing to do, it felt like time had slowed to a crawl. Manny kept pacing up and down, searching for a boat, a sign, anything that we had been spotted. I think two or three hours must have passed before we saw anything at all.

"There, a boat, see?" said Manny. "Is it heading our way?"

I squinted against the gale and saw what Manny had noticed before any of us. Rising and falling with the ocean there was a boat, although it was impossible to know if it was coming our way or just passing by. It looked a little like a tanker, long and gray, with no clear sign of life. We watched it for a while, all of us hoping it was heading south. After a while it became evident that it hadn't seen us. It may have just been adrift itself. When it disappeared Manny became more withdrawn, disillusioned with our lot.

"Luke, what if nothing comes?" asked Pippa. "What if..?"

"*Don't*," I replied. "Don't Pippa. There are others out there. We just have to be patient."

The *Tukino* was a wreck, destined to be torn apart over time as the ocean rusted it. Its silent presence was an unfortunate reminder of how close we were to death too. It was hard clinging onto hope when there was nothing to see, nothing but the water and the sky surrounding us.

It could have been a few minutes or an hour. I really did lose all track of time. But finally, eventually, Manny spotted another boat. This was different, much smaller than the tanker. I didn't want to get my hopes up, but it was starting to get dark. Soon it would be cold and we had no shelter. I wasn't sure we could survive the night out here, and we had no food or water either. This felt like our last chance.

"I saw it a while ago, but I didn't want to say anything in case I jinxed it. I think it's heading our way. I really do," said Manny.

I detected optimism in his voice, and I hoped it wasn't misplaced. Still, as we watched the boat it did appear to be coming for us. It got larger and larger, struggling against the large waves, until finally it was close enough to see clearly. When I saw the name on the side I couldn't help but smile.

"You're right, Manny. I think it's coming for us. I think it's Douglas."

"Douglas?" Manny's face was blank. "Do we..?"

"Is that who you told me about?" asked Pippa, clutching my arm. "Is that them?"

I nodded. "Douglas and Honey. It has to be. I recognize that name, the *Bella*. It's their boat for sure."

As the yacht neared the sandbank I suddenly worried that it might hit something too. How close would they be able to get? It was such a large yacht that it surely couldn't get any closer to us than the *Tukino*.

"They're going to pick us up, right? They're good people, aren't they?" asked Pippa.

I knew she was concerned, but I also knew that they would help. Even from the small amount of time we had spoken to them I could tell they were on the level. "Yeah, we'll be fine, just as long as they can get close enough to pick us up."

Pippa gripped me tighter. "But what about..?"

"He can see what happened to us," I said. "He'll know to avoid the shallow water. Trust me, they don't want to end up beached like we were."

"I wasn't worried about them hitting the sandbank," said Pippa quietly.

And then it dawned on me: the shark. Pippa was worried that it was still out there. I had to admit it could be. How long would it hang around? We hadn't seen any sign of it for hours. Would it really wait that long?

"Surely it's long gone?" said Manny.

There was that hope again, springing up out of him like an uncapped well.

"It must have better things to do than wait for us to be stupid enough to get back in the water."

I watched the superyacht get close, slow, and then stop. I waited for a sign, for Douglas or Honey to come out and give us a big grin, but nothing happened. The yacht just sat there.

"What's he waiting for? Send over the rescue party already," said Manny.

"Luke?"

Pippa didn't need to say any more. I could sense it too. Something told me that there was something wrong. It was just a feeling that this wasn't right. Why weren't they coming out to help us?

"This is stupid," said Manny. "How do they expect us to get to them? What are they waiting for?"

Weir marched into the surf, letting the water reach his knees. "Come on, join the party. What is this, a peep-show?"

Whether his words had an effect or not, I don't know. I suspected Douglas was just watching us, carefully, as Weir's words would have been swept away on the howling wind. Whilst it was an uncomfortable feeling being watched like that, I guess it made sense. Douglas had no idea who had fired the flare, and given the nature of the seas, he had every reason to be cautious.

Chelsea shivered visibly, reminding me of how cold and miserable I felt. We were all physically suffering and it was a relief when Douglas appeared on deck. He waved at us and then disappeared. From around the back of the yacht a few seconds later came a small single-engine boat, no bigger than a bath-tub. At least we weren't going to have to swim for it.

As the boat drew closer, its little engine straining against the storm, I saw it was Honey who had come out to rescue us. She looked the same, her arms so thin, yet now draped in a brown oilskin that flapped in the wind. Honey brought the boat right up to the sand, stopping a couple of feet short of Weir.

"Thank Christ for that," said Pippa. "Chelsea, let's go."

I could see we weren't all going to fit. The small boat would only fit three or four of us alongside Honey so she was going to have to make two trips to ferry us back and forth. We all approached nervously, desperate to get off the sandbank, and yet fearful of the ocean. The storm and shark had made us wary of the treacherous water surrounding us, yet we had no choice. We had to sink or swim.

I was in no mood for another fight, so I was pleased when Manny stepped forward. Weir had reached for the boat first and was about to clamber aboard when Manny tugged him back.

"*You* get to wait," said Manny.

Manny helped Ava, Chelsea and Pippa climb in, and then Estelle squeezed in beside them. I tried to catch Honey's eyes, to say hi, but she kept her head down and said very little. I guess it was difficult with the storm, and it was awkward just keeping the boat steady. Manny and I held onto it until the women were all in and then they were off. I watched Honey zip back to the yacht and waited patiently for her to return.

"She say much to you?" I asked Manny. "She didn't seem too happy about being out here."

"Do you blame her?" Manny sniffed. "I think I'm getting the flu. We're damn lucky they spotted our flare."

"True." I looked at the *Bella*. It was an imposing vessel, larger than I remembered, yet it was the most beautiful thing I had seen all day. To know that we would soon be safe, dry and warm made me feel something approaching happiness. There was still no sign of the shark. It was gone, off to terrorize someone else. The yacht would be home for a short while, but I knew Pippa wouldn't want to hang around too long. No matter how comfortable it was, it wasn't home. It wasn't ours. "What do you think, Manny? Douglas and Honey weren't too well off last time we met. They're going to need our help. How are you finding this life out on the ocean? Something you could get used to?"

Manny shook his head and gave me a look that suggested I had flipped. "Giant sharks chasing us? Are you crazy? No, this is just a rest-stop until we get back on track. We need to find *dry* land, man. You hear me? Dry land."

I glanced at Weir. He kept his distance from us, a few feet back, and said nothing. He was just waiting to get onto the yacht. I suspected that once he was safely on board, that would be the last we'd see of him. He wanted nothing to do with us, and that was fine by me. He'd made his own choices.

"I hear you. Pippa wants to find a place for her and Chelsea. Start over. I don't know how easy that's going to be. The mainland seems to get further away every day. And so much of the land is under water now that I don't know how they'd find food or fresh water. I doubt much still grows. I want to help her, I *will*, but I just don't know where to start."

The little boat returned from behind the yacht, Honey driving it straight toward us.

"You sound like you're not planning on joining her." Manny folded his arms. "Don't tell me Uncle Luke is thinking of breaking the family ties? I thought you and Pippa were joined at the hip."

"Yeah, well, I figured maybe she was right. She said a few things to me on the trawler, made me see things a bit differently. I don't know anymore, Manny. I'm not sure I can keep doing this. I mean I love my sister, and Chelsea, but… but I'm missing something. I'm missing out on my own family. Shoot, I sound like an idiot. I have no idea what's going to happen. But Pippa needs the chance to raise Chelsea without me interfering all the time."

"I'd hardly call it interfering. I know what you do for them, Luke. Still, if you want some help you know I've got your back. Chelsea's a great kid. She'll miss you like crazy if you go your own way."

"I know." Was I really contemplating leaving them? I had lived with Pippa and Chelsea for so long that I didn't know any other life. Yet, faced with getting on this huge yacht it felt like I had a decision to make. How long could I keep following them, trying to please Pippa and bring up Chelsea when she was my niece, not my daughter? Thinking about them I felt proud; proud of everything they had done and everything they had become. I had played my part, but they could cope without me. Pippa was stronger than she let on, and Chelsea was hardly a little kid anymore. She would be seventeen soon. It was time for a clean break. Once we found somewhere safe for them to live, I would tell Pippa. I wasn't going to abandon them, and I wasn't going anywhere without them until I knew they had their own place to call home; I had to create my own life instead of living it through someone else. As I watched Honey approach, I knew what I wanted. I liked being out on the ocean, even if it did mean you had to watch your backs from being hunted by giant sharks. The Megalodon couldn't be everywhere at once though. If we were clever we could avoid it, I was sure of that. To start my life over I just needed a chance to talk to Ava. She might be annoyed at me, but I knew there was something between us. If I could just talk to her, I could talk her round. I could really get to know her and if she got to know me better, I was certain things would work out.

"Finally," said Weir, as Honey drew the boat up to us. He grabbed the side of the hull and leapt in.

"I'm not sorry to see the back of this garbage dump," said Manny, as he jumped in behind me. "I never was one for the beach."

The boat was cramped and water sloshed around the interior around our feet. I thanked Honey as I sat down and she grunted at me, but kept her eyes averted. With the ocean spray, it was hard to have a conversation anyway, and the second we were in she turned the boat around and headed for the yacht. As we got closer it looked even more impressive. I wondered if Douglas and Honey really owned the boat, or if they had just been lucky. Perhaps they had inherited it, or perhaps they'd stolen it. I didn't care, quite frankly. I was just grateful they had come along when they had. I took one final look at the sandbank and the *Tukino*. She was stuck fast and half of the boat was under the ocean. It was pure luck that we hadn't all been killed. Seeing the trawler like that reminded me of Jonah. He probably thought he would die on that ship, probably years from now. I felt bad for him, sorry that I couldn't have done more. I looked to the *Bella* as we shuttled away from the sandbank. No more looking back. I had to look forward to the future now. There was a lot to sort out and a lot to discuss; thanking Douglas and Honey was number one on the list. After that they would have to get in line. Pippa and Chelsea had to talk to me about where they wanted to settle and where was realistic. They had to realize finding a new home wasn't going to be easy. I had no idea what Estelle wanted, but I was fairly certain she would go wherever we went. She seemed to be getting along with us just fine, and being on her own, would be a fool to turn down an offer of help. Manny too. Weir would probably want to be dropped off at the first place we came to, where he could get his own boat. The feelings of dread left me as we neared the yacht. I saw Chelsea and Pippa waving at me, smiling. For the first time in a long time, I began to feel excited for the future. A fresh start. We all needed it, something to believe in and look forward to. As I looked at Ava, I knew where my future lay.

Honey pulled up alongside the yacht and Douglas appeared suddenly, his hands reaching down to grab us. He threw a rope to Honey and they quickly secured the boat. I couldn't wait to get my feet onto the deck, onto something solid and dry. Douglas said nothing but helped me up, and together we hauled Manny up. Weir shoved my offer of help aside and pulled himself up.

"We did it," said Ava, as she threw her arms around me. "I didn't think... I thought we were done for."

I hugged her and looked at the others, cold and wet, yet all grateful to be back on a boat. Relief was the overriding emotion.

"Douglas. Thank goodness you found us," I said, shaking his hand. "I thought you were heading north? I guess lucky for us you changed your mind."

He grimaced as I shook his hand. "We were heading for Kiawah Island when I saw you. The resort is still there, well most of it, and you got lucky with that flare you sent up. I figured I couldn't just leave you."

"I'm Luke," I said. "This is my sister, Pippa and her daughter Chelsea." I made brief introductions. Everyone thanked Douglas and Honey, apart from Weir. He simply grunted and looked out at the ocean. I don't know if he was worried about the Megalodon returning, or just feeling embarrassed at having to be rescued. His attitude didn't concern me too much. I knew he would jump ship at the first opportunity.

"Douglas, we don't have time for this. We should get going." Honey touched his shoulder and he jumped as if she had hit him with an electric current. "We're behind schedule."

"Okay, okay, I know. You don't have to remind me," he replied impatiently.

Douglas let go of my hand and pointed to a glass door nearby that led into what looked like a lounge. I could see reclining sofas inside, potted plants and what looked like a bar. Although the glass in the room's windows were broken, the furniture looked comfortable. We were all so desperately tired, cold and wet, that we would've been grateful for a bare cell if it got us out of the rain.

"You should all get inside and warm up," said Douglas. "There are blankets and some spare clothes around. Help yourself to a drink. We have food set aside too, but we can arrange that later. Right now, I should get us moving."

"Douglas, we need to *go*." Honey prodded him impatiently.

Douglas offered a wan smile. "Luke, you want to join me upstairs?"

I nodded and ushered the others toward the open door. Honey began to climb a staircase to the upper deck and Douglas followed her, pausing and beckoning me to follow.

"Are these two on the level?" asked Ava, before she left. "They seem a little off."

"You prefer the company of sharks? Yeah, they're on the level. Jonah knew it as soon as he saw them."

"But they seem a bit, I don't know, preoccupied. Like they don't really want to be here. You heard how Honey kept saying we had to go."

I cupped my hands around Ava's face. "We just have to trust them, right? What choice do we have? They seem nice to me. Let's go with it. I'll go talk to Douglas and join you soon. I figure he just wants to know who he's dealing with. Would you watch over Chelsea for me? I'm worried about her. She'd never say anything, but after the ordeal with the *Tukino* and nearly drowning earlier, she needs a good rest and a friend to talk to."

Ava leant in and gently kissed me. "Deal."

She smiled and slipped away from me. With the others starting to make themselves at home I followed Douglas up the metal staircase. He said nothing but led me up the steps until we reached a black door. With the rain still falling he hesitated in front of it and looked down at me a few steps below.

"Luke, I know you helped me before. I'm sorry about your boat. I wish things could be different."

"Forget it," I replied. "Let's just get inside and figure out where to next. If you still want to get down to Kiawah then I'm all for it. This is your ship, Douglas. You're in charge."

"Right. Yes, of course."

Douglas looked out at the ocean. There was nothing to see, just waves crashing into each other and a gray sky filled with rain. I followed his eyes in case he had seen the shark, but it had gone. There was no fin, no sandbank, and no land; just endless water as far as the eye could see. I took a step up closer to Douglas. I could see no reason for him to wait out here in the cold. Honey had intimated they should get moving quickly and I was inclined to agree with her.

"I'm pretty exhausted, you know. Shall we go in?" I glanced at the black door, which I guessed led to the bridge. "Everything all right, Douglas?"

"Yeah, yeah, I just… never mind." Douglas glanced through the small square window in the door and sighed. "This is the bridge. You'll find everything you need in here. Let's go."

Douglas pushed the door open and we marched into the bridge. It was a large room, warm and dry, and the glass panels offered an almost 360 degree view. The yacht was magnificent. With all the instruments and computer technology on display in front of me it was clear that Douglas knew what he was doing. It meant nothing to me, but Jonah would probably have given his right arm to have this sort of equipment.

Douglas slammed the door shut behind me and went over to Honey who was pushing buttons into a console, presumably charting a path out of the shallows, south to the resort where they'd been going before stopping to save us.

There was another man next to her, bending over the console. I guessed it took a large crew to run a yacht this large, although it was odd Douglas hadn't mentioned him before. When we'd encountered each other earlier it felt as if they were alone, just the two of them. I wondered if he was their son. He was dressed in black jeans with a tight charcoal T-shirt hugging his slight frame. Even with his back to me I could tell he was young. I cleared my throat and the man turned around as I approached.

"Luke," I said holding out my hand. "Thank you for—"

"Don't mention it."

The man whirled around and pointed a gun at me. It looked like a pistol, but I was no expert. He wasn't their son, and he wasn't part of the crew. This man was different. He had a hold over them. Despite his obvious youth, he was serious and glared at me as he lifted the gun and aimed it at my head. His face was young and he had piercing blue eyes. He swept floppy blonde hair from his face and smiled maliciously. I knew then he wasn't Douglas and Honey's son. He looked familiar, although I was sure I had never seen him before.

"Luke, I'm sorry," sighed Douglas. His shoulders literally slumped when he saw the gun pointed at me. "This is Lance. He's in charge here. I'm sorry to drag you into this. He's with McKade."

CHAPTER 17

"Are we done here?" Lance shoved Douglas in the back. "Well?"

"Yes, we're done. We'll be back to your boss soon."

The yacht surged away from the sandbank and suddenly the luxury ship didn't feel so safe or welcoming. Lance had ordered Douglas to set a course back to Mckade's ship, and I understood why Honey and Douglas had been so reticent about helping us. They were dragging us deeper into trouble.

"Where is he?" I asked. "Where is Mckade? Hiding out while you do the hard work?" It struck me then why I thought I recognized him. He was Ava's brother. He had the same eyes, the same naturally blonde hair. What he didn't have was her warmth and charisma. He spoke with bitterness and a toxicity that practically oozed from his pores. They might share the same blood, but they were worlds apart in personality. "Did he send you here?"

"Luke, yeah? When I need your opinion I'll ask for it." Lance glared at Douglas. "You and Honey stay here. You'd better get us back to Mckade in fifteen minutes."

Douglas rolled his eyes. "Look, we've done what you asked. We followed them and found them. We haven't done anything to you, so why don't you just let us go? This is unnecessary."

"Unnecessary?" Lance ran a hand through his shaggy hair. "I'll tell you what this is, Douglas. This is a job. This is something you're doing for us in return for us letting you live. You get that, right? I mean, when Mckade gave you a chance this is what you chose. I distinctly remember you choosing to help us, or am I wrong?"

"Some choice. I let you take our boat and you leave us out in the ocean to drown, or we work for you with a gun pointed in our faces."

Lance smiled, but there was no warmth in it. "I'm not here to argue. Or do you have a *problem* with our arrangement? I'm sure Donovan would be happy to come up here and explain things."

Lance raised a small hand-held radio to his mouth.

"No, no, it's fine. Everything is fine," said Douglas quickly. He sank back against the console and grabbed Honey's hand. "We're okay, right?"

I noticed at the mention of Donovan that Honey slid away from Lance. Until then she had been quiet, but suddenly she seemed nervous.

Lance lowered the radio. "Okay, Douglas. Okay. So, why don't you explain to our friend here what's going on? I mean, I assume you brought him up here for a reason?"

"I think I've figured out much of it already," I said. "Douglas and Honey were heading north, trying to get away from you. Yet, somehow Mckade caught up with them. Quite why you follow him I don't get. You're nothing like your sister."

For a moment Lance's bravado faded and he looked puzzled. "You know Ava?"

"I know that you abandoned her to follow that lunatic. I know that Mckade is bad news and if you're in with him, then you've chosen the wrong side. I don't know what's going on here, Lance, but you have an opportunity. You talked about giving Douglas choices, well now I'm giving you one. Stop this. Whatever hold Mckade has over you isn't worth this. Why go back to him? Join us. My family are downstairs. I know Ava would love to see you again. Douglas and Honey are good people. This boat clearly has ample room for us all. Join us before Mckade makes you do something you really regret."

Lance puffed out his cheeks and exhaled. "Wow, that was quite a speech. Coming from someone I gave a shit about, it might actually mean something. But, you see, I don't know *you* or your family. And I don't know how you know Ava, but I'm not going to give this up for her, or anyone else. Mckade is going places. He's gathering an army to run his armada, and I know what side to be on. It sure ain't yours."

"Listen to him," said Douglas quietly. "We can take you wherever you want. You don't *have* to go back to him. I've seen how Mckade operates. He's just using you. And when he's done he'll drop you in the ocean with a bullet in your head. You're not a stupid kid, Lance, so—"

Lance whipped the butt of the gun across Douglas' nose. He instantly cried out in pain and brought his hands up to his face. Blood spurted between his fingers and he fell to his knees. Honey fell with him, crying.

"Leave them alone. What is this?" I couldn't believe he was so different to Ava. "There's no need for this, Lance."

"You shut your damn mouth," said Lance, turning the gun toward me. "This is *not* up for discussion. Mckade has given me orders to bring you back to him. We saw your trawler. Shame we lost the boat, but your family can still help. Like I said, he needs workers. We wouldn't have needed Douggy and his yacht, except you went into the shallow water. It was far too dangerous to follow you in there ourselves. So, we are going back to him and that's that."

"And my family? My friends?" I began to realize Lance's mind was made up. He wasn't for turning. I wondered if there was a chance I could convince him to abandon his foolish plan if he met with Ava. "Why don't we go down and talk to them. You'll see, Lance, that there are other ways of surviving out here."

"You know, that's the first thing you've said to me that makes sense. Why don't we go downstairs?"

"No." Douglas looked up at Lance as Honey clung to his shoulders. "No, we need to stay up here and make sure the *Bella* stays on course. This weather could turn worse at any moment. You've seen how wild it is out there. If it gets any—"

"Jesus, quit your whining." Lance sighed. "Look, I need to report back to Mckade what we're bringing him. So, I need to know who is down there."

"Just radio your friend. Donovan can tell you, right?" pleaded Douglas. "Or Luke can tell you exactly who is here."

"Enough!" shouted Lance. "Get on your feet. We're all going down there. I am over your shit. Douglas, you're staying here to make sure we stay on course. Luke and Honey are coming with me. A little insurance policy to make sure you don't get any funny ideas."

"No," insisted Douglas. "You *know* what Donovan did to Honey. I'm not putting her in that position again. What he did, what he would do... no, I can't allow that and you know it."

"On your feet," said Lance slowly. He pointed the gun at Douglas. "I'm going to count to five. Then Donovan will be the least of your worries. One."

"Lance, look, I'll tell you who is down there." I racked my brain to think of a way out of this. Clearly Honey was terrified of this man called Donovan, and Douglas had no intention of going down to the lower levels to face him again.

"Two," said Lance, ignoring me.

I looked around the room. The bridge was full of equipment to manage the boat, but nothing I could use to fight him.

"Three."

I thought about rushing him and making a grab for the gun. But there was too much space between us. If I made a move I might startle him and he would be able to get at least one shot off before I reached him.

"Four."

Douglas showed no sign of moving. He and Honey sat on the wooden floor looking up at him defiantly.

"Lance, you know what Donovan did to my wife. I am not going to let him near her again. I'll take you to Mckade. You can have this boat. You can take anything, but Honey is—"

"Five."

Lance moved the gun at the last moment and when he pulled the trigger I staggered back, too shocked at first to realize what he'd done. Blood splattered all over the console and Douglas's face, as Honey's head exploded. The bullet entered through one eye and shattered her skull. Grisly lumps of her brain and skin dripped down the side of Douglas. Some of her blood splattered my bare feet. There was no time to scream or react. Her lifeless body slumped and then Lance sprang into action. He grabbed Douglas and hauled him to his feet. He shoved the hot muzzle of the gun under Douglas's chin, his finger twitching on the trigger.

"Stay here, point your damn ship in the right direction, and get us to Mckade. You fucking understand me?"

Lance shoved Douglas forward and he crashed into a control panel. With the two of them preoccupied I took a couple of steps back. I was close to the door now and I had to warn the others. I had to warn Ava. I had to get down and make sure this Donovan hadn't done anything to them. I had to get out of here. The bridge stank of death. Honey's face was a bloody mess, blown apart beyond recognition. The sound of the gun still rang in my ears, and I couldn't imagine what Douglas was going through.

Douglas glanced at his dead wife's body and then the blood on his hands. "What have you done? Honey? This isn't… this isn't happening. Honey… Honey, get up. Honey?"

As Douglas tried to bend down to his wife, Lance pushed him away. "Focus, Douglas. The boat." Lance swung the gun in my direction and I froze. "Don't make me count to five again."

I held up my hands. "Douglas, I'm sorry but you have to do it. Stay here. Take us to Mckade."

Douglas swayed on his feet as if he was dizzy. "But… but—"

"One, Douglas," said Lance. "In fact that's one, two, and three for wasting my time. Next comes four and then a big bang. You want that? Or you going to start listening to me?"

The ringing noise in my ears still reverberated around like a school bell and I felt sick. Honey was dead. Lance had killed her in front of us as if it meant nothing. Could this really be Ava's brother? What kind of psychopath was Mckade who could convince a young boy to commit cold-blooded murder?

Lance's radio crackled. "Pick up, Lance. What's going on? I heard a shot."

Lance kept the gun trained on me and with his free hand raised the radio to his mouth. "Donovan, we're coming down. I just had to focus Douglas' mind. Let's just say your friend Honey won't be joining us."

There was a chuckle on the other end of the radio that made my skin crawl. This was a man who right now had my family and Ava at his mercy. I assumed he had a gun too but hoped he wasn't stupid enough to use it.

Lance glanced at me and then back to Douglas. "If I'm not down there in sixty seconds, pick one of the survivors out and throw them overboard. I can tell we're going to have trouble with this crew."

Lance lowered the radio and I gritted my teeth. How could he act so callously? He had already become so twisted and bitter, so malevolent, that it was hard to accept he was so young.

"Four, Douglas. Remember what happens next?" Lance prodded Douglas in the arm.

"Douglas, for Christ sake answer him." I snapped. I know the man had just lost his wife, his boat, everything that meant anything to him in the world, but he had to realize he was putting me in danger. "Just take him to Mckade and get this over with. Honey is gone. Just do what he says."

Just as I thought Lance was about to pull the trigger, Douglas began to nod his head. He mumbled something inaudible and then put his hands on the control.

"Say that again, Douglas?" asked Lance.

"I'll take us to Mckade," muttered Douglas.

"Good enough." Lance punched Douglas on the side of the head. It wasn't enough to really hurt him, just a shock that made him look up. "Any funny business and I start making more banging noises. Got it?"

Lance grinned and turned to me. "So, Luke, what do you say we go join the others? I need to find out who we've snagged for the captain. The weather seems to have taken a turn for the worst so we'll take the scenic route. This really is a beautiful ship. On the way down you can tell me how the hell you know my sister."

Lance grabbed my collar and twisted me around. There was another door that led to the interior of the ship. I felt the gun in between my shoulder blades, and then Lance's warm breath in my ear.

"Same goes for you, Lukey. I think you're trying anything and this goes boom."

I let Lance shove me forward and we left Douglas behind on the bridge. I think he knew better than to do anything stupid, and as we made our way into the bowels of the ship I began to wonder just how we were going to get out of this one. If Donovan was anything like Lance we were in trouble. Mckade's men were under orders and we were obviously expected shortly. Quite why he thought we would join his crew I don't know. If Mckade was assembling an army he needed men, sailors, people like Gills and Weir; he would have little use for women like Chelsea and Ava. Then it dawned on me that he would have *plenty* of use for

Chelsea and Ava. I felt my stomach flip and knew exactly what he had planned for us.

"Down there," said Lance. "There's another door at the end of the corridor that leads to a staircase. We'll find Donovan at the bottom of it, and whoever else was with you, Luke."

We passed several rooms that looked as if they had been ransacked. I saw bedrooms that once must have been the height of luxury. Now the sheets were tossed aside, and the contents of every cupboard and drawer had been turned inside out.

"Lance, do you know why our boat crashed? Do you know what's out there?" I had to try something, make him understand that we weren't just battling the elements or Mckade. "Have you seen what's out there in the ocean?"

"Yeah, Mckade. He's the king in these parts and his empire is spreading. There's no need to worry though, unless you want to be a little bitch like Douglas. He needs men. Play this right and you can join us. I'm not just saying that. This is a great opportunity for you."

I opened the door and found a set of steps leading down. "An opportunity to join a bunch of murdering pirates? I don't think so."

Lance laughed and we stopped at the top of the staircase. "Pirates? I think we're a little more advanced than that."

I put one hand on the rail and turned to face him. His blue eyes blazed. He was getting off on the power that the gun gave him. Without it, I had no doubt he would be another lost soul searching for something to give his life meaning.

"America is gone," said Lance. "The mainland is swamped with disease. The food's running out and the water is still rising. The future is on the water. Mckade figured that out a while ago. You refuse to join him, you might as well be dead."

"So, what if we don't decide to join him? What if none of us do? Are you going to kill us all?"

Lance shrugged. "Probably. Mckade has no time for losers. He took over the oil depot a few days ago. Killed the woman who ran it. I saw him do it with my own eyes. When we get close enough I'm going to radio in just who we picked up and he'll tell me what to do. If he thinks you're of no use then it's *sayonara*, Lukey."

The yacht was warm and yet far from comfortable. It swayed violently as the growing storm battered us. Lance put one hand on the rail next to me and I leaned in to see his face clearly. I had to believe there was still some humanity inside him.

"Does that include Ava? You going to kill her too?"

Lance looked at me and said nothing. He was sizing me up, trying to decide if I was playing games.

"Bullshit. She's not here. You're stalling."

"You think I'd want to stall, knowing that Ava is down there with this Donovan guy?" That seemed to get Lance's attention. He caught his breath and waited for me to explain. "I fell in with her crew a few days ago. My family and a couple of friends are with her down there. We're not looking for trouble Lance, just a ride. You could easily call into Mckade and tell him there was nobody left alive. Our boat crashed, you saw it. Tell him there was nobody around to pick us up; that we all drowned. Hell, I don't care, tell him we were all eaten by a giant prehistoric shark. Just let us go. Let Ava go."

Lance shook his head. "You must think I'm dumb."

He pushed me and I took a step backward. It wasn't enough to send me flying down the stairs, but the meaning was clear.

"Move it," said Lance menacingly. "I need to talk to Donovan."

I began to descend the staircase with Lance behind me. The gun was quickly at my back and pressed between my shoulder blades.

"Just think about it, Lance. We can help you. You can come with us if you want. There's more at play here than Mckade. The ocean isn't safe. It isn't our future. The Megalodon is out there and—"

"The *what*? Don't tell me you saw one?"

"The Megalodon? With my own eyes. Too close, I can tell you. What do you think ripped a big hole in the hull of our ship?"

"Now I know you're full of it," said Lance. "Mckade says they're stories designed to keep people out of the water. The government invented them as a way of keeping people on the dying mainland, a desperate last ploy to keep control when we all know they've lost it. Get your ass down to the lounge and I'll find out just what else you've been lying to me about."

I reached the bottom of the stairs and put my hand on the door. I couldn't hear any chatter or noise from the other side and guessed that Donovan had them under control. "Fine. Have it your way." I pushed open the door and walked into the lounge, recognizing the room immediately. It was the same one that I'd seen when getting aboard the yacht a few minutes earlier. The outer doors were closed now and everyone was sat on the couches and chairs. I caught Pippa's eye, but said nothing. In the center of the room was a heavy-set man, thick hands holding a gun similar to Lance's. He swung it toward me as I entered the room.

"Lance, you had about ten seconds left before I was going to throw the black guy overboard. What took you so long?"

The man who I assumed to be Donovan wore a flannel shirt and grubby jeans with frayed heels. He had steel-capped boots and a look in his eyes that told me not to say anything, or I would end up just like Honey.

"This piss-ant's been trying to convince me there's a giant shark out here with us."

"Yeah, I heard those stories too. Total BS." Donovan scratched the stubble that ringed his face. "We should be within range any moment. Let's radio Mckade and tell him what we got here."

Donovan raised the radio to his mouth and then Ava sprang up as Lance came out from behind me into the room.

"Lance?"

He looked at me with disbelief and then at Ava before breaking out into a laugh. "I thought you were full of shit. Ava?"

She began to smile and approached us. But before she could cross the room Donovan grabbed her arm. "Sit down."

"Sorry, sis. Better do what he says," said Lance.

"But Lance, you can tell them to leave us alone, right?" Ava sat back down next to Manny. "Explain to him who I am. Tell him."

Lance ran a hand through his hair and sighed. "Sorry, you made your choice. You had a chance to join me, to join Mckade on your own terms, but there's nothing I can do now." Lance quickly scanned the room and then turned to Donovan. "Get the boss on the radio. Tell him we've got seven survivors, including four women. Pretty good haul, I'd say."

Donovan licked his lips. "Damn good haul." He let his eyes drift over to Chelsea. "I'm looking forward to getting back. We're going to have some real good fun tonight."

CHAPTER 18

"Nothing. Must be the storm." Donovan lowered the silent radio. "I'll try again in a minute."

Lance wandered over to the bar and began to pour a bottle of open whisky into a glass. "Luke, take a seat. We may as well get to know one another. I'm sure the captain will have his own questions."

"I've got a few questions for him myself," I said, as I went to stand next to Pippa and Chelsea. I wanted to try and put myself in between them and Donovan. I didn't like the way he was looking at them. "But let's start with you."

"Me?" Lance drank from a glass tumbler and then threw the glass behind the bar where it smashed on the tiles. "Oh no, I think it's time for a family reunion. Think of the tears, the joy; the drama!" Lance wandered back into the center of the room. "How about it Ava?"

I was pleased that Ava was close to Manny. If anything happened he would stand up for her. Weir and Estelle had their own chairs around the side of the room. Douglas' yacht was furnished with expensive niceties and artwork that oozed money, and yet many of the windows were broken or cracked. I remembered how the side of the boat had been scratched and dented. Mckade must have let Douglas go to follow him, fooling him into thinking they had escaped when he had just been a decoy to round up more survivors.

"Lance, what the hell is wrong with you?" Ava asked angrily. "You wave a gun in my face and expect me to be ok with that? And what happened upstairs? Donovan said you had some trouble with Douglas and Honey."

"It's all sorted now. They just needed teaching a lesson. Forget them. Let's talk about you. Let's talk about how you abandoned me."

Ava leant forward and stared at Lance. "Abandoned you? Are you crazy? Jesus, Jonah offered us a place and you threw it back in his face. You left me, Lance, left me alone and—"

"You were with Jonah. You were *safe*. I had to leave and you know it. He hated me. Jonah treated me like dirt, not like Mckade does. Jonah was a stupid old man who didn't respect me, didn't see my potential. Where is the old fart anyway?"

"Jonah's dead, Lance. And he treated you fairly, the same as me. You were just too stubborn to see it. Jonah helped me and he would've helped you too, if you'd given him half a chance. Now he's gone and these people are all I have left. The *Tukino* sank and... look, it hardly matters now anyway. What are you playing at with Mckade? He's bad news and he's going to get you into trouble. More trouble than you're already in. You don't know what you're doing. You don't know what's out here or you wouldn't be messing around with him."

"Enlighten me. What's out here that I should be so scared of?"

Ava looked at me and I silently nodded my head.

"A shark," she explained. "A Megalodon. It's big enough to chew this boat up and tear it in half. And believe me, you don't want to piss it off. So, where exactly are you taking us?"

Lance looked at Donovan and then the two of them chuckled. It was forced, for our show only. They weren't giving anything away.

"You know, I don't believe in monsters, Ava." Lance walked across the tiled floor to his sister. "But maybe *you* should. Mckade is going to put you to work. He's the captain I follow, the man who is sorting this crap out. He's waiting for us now on his boat and it puts this one to shame. It's got a helicopter landing pad, three bars, a heap of bedrooms; everything you could possibly want and everything you never knew you wanted. It's a floating palace. You think I want to scrounge out a living on a trawler, fishing for scraps when I could be living in luxury? Dream on, Ava. If you know what's good for you, then you'll sign up. There's a lot of hard work involved, but nothing's for free, right? Someone like you will be of use to him. I'm sure he can think of a *service* you'll be able to perform. You and the other girls are *very* welcome on our ship. Luke and you men here can sign up or swim back to the mainland. There's no in-between anymore. Mckade has control of all the diesel depots down the eastern seaboard and he's expanding. He needs willing workers." Lance whirled around to talk to the room. "That goes for *all* of you. This is an opportunity for you. Take it. Or not. There are plenty of bullets to go round."

"Okay, tone it down, buddy," said Manny. "We're just trying to get a handle on the situation. There's no need for threats."

"Threats? Oh, I haven't even started. Donovan, you got anything on that radio yet?"

I bristled as Donovan tried the radio again. He was a large man and rushing him would probably be a very bad idea. But waiting to face Mckade seemed like an even worse option. It was clear that his operation was run on fear of death. I had no intention of joining up and was quite sure nobody else would either. The inference from Lance was all too clear about what fate the women would have, and I would do anything in my power to stop Mckade getting his hands on my family and Ava. I glanced at Manny and wondered if he could read my mind. Donovan was close enough to me that I could rush him, maybe not enough to stop him shooting me, but it would give the others a chance. Manny was behind Lance and had the same chance. If we went together then maybe, just *maybe*, we could overpower them. Quite how I was going to communicate my idea to Manny escaped me. If what Lance said was true, then it would only be a few minutes before we reached their ship. If we let them take us on board then it was over. He would have the numbers to do whatever he wanted. I might not be able to stop Mckade, but I could stop Lance and Donovan.

"Come in, this is Donovan. Are you picking me up? We've picked up seven lowlifes. Come in, come in," said Donovan, as the radio finally crackled into life. It hissed and spluttered, and then a male voice came over clearly.

"*Donovan, that you? Where you been?*"

The big man smiled. "Harry, where've you been my whole life? Is Mckade with you? This weather held us up a while. Don't worry, it's all under control now. Lance had to off the bitch, but we got seven more people now."

"*Mckade is here. He wants to know exactly who you picked up.*"

"We got three men and four women. Oh, and a special guest star: Lance's sister."

"*Ava? She as pretty as I remember?*"

Donovan let a salacious smile creep over his face as he leered at her. "You bet. But I got dibs."

I looked at Ava who had no reaction. She had met these people before, and knew how they operated. They seemed to enjoy shock and fear tactics, yet I was worried that before we even got back to Mckade's ship that these two men might take matters into their own hands. Lance had no reaction when Donovan looked at his sister. I couldn't understand how he could be so cold. If anybody had said anything like that about her, or my own sister, I would be beyond angry. There was nothing I wouldn't do to protect Pippa. It had been that way since we were young, and probably a big part of why I had stuck around after her ex had taken off.

Lance simply pointed his gun around the room as if picking out a target. The conversation over the radio meant nothing to him. Suddenly, the radio crackled and then a different voice came on that seemed to scare Donovan.

"*Donovan, put Lance on.*"

"Mckade? Yes, Captain." Donovan held out the radio at arm's length, as if it were radioactive. "Lance, he wants to speak to you."

"No shit," said Lance snatching the radio from Donovan. "Captain, this is Lance. Everything is under control. We're on our way back now."

"*Good. Men and women. They'll be a good addition to the crew, especially as I hear we lost Honey. I'm pleased to hear that Douglas came through.*"

"He's charting a path to you right now, Captain."

I studied Lance's face, trying to gauge whether he was as scared of Mckade as Donovan so clearly was. There was definitely a nervousness in his voice, but he was a lot calmer than I expected he might be. After killing Honey and finding his sister, he could've been forgiven for being in shock. But he appeared to let it all slide off him. If anything, listening to him talk to Mckade, I got the impression he was in awe. Lance wanted to please him, as if Mckade was his father. I listened to the radio intently, trying to pick up any useful information I could. There was no background noise, and Mckade's voice kept faltering, as if the radio signal was weak. He had an accent that I couldn't place, perhaps Irish or Scottish. The crackling was intermittent, and all I could do was listen and focus to find out what was going to happen next.

"You want us to tie them up, Captain?" asked Lance. "Douglas has plenty of rope if you—"

"*No, that won't be necessary, unless they give you any trouble. When you reach us get everyone aboard. You still have the weapons and grenades, I assume?*"

"Of course."

"*Then we'll leave Douglas a parting gift to say thank you. I don't want that boat falling into anyone else's hands. Have you found out if we have any sailors amongst the people you picked up? Anyone who might be willing and able to get straight into things for me?*"

Lance hesitated and I detected a ripple of fear in him for the first time.

"Um, no, I hadn't found the time to talk to them all yet. I've—"

"*You're not going weak on me are you, Lance? Try. Now.*"

Lance lowered the radio briefly and looked around the room. "I know Ava can't sail for shit, but how about the rest of you? Volunteers? Who knows their port from their starboard?"

With Gills dead, there was only one man left from Jonah's crew. None of us otherwise had any experience on the ocean, certainly nothing we could offer to help or use for bargaining.

"I know these seas," said Weir slowly, getting up. "I've lived on a trawler longer than I've lived on land."

"Sit down, Weir, you can't be serious," said Ava. "You're not going to join these pirates. Mckade is a psychopath. He doesn't run an army, just a bunch of madmen who go around raping and killing people for sport. He's the only one who needs a bullet. Give me a gun and I'll do it myself. Sit down while you still can, Weir. We're on your side. No matter what you're thinking, you don't have to do this."

Weir ignored her and took a few steps forward. As usual there was no fear in him, and as he approached Lance I almost felt sorry for the boy. Was it better to have Weir as a friend or an enemy?

"Mr. Weir? You up for it?" asked Lance. He pointed his gun at Weir's chest. "This is no time for tricks or games."

"Does it look like I'm playing games, boy?"

There was no doubt in my mind that Weir was serious. Even after everything, after our disagreements and fights, I couldn't believe he was siding with Mckade. He had to understand what it meant, or maybe the death of Jonah and Gills had hit him harder than I'd realized. Losing the *Tukino* had been the final straw. He had nothing left and this was his way back in, back to the only life he knew. It crossed my mind to warn him, to dissuade him from making another stupid decision, but he wouldn't listen to me. Anything I said to him was only liable to push him further away.

"One, Captain," said Lance. "The rest look pretty beat up. Don't know if they're much use. Two guys who look like they'd be more at home down below with the rest of the women if you ask me."

"*I'm not asking you, Lance. I thought we had—*"

I heard Mckade sigh and then his voice faded to gray. The radio popped and fizzed, and Lance fiddled with the controls until his captain's voice returned.

"*—to prove it. Don't you think, Lance?*"

"Sorry, Captain, you cut out, repeat please?"

"*Lance, I need you to listen carefully. I'm getting tired of your immaturity. I thought you were on my team. Your sister will not align herself with us. I heard she is with you and what she had to say. Put Donovan back on.*"

Pippa reached a hand over to me and squeezed my knee. "What is this, Luke?" she whispered. "Why are they doing this?"

"Boys and their toys, mom," said Chelsea. She rolled her eyes. "Put a gun in a little boy's hand and he thinks he's the king of the world."

I could feel the dread and resignation in both of their voices and it filled me with anger. This wasn't right, wasn't fair; Mckade also had a problem with Ava and I wasn't sure how that would play out. All I knew was that every second we wasted getting away from the shoals meant that the shark could return at any time. Estelle had kept quiet so far, and I wondered how much of what was going on she understood. She was afraid, that much was clear, but beyond that I couldn't tell what she was thinking. I looked at Manny to see if he might be prepared to attack the two men, but I couldn't catch his eye. For now, we had to go along with them.

"This is Donovan."

He took the radio from Lance as Weir shot me a look. I couldn't tell if he was trying to tell me I was doomed or if he was just pleased to have some sort of control back. I thought he might come around, but I could tell he was too far gone now. The radio crackled and hissed, and then Mckade's voice came back.

"*Donovan, are you listening? How many times am I going to have to repeat myself?*"

"Captain, sir, yes, sorry the radio signal keeps dropping out. I've got you now. Go ahead," said Donovan nervously.

"*I need to ensure the safety of my crew. I cannot afford bringing anyone on board who will jeopardize that, or compromise the integrity of my crew. Do you understand?*"

"Absolutely."

"*Very good. Then take the gun off Lance. Now. Then give him your knife.*"

Slowly, Donovan lowered the radio and walked over to Lance. The confusion on both men's faces was apparent.

"Sorry, man, orders are orders," said Donovan, holding out an open hand.

Lance reluctantly handed over the gun. "What is this about?"

Donovan shrugged and reached down into his boots, retrieving a sharp knife before handing it to Lance.

"Is this some sort of test?" whispered Pippa to me.

"I don't know," I replied. "Just sit tight and let it play out. Until they try to hurt one of us we'll let them argue amongst themselves."

Lance held the knife and turned it over in his hands. "This is bullshit. What am I supposed to do with this?"

"*Donovan?*"

The big man tucked Lance's gun into his waistband and raised the radio to his lips. "It's done, Captain. You want us to—?"

"Can everyone hear me?" asked Mckade.

Donovan looked at Lance. "Yes, Captain. Everybody is here."

"Good. As I said, I can't risk bringing anyone on board who is going to be a disruption to our plans. Everyone needs to understand that there is only one way to get on in this world, and that is my way. You don't like it? Tough. I need you all to understand how things operate, so here's what's going to happen before I can let any of you back on my ship. Donovan, leave the radio on so I can hear everything. I'm sure that if things go as I say I'll be able to tell from the reaction in the room. And if you dare show up without following my orders to the letter then we'll simply blow you out of the water. You know how much firepower we have. So, here's the deal. The only way I am going to accept you back into the fold is with a sign of allegiance. We need to clear the path. I need to open the door to you and the others you've found, but I can't do that based on trust. Look where that got Douglas and Honey. So, I'll say this only once, and I expect it done. Lance, take the knife Donovan gave you and go over to your sister. Slit her throat. I want her dead. And Donovan – if he doesn't do it - shoot him."

I stood up immediately. "Donovan turn that crap off. This isn't happening. Even *you* must—"

"Sit the fuck down." Donovan whipped around and pointed his gun at me.

"Jesus, man, listen to him. Your boss is insane." Manny stood up and held his hands up. "I'm not letting you do this."

Pippa and Chelsea were next to chip in, and even Estelle began to mutter something in Spanish. Quickly the whole room was in uproar and it was only Donovan putting a bullet in the ceiling that stopped the mutiny.

"All of you, back off!" Donovan's face had turned deep red and he looked over at Lance. "I've got you covered. Do it. Off the girl and we can go home."

Lance said nothing as he walked across to Ava.

"Lance, you stop, right now," I said, but of course he didn't.

Ava stood up and wiped her damp hair from her face. She looked up at her brother and smiled. She actually smiled and I was dumbstruck by how stunning she looked. In her position I think I would have run or fought him, but she simply stood there waiting.

"So, it's come to this, brother."

Lance was only a couple of feet in front of Ava now. I had no idea what he would do. Surely, even he wouldn't stoop so low as to kill his own sister?

"Ava. Why?" Lance looked up. "Why did you have to leave me?"

All I could see was the back of his head. Was he upset, angry, remorseful; I couldn't believe he was going through with it. I frantically looked around the room for a weapon, but drew a blank.

"We've been over this," said Ava calmly. "You left me. You fell in with these scum. I made the right choice. What are you going to do now? You going to kill me? Your own blood?"

I saw Lance's arm raise and couldn't stand it any longer. I wasn't prepared to sit back and wait to see what he would do. I'd already seen that he was capable of killing. I sprang up and lunged for Donovan. I had to get the gun off him to stop this madness.

"Stop!"

Donovan was surprised but he had the advantage on me and as I lunged for him he fired the gun. I heard the bang and felt a pain surge across my chest, but I had no idea where I'd been hit. All I knew was that I was still standing and I had to continue fighting for my family. My hands reached Donovan and I grabbed him. Somewhere between us was his gun, and grappling with him was like fighting a bear. The man was a mountain. I aimed a punch at his kidneys as he gripped me in his huge arms. We fell to the floor, smacking into the hard tiles painfully, him on top of me. I tried to roll him off as the air was squeezed from my lungs. I heard shouting and screaming, but all I was concerned with was Donovan. Blood began to seep inside my shirt and then Donovan landed a punch on the side of my head that made me see stars. I tried to find his gun, to wrestle it away from him, but he was too strong. Another bang exploded around my head and I knew the gun had gone off again. I'd failed.

CHAPTER 19

I rolled Donovan off me and clawed across the tiled floor, his blood all over me. I quickly reached a sofa and looked at his lifeless body. I felt sick. His head had been blown wide open, and his brains were spread out over the floor like an oil slick. Crimson liquid ran into the grooves of the tiles, mingling with cold seawater to create a thick soup of foul blood.

"That's enough!" yelled Lance. "Everyone, just back off."

I looked up at the smoking gun in Chelsea's hand. She was trembling and still had it pointed at Donovan. Pippa had her hands over her mouth, tears streaming from her eyes. I watched as Manny reached an arm out to Chelsea gently and told her to lower the gun.

"That was a stupid thing to do," said Lance, holding a knife to Ava's throat. "*Real* stupid."

I clutched the sofa and got to my knees. I was battered and bruised but Chelsea had saved me. I realized then that Lance's gun that Donovan had tucked into his waistband, must have come free when we were fighting. Chelsea had saved me, but at what cost?

"Por favor—"

Estelle's arms reached down and she helped me up. She was clearly shocked by events, but she understood what was happening. She stood next to me and I looked at Lance. He had Ava in front of him and the knife was at her throat.

"Quit moving," said Lance. "All of you had just better back off."

"Lance, think about what you're doing," said Manny. "That's your sister. Your *sister*."

Lance's eyes were wild, his confidence shattered, his illusion of safety gone like Donovan's skull. I caught my breath trying to block out the pain in my jaw from Donovan's heavy punches. My broken nose was sore, but I had been lucky. If Chelsea hadn't shot Donovan I don't know that I would've been able to fight him off. The room was almost silent now. I could hear Pippa sobbing and the wind howling all around us, and the rain was still pelting the deck as we made our way to the rendezvous with Mckade. This was the chance I had wanted. This was the last opportunity to get out of it, to save my family and Ava from Mckade and his murdering bunch of thugs.

"Lance," I said quietly. "Look at Ava. She's scared. You don't want to do this."

He pressed the knife against her throat and she screwed up her eyes as the blade dug into her skin. A thin trickle of blood ran down the hilt of the knife and across Lance's fingers. I resisted the urge to run for him. He was six or seven feet away from me, and could easily jam the knife into her before I made it to him. I was going to have to talk him down.

"You're crazy, all of you," said Lance. "I gave you a chance, a chance to do something with your lives. Mckade can give you shelter, a purpose, food and water. He's not going to do that now, not after what you did to Donovan. He's going to kill all of you."

Something in his tone told me he was right. There was no going back from this. Yet he sounded scared too, as if Mckade might not be the wonderful benefactor that Lance made him out to be. Lance was clearly supposed to be in charge of this operation and so far, he was returning with two dead bodies. How would Mckade view that?

"You're right, he probably will. I'm sorry about your friend. It wasn't our intention to kill him, but he kinda brought that on himself. We're just defending ourselves, Lance, you know that. I was defending my family, my friends; Ava. I know you don't want to hurt her, so put the knife down. We can talk this through, but we have to do it now. We're going to be with Mckade any minute, right? So, how about we all calm down and deal with this before the situation gets any worse?" I could see that Lance's grip on his knife had relaxed slightly. I looked at Ava and she stared right back at me. Her blue eyes were full of fear. I wanted so desperately to hold her, to make this right, but Lance still hadn't let her go. "Lance, your sister needs you. She misses you. You can join us if you want, you can be the captain of your own ship. You don't have to do what Mckade tells you to. I can see you're a strong man. Make your own way. Forget Mckade."

"Ha, yeah right." Lance's eyes looked at Donovan and then roamed around the room. "He's heard everything, you know."

I followed Lance's eyes to the edge of the sofa where I saw the forgotten radio. "It doesn't matter. He's not here. He can't hurt you if he doesn't know where you are."

"He knows everything." Lance tensed up again. "Mckade won't let me go. I work for him. You don't just quit a job like that. I have orders and… and this is what's going to happen. First of all, that bitch is going to get rid of the gun."

I looked at Chelsea. She still had it in her hands. "Lose it, Chelsea. Put it down."

I gave Manny a nod and he took it from her. Her fingers let go of the gun easily and when it was gone she collapsed into Pippa's arms. Manny threw the gun over to the far side of the room.

"There. Gone. See? We can do this all friendly like," I said. "How about you let Ava go and talk to me? You still have the knife and you have my word that no one is going to try anything."

Lance slowly shook his head. "No. Like I said, I have a job to do. Mckade wants Ava gone." Lance's eyes darted furiously from side to side and then picked me out. "I have to prove this wasn't my fault. He'll kill all of you, but not me. Not me. I can still recover this."

"Lance, slow down." I took a tentative step toward him. "Talk to me."

"No," whispered Estelle. "Es demasiado peligroso."

She put a hand on my shoulder and tried to pull me back, but I resisted. I got a couple of steps and then stopped. A tear fell from Ava's eyes.

"Lance, will you please talk to me?" pleaded Ava. "It's been so long. We haven't even had a chance to catch up. Mckade will understand. He's not here with you. If he was, he would understand the pressure that you're under."

Lance closed his eyes and I wondered if she was getting through to him.

"I think it's a test," said Ava, her voice wobbling. "I think he wants you back. I think he wants you to bring us all back to him. We can do so much together. You're my brother. Come on, Lance, just let me go and—"

"No."

Ava tried to free herself from his grip, but as she did so Lance opened his eyes again and held her tighter. "No, you're full of it, Ava. Just like dad. All you ever do is control me and tell me what to do. Well, not anymore. I'm *somebody* now. I don't need to scrounge around in the dirt looking for food. You fell in with the wrong crowd, Ava. You're not my problem anymore."

I saw Lance press the blade against Ava again and the thin line of blood became thicker. Ava cried out in pain and I winced, knowing the pain and terror she must be feeling.

"Wait." Weir had been watching the whole time and suddenly strode purposefully toward Lance. "Hold up a second."

"Woah, what are you doing?" Lance shuffled to face Weir. "Don't tell me you think this is a dumb idea too? I thought you were different from the rest."

"Me?" Weir ran a hand over his strong stubbly jaw. "I'm not with these assholes. I already said I wanted to join him. But like you said, Mckade is going to want to kill us all for what happened to Donovan. So, *I* need to prove myself. Let me do it." Weir looked at Ava and smiled. "I've hated that bitch from the first day I met her. If you remember rightly I didn't take too well to you either. I thought you were soft in the head. I can see I was wrong about that. I need to do this, Lance. Forget Donovan. I can vouch for you, tell Mckade this wasn't your doing. Let me deal with Ava. I'll do it quick and painlessly."

"What the fuck, Weir?" I screamed at him. "What the hell are you doing?"

Weir gave me a wry smile. "Don't worry, grease-monkey. You're next."

Weir walked right up to Lance and held out his hand, his palm open. "Give me the knife and I'll do her right now. Then you and me can see to the others and get off this boat, talk to Mckade and make this right. What do you say?"

I held my breath. Surely Lance would see that he needed to let this madness end, to let Ava walk away.

"Lance, look at me," I said. "If you give Weir the knife this is all over. There won't be any more chances."

"I need that gun," said Lance. He lowered the knife a few inches away from Ava's neck and she breathed out. "My gear is up in the bridge. I need my gun to go and get it."

Weir nodded. "Sure, buddy. So, let me take care of the girl and you go get your shit."

Lance lowered the knife a little more, but didn't let go of Ava. He still had one arm around her and he held onto her tightly. "You're not dicking around?"

Weir let out a long sigh. "Luke, you want to tell him how we're best friends?"

I was freezing cold and could sense the situation spinning out of control. Adrenalin rushed through my body but it was fading now, and I was tired. This was the last I could do. I had to make Lance see sense.

"Tell him, *boy*."

I glanced back at Estelle. She was right behind me. If Weir got that knife and killed Ava who would be next? Her? Would he turn on me, or Pippa or Chelsea? Manny would fight, as would I, but the gun was far out of reach. We were unarmed and he was the dangerous one. "Lance, Weir is *not* our friend. He's been looking for a way to get rid of us for some time, and you're his ticket out of here. If you give him that knife your sister is dead. I never thought he would sink so low, but I guess I misread him. You need to ignore him and listen to me. Listen to your sister. She just wants a chance to make amends. We're not your enemies, Lance. Don't do anything you're going to regret for the rest of your life."

"It's true," said Manny. "Listen to him, buddy."

"They will suck you dry," said Weir. "If you don't give me that knife, Mckade is going to tear you a new one. Let's get this over with and move on. You need to get your shit and I need to get off this boat. Time's up, Lance."

Weir extended his hand and reached for the knife. A shiver ran up my spine as Lance relaxed his grip on it. Weir slowly took it from him.

"Do it quickly," said Lance quietly, as he let go of the knife.

"You did the right thing, Lance," said Weir. He looked triumphant. "You've proven you're with Mckade. I know what I have to do now."

The boat swayed and I felt my stomach lurch as Weir twisted the knife around in his thick fingers. How many times had he skinned and gutted a fish? He knew how to handle a blade, and before I could move, he darted forward. Ava screamed and my heart blasted a sonic boom to my head. I ran to her hoping for a miracle, yet knowing I was going to be too late as Weir thrust the knife powerfully forward.

Blood spurted out furiously, as if the artery was a broken faucet that couldn't be turned off. Weir jammed the knife into the neck further, right up to the hilt, and opening up a huge mortal wound as blood sprayed over his face. He said nothing as he killed mercilessly, and I felt my knees weaken as the screaming started.

"No, no, no!" Ava screamed. "Stop it!"

"It's okay." I pulled her away from Weir as he continued to sever Lance's head from his body. "You're okay, Ava."

We fell to our knees, my arms around her. I fought down the bile rising from my stomach to my throat as I watched Weir kill Lance. He caught me off guard with his move, and more importantly, Lance. They stumbled back to the open doorway together, one of Weir's strong arms holding Lance up, the other holding the knife in Ava's brother's throat. Lance made horrible gurgling noises as blood poured from his mouth and stained his yellow teeth. I could see that Weir took no pleasure in the act of killing, but I understood. He had fooled us all, me included. I thought he was going to kill Ava in front of me, but it had all been a ruse. How long had he been planning and plotting a way out of this mess? How far back had he realized what was happening? Perhaps agreeing to join Mckade had been the start of it, or perhaps he had changed his mind at the last moment. Whatever he had done, I was just glad he had chosen the right side for once. I held Ava in my arms, pleased she was alive. I took no satisfaction in watching Lance die, yet I felt unable to avert my eyes.

"No, please, no." Ava's words turned into sobs as she watched Lance fade away.

I gritted my teeth and watched Weir finish the job. I wanted to see it done, needed to know it was finished. There was no other way now. Once Lance had started the killing there could be no other outcome than death for all of us onboard. If Weir hadn't seen the light when he had, then I had no doubt Ava would have been next. Lance's blue eyes bulged from his head and he strained to free himself from Weir in vain. Weir was far too strong and committed. They staggered further back to the open doorway as the wind swept cold air and rain inside.

"Let him go, Weir," said Manny, walking past me. "He's done. The boy's done."

Lance's arms fell to his side and the gurgling noises stopped.

"Almost," said Weir roughly. "There's still some fight left in him. I'm not taking any chances with this fucker."

Abruptly Weir yanked the knife out of Lance's neck and passed it back to Manny. "Hold this."

Manny had no choice but to take the bloody knife as Weir put Lance in a bear-hug. He lifted the boy up and carried him over the threshold to the deck outside.

"Weir?" Manny turned the knife over in his hands and then tossed it onto an empty sofa. He wiped his bloody hands on his legs. "Weir, what are you..?"

I held Ava to me as she sobbed in my arms, her brother's blood pooling around us, and we watched Weir lift Lance up into the air like a paper plane. He walked to the edge of the boat and without a sound tossed Lance overboard.

"Jesus," said Manny quietly, as he turned to me. "I don't think he was even dead yet, he was just—"

I shook my head and Manny shut up. Weir marched back into the room, the rain having washed much of the blood from his face.

"She okay?"

Weir's words shocked me more than anything else he had said. There was genuine concern in his voice, and I was taken aback.

"Er, sure. Well, I mean... she will be."

Weir nodded and held his hands out in front of him. Even from where I sat on the floor I could see they were shaking.

"Good."

Manny rolled his neck around his head and looked up at the ceiling. "Shit, Weir, I thought—"

"You thought what? That I was going to kill that poor girl? That I would abandon you to pirates and go on a killing spree? I know I'm an asshole, but I'm not like that." Weir held the back of his hand to his lips and suppressed the nausea growing inside of him. "I've never killed a man before, but Lance was not going to back down. That boy was bad news. I saw it the moment we took him in. Ava worked hard, made something of herself, joined in and learnt how to run on the *Tukino* with us. She might not have been my choice to join the crew, but she certainly put the effort in, I can't knock her for that. Lance was a slacker. He thought the world owed him everything. He was a waste of breath. He joined up with those pirates at the first opportunity. He knew what he was getting into. We all tried to warn him off. Jonah did everything he could for the kid, but Lance threw it back in his face. I wasn't about to let him kill Ava. His own sister? What kind of screwed up fuck-head *does* that? Given the chance he would have let us all die. I couldn't stand by and watch him do that. I've made my own mistakes, but that's what they were. Mistakes. I didn't intentionally ground the boat. I didn't mean to hurt you all. I just… with Jonah gone I guess I let my ego and temper get the better of me. I'm sorry for the trouble I caused you. Things got out of hand and for a while there I lost it. I would've explained earlier, but I knew Lance would believe me if *you* believed me. He'd believe the sun was green if you told him it was so. It was all I could do to make him believe I would sign up to join Mckade's crew. Mckade is—"

I looked at the radio still lying on the floor close to Donovan's lifeless body. "Oh, shoot. Mckade. Do you think..?"

"Yeah, probably." Manny picked the radio up. "You still listening, Mckade? You there?"

"*Who is this? Put Lance back on. I did not tell you to start shooting.*"

"It's finished. Your men are dead. Goodbye, Mckade."

"*Wait—*"

Manny clicked the radio off. "He heard what he needed to. We gain nothing by talking to that asshole."

"But, if Lance was right then he's going to be right on us any second." I felt Ava's arms wrap around my waist. The tears had slowed, but her body was shaking. "We need to tell Douglas to change course. If it's not too late. We can't afford to run into Mckade."

"On it." Weir marched across the room and picked up the discarded gun. "Just in case our friend Douglas isn't as co-operative as I need him to be."

"You'd better go with him, Manny," I said. I couldn't leave Ava. I had to stay with her. "Get us the hell out of here and as far away from Mckade's ship as possible."

Manny and Weir headed through the door and up the stairs. I looked around the room. It was a mess. Pippa and Chelsea were away from me and Donovan's body lay between us. I was going to have to move it, throw it overboard. I could guess what he had done to Honey. The man deserved no respect.

"Estelle, would you help please?"

I slowly pulled myself up and with Estelle's help we got Ava onto the nearest sofa where she curled up into a ball and held a cushion to her chest. She reached out a hand to me and I took it.

"I just have to do something, then I'll be right back."

"He's gone, isn't he? Lance?"

I nodded. "I'm sorry."

Ava buried her face in the cushion and I let her go. My head was pounding but I still had no time to rest. I wanted to stay with Ava and curl up into a ball next to her, but there was so much to do. Weir's beating and Donovan's punches were starting to hit me, and I felt dizzy.

"Pippa, why don't you take Chelsea and Estelle, and check out the ship? Manny and Weir will help Douglas get us out of here. Maybe you can get some rest."

Pippa looked at me. "What about you, Luke? You can't keep going like this. How long is it since you slept? Let me take care of Ava. You need—"

"I need to tidy up." I glanced at Donovan's body. "I'll catch up with you later."

Pippa realized what I was doing. "Right. Of course. Come on, Chelsea." She led Chelsea by the hand to the staircase and beckoned for Estelle to follow her. "Meet you in the bridge in a few minutes, yeah? I'm not going to be able to rest until I know we're well away from this lunatic Mckade."

"Sure." I waited for Pippa, Chelsea, and Estelle to leave, and then looked at Donovan's body. He wasn't going to be as easy to lift as Lance. I put my arms under his shoulders, trying to avoid looking at the remnants of his mangled face. I lifted him up, but he was simply too heavy for me. My energy levels were zero, so I simply grabbed a hold of his arms and dragged him across the room. I managed to get him to the doorway before I had to stop and take a rest. My breath collided with the cold rain blowing in and my head spun. I dragged Donovan out onto the deck as the swirling wind howled around me. The storm clouds gathered above us didn't look like abating anytime soon, and as I got the body to the edge of the boat, I looked for Mckade. My eyes scanned every inch of the seething ocean, but I saw no sign of his boat. Roiling waves crashed against the deck and I hoisted Donovan onto a railing. His legs dangled over the side and with one last shove I forced his dead body over into the rough water. Instantly, my legs buckled and I hit the wooden deck. One hand grabbed the safety rail and I pressed my forehead against the cold, wet deck. We had all been so close to death. The *Tukino*, the Megalodon, Mckade's men; it all seemed surreal. I thought of the giant shark swimming around the ocean. Was it still out there, close by, watching and waiting for us? I wanted so desperately to talk to Pippa and Chelsea, to promise I would do everything I could to look after them, but just lifting my head up felt like it was beyond my power. I thought of Ava curled up on the sofa mourning her brother. Rest. That was what we all needed. I heard a soft voice call my name from somewhere inside the boat, but the storm had sapped the last of my energy. I let my head rest on the deck, just for a moment, allowing the cool sea water to cool my brain. The bracing wind howled and whistled around me. I just needed a moment to gather myself, to think what would come next. I just needed a chance to breathe, to let my wounds heal. I needed sleep. With my eyes closed I could properly rest. I heard my name again but it sounded like a dream, as if mom was calling me from downstairs. She had to wait. They all had to wait. I needed peace. And as my hand slipped from the safety rail I embraced it, delving into the quiet darkness without thinking about anything.

CHAPTER 20

When I came around I was still cloaked in darkness, only I was warm and dry. I could hear the ocean and feel the rocking motion of the boat, but the deck was gone and in its place a soft bed. Muted noises came softly from a room above me, the chatter of conversation and faint hum of an engine. I had only rested my head for a moment, so how had I ended up here? Had I been sleeping?

I forced myself upright and rubbed my eyes, half expecting to hit my head on a ceiling. The room was dark but there was a small rectangular window above me allowing a little light in. The room was small and functional, furnished with an oak writing desk in one corner and some kind of built-in wardrobe in the other. A red leather chair was tucked under the desk, and across the cream-colored walls were certificates and charts. The plain brown door across the room from me was closed. I touched my head and felt a bump just above my right ear. I no doubt had some bruising and cuts, but I felt surprisingly well. Perhaps sleep was what I had needed after all. The cotton sheets beneath me were a shade of deep blue and the quilt covering me was adorned with red and gold circles. There appeared to be no central motif to the room and I couldn't figure out where I was. I stretched and yawned, and as I slid my hand over the quilt I felt something move in the bed next to me.

"Woah!" I jerked back, confused and wary, and then pulled the quilt back.

"Hey, how are you doing?" asked Ava. She sat up and tugged her top down. She had changed into a tight white T-shirt and cargo shorts. "Sorry. I'm supposed to be watching you, but you looked so peaceful I couldn't help but climb onto the bed next to you. I must have gone out like a light. Damn."

"Ava?" I reached my hand out in the gloomy room and touched her cheek. "Are you all right?"

Ava took my hand in hers. She was warm and I pressed my hand into hers firmly. She squeezed my hand back and smiled. "I guess. What happened… was out of my control. And yours. I can't excuse what Lance did and I can't turn back the clock. We just have to deal with what's presented to us, right?"

"And what exactly happened? I thought you were on the sofa and I… I was outside. But… I don't remember. Donovan was heavy and—"

"You passed out," said Ava. "I got Manny to help me drag you in here. We found some dry clothes, for all of us, and let you sleep it off."

I realized then that I was in strange clothes. In a stranger's clothes to be precise. The pants were a little big on me and the collared shirt I wore was unbuttoned, but at least it was dry. I felt a little odd knowing that Ava had helped undress me. "So you… helped to change my clothes?"

"No, Manny did that. I was too busy finding some water. Over on the table, by the way, when you're ready. There's not a lot to go around, but enough for now."

"Right." I still had my hand enclosed around Ava's and the light above me threw shadows from the clouds outside that danced across her face. Looking into her blue eyes I couldn't imagine what she was feeling. Losing her brother like that must have been devastating.

"It's okay, Luke. Don't stress. Mckade is history. Douglas never even set a path for him. That's why the radio kept crapping out. The whole time we were with Lance he was taking us north, away from danger."

"I hate to tell you this, Ava, but lying in a bed with me, you're still in danger."

She laughed and raised her free hand to her mouth.

"You don't need to do that anymore," I said, and before I even knew what I was doing I was kissing her. I ran my hands through her long blonde hair and she kissed me back. Drawing her close I pressed her body next to mine, and for the first time in days, I felt truly alive again. I felt hope. I felt pure raw energy rush through my body and time slowed as I held her. I forgot about everything but how amazing she was.

"Luke," said Ava breathlessly, "we have to stop."

"Do we?"

Ava giggled. "For now." She suddenly swung her legs off the bed and got up. "I don't know how long we've slept, but we should go to the others. They'll want to know how you are. Pippa was beside herself with worry."

"You're right, of course." I stretched and clambered off the bed, reluctant to leave, yet knowing it was the right thing to do. "How is she? Is Chelsea..?"

"They're both fine. Chelsea was shaken up by the whole thing, but I think they were more worried about you."

I had to admit I was beginning to feel bad for sleeping for so long. "What about Manny? Did he and Weir get Douglas to..?"

Ava pressed a finger against my lips. "Why don't you stop asking me a million questions and talk to them yourself? Everyone is fine. Even Weir. I think he left the dark side and joined us. You know, you were out for quite a while. We had to make plans and do something. Weir was really helpful."

Ava opened the bedroom door and I followed her out. I instantly recognized the corridor where Lance had frog-marched me earlier out of the bridge. As we made our way to the bridge the boat felt calm. It rolled from side to side, but it felt like the storm had dissipated.

"Actually, I'm not sure without him we would've made it this far," said Ava, taking my hand. "Douglas had to take care of his wife. He wasn't much good after that."

"Poor guy." I didn't need to remind Ava how Douglas' wife had died. "And you? How are you holding up?" I stopped Ava in front of the door to the bridge and looked at her. I examined her neck, running a finger gently over the dressing that had been applied over her cut.

"I'll be okay now," she said, and she leant in and kissed me. "Estelle helped me with this," she said rubbing the bandage around her neck. "She's really quite sweet. I think she was going to help your sister find some food. At least that was the plan when I left them. God knows how long we've been sleeping. You'd best go in there. Manny will want to talk to you. I'll go round up the others and let them know that you're back on your feet."

I turned to the doorway as Ava left me, and I wondered just what Weir had done. Where had he led us? Could we really trust him? As I entered the bridge I was surprised to find him and Manny leaning over the control center. Douglas was nowhere to be seen, and thankfully neither was Honey. They had cleaned up well.

"Well, if it isn't my favorite grease-monkey," said Weir. "You're just in time."

"For what?" I shook Manny's hand as he greeted me. He looked a little tired but was in good spirits. "You okay?"

"I'm good," he replied. "I mean, I haven't had fourteen hours sleep like some people, but I'm good."

"I was out *that* long?" Looking out of the tall windows on the bridge I noticed the sun was rising in the east. I must have slept overnight. A new day was dawning. How much had I missed out on? "Where are we? What about Mckade?"

"Always the worrier," muttered Weir. "We lost Mckade. Douglas took us away from him and we haven't seen him since. I don't doubt he's royally pissed off, and trying to track us, but luckily we seem to have lost him."

"And you can manage this ship, Weir? You can read all of this... stuff?" The array of controls in front of me was bewildering. I had no idea how he understood any of it. "It's nothing like the *Tukino*."

"Give me some credit," replied Weir. "Douglas gave us a rundown of how things work. Manny's been helping me while you found a nice warm bed to crash in."

"Okay, okay, I get it. I'm a lazy ass."

"Don't sweat it, Luke," said Manny smiling. "It worked out okay. This really is an upgrade from the *Tukino* to be fair. Enough room for all of us and plenty of power to get us north and away from Mckade's men."

"North? I thought we were heading south?"

"Yeah, about that." Weir flicked a switch and then looked at me. "There are two good reasons we changed course. First one is Mckade. He has control of the whole south-eastern seaboard now. We couldn't risk staying in that area and letting him find us."

"And two?"

"Two?" Weir sniffed nervously and glanced at Manny. "Two is the Megalodons. I'm sure you don't need reminding what happened to us down there. The way I figure it, they prefer warmer waters. It's essentially a shark, so let's treat it like one. They go where the food is. So, it just made sense for us to head north. We have to play the odds, and odds are we'll keep out of their way if we head north."

"They?" I asked.

Weir shrugged. "Stands to reason there's more than one of them."

"And on that bombshell, Luke, I suggest you forget trying to wrap your head around that wonderful news and follow me," said Manny. "I was hoping you'd be up in time to see this. Like I said, you're just in time."

Weir grinned. "Go on. I've got this."

Confused, I followed Manny outside where the fresh morning air startled me. He led me around to the port side that was still in shadow and smiled as if we were on a carnival cruise instead of running for our lives.

"Look. We're home."

Manny pointed west and I couldn't believe it. We were home. New York spread out before us, its skyline illuminated by a warm glow. It was nothing like it used to be before the oceans rose, but it was still something. The city that never sleeps appeared to be just taking a nap. It felt good to be home.

"You want to check out the old apartment?" I teased Manny. "Maybe grab those beers you lost?"

"Oh, sure. I could do with a whole heap of things if we're running by. There are some Twinkies I was saving and I was halfway through The Stand too. I never did get to finish it. Maybe we can swing by and pick it up?"

I punched Manny in the arm playfully. "Twinkies? You were holding out on me!"

I watched the sunrise burn away the shadows over the city. It felt like a second chance. It felt like things were clicking into place, finally. Ava was on side and even Weir seemed to have come around. As long as Douglas was happy with some help on his superyacht, then we were in no rush to find a new home. I still needed to catch up with Douglas and thank him before I scoured my brain to think of somewhere safe for Pippa and Chelsea.

The very top of the Statue of Liberty was still above the water. Just like the city she guarded, she was barely visible, just the last visible parts reaching up toward the sky, clinging onto life before the ocean claimed her forever. I saw the upper tips of the crown and then the torch appeared. What looked like a thousand seagulls had nested on it, although the rest of the body was submerged. Further north I could see the tip of the World Trade Center, its lonely spire poking up into the sky like a symbol of hope. The hotels, offices, apartments and galleries beneath it were all gone, buried beneath an ocean of mistakes. The land it was built on was soft now, and I wondered how long it would remain standing. The Financial District was a distant memory, stocks and shares usurped in importance by how we could find fresh drinking water. Yet those monoliths we'd built so many years ago were, for the most part, still there, waiting and hoping they would have a use once more. Manhattan had been my home for years and I loved the city. Yet, it was time to move on. In a few months, or years, it would be gone completely. The encroaching Atlantic would soon spread its icy fingers further and take the city, drowning it along with the other cities it had already taken.

"Snap out of it, Luke," said Manny. "You always get misty eyed when you look at New York. Forget the past. I just wanted to show it to you for the last time. Who knows when we'll be back here? *If* we'll ever be back here."

"Weir say anything to you about where he's headed?" I asked, relaxing over the rail as we sailed past the city.

"North. Away from Mckade and away from trouble. There's a chance Mckade is going to come after us for some payback, but we've seen no sign of him. Weir reckons he's given up and stayed south where he's in control. Weir also thinks the Megalodon probably prefers warmer water. Figures it's safer for us to stay north for now. He says there's good fishing up there."

"And was this Weir suggesting or telling us what to do?"

"To be fair, he let us all have a say. Even Ava. He apologized again for letting his temper get the better of him. You know, I'm beginning to warm to the guy. He's no angel, but I'm pleased he stuck with us. We had a chat about things, and decided he was best placed to run the ship. While you were sleeping, we all agreed it felt safer to head north." Manny shrugged. "Seemed little point in continuing south. For now, Weir's our best shot at surviving, right? He knows how to hunt, how to sail, and how to be an absolute ass. We need him and he needs us. He's realized that now."

"And Pippa and Chelsea? They were okay with this?" I couldn't but wonder if Pippa was just going along with it. She didn't want a future for Chelsea out here on the water. No matter where we went there would always be danger.

"She said she wanted to talk to you, but yeah. Essentially, I think she was okay with it. The only question mark was you. It's not like we could pull up to the nearest hospital. You look pretty beat up. You sure you're all right?"

I guess I had to go and talk to Pippa, put her mind at rest. I wanted to see Chelsea too. I had to thank her for what she did. If she hadn't shot Donovan, things could be a whole lot worse for all of us. I hated that she was put into that position, forced into doing something horrible, but I was proud of her for making the choice she did. It can't have been easy. It had been a rough few days. Heading north sounded fine to me. Anywhere that we could regroup, refresh, and come up with a strategy of how we were going to live, was fine with me.

"I'm pleased you're here, Manny. We should—"

Before I could finish, something in the water caught my eye. Debris littered the ocean, but this was different. There was something there, something moving with a purpose. It was just below the surface, but large enough that it was pushing the water upward as it came toward us. At first glance, I assumed it was one of the planes from the airports. What appeared to be a tail fin poked up above the crest of the largest wave, and yet the speed with which it was approaching us suggested it had an engine. It couldn't be a plane, or another boat.

"Manny, is that..?"

I pointed at the oncoming wall of water which was still rising steadily, blocking out the view of the city. A tapered silhouette danced just beneath the surface until the dorsal fin appeared, rising up out of the sea like a dormant volcano forced up as it erupted. Suddenly, the fin extended higher and revealed the glistening gray skin wrapped around it. The monster was streamlined and built to perform the perfect attack, completely at home in the water. The predator was at the top of its game and the top of the food chain. We stood little chance against it.

"The Megalodon," whispered Manny. "No. It can't be."

It had to be a mile away, yet I could already make out the shape of the shark as it powered toward us. If it struck us head on it would destroy the yacht in seconds. I had to get Weir to turn us away, perhaps outrun it.

"Come on, we don't have long." I grabbed Manny and ran back to the bridge, running as fast as I could. As I flung open the door and burst into the bridge, Weir turned to greet me.

"Luke, I was just—"

"It's here. The shark. The *Megalodon*. It'll be on us in seconds. You've got to move this boat, Weir. Get us the hell out of here, or we're all dead."

CHAPTER 21

I raced back to the door and pushed it open. Staring out at the approaching shark I waited for the impact. There were only seconds and no way that Weir could move the boat out of the approaching monster's way in time. The massive beast was finally going to get us. The swell of water came at us fast and I prayed the end would be quick. Although Weir sped the yacht forward, the huge wave of water crashed into us and knocked Manny off his feet. I clung onto the doorframe with both hands and held my breath, awaiting the crunch of the hull as the Megalodon sank its teeth into the boat. But there was no sound, no sign the shark had actually hit us. Where was the teeth enveloping us? Where was the boom as the yacht disintegrated? Instead, the shark seemed to miss us. Still clutching the doorframe, I looked out at the sea and I saw the fin descend into the ocean. The monster swam right beneath us. The yacht was tossed around as the water rocked us back and forth, but there was no contact with the shark.

"The bitch is playing with us," muttered Weir.

"Let's skip the games and get as far away from here as we can," said Manny, as he got to his feet. He went to the forward windows and peered out. "I can't see it."

"She's out there." Weir began to turn the boat. "And next time she won't miss. She was checking us out, seeing if we were worth eating."

New York came back into view and I suddenly realized Weir was taking us right toward it. We sped up quickly and I was looking right at the torch of the Statue of Liberty again as it loomed larger on the horizon. The mass of gulls around it were darting in and out of the water, evidently having found a school of fish to feast upon.

"Weir, don't, we can't go back to the city. It's too dangerous." I staggered back over the uneven floor to the controls. "There are a million things we could crash into hidden beneath the water. Not to mention the crumbling buildings. You know the foundations are—"

"I see it." Manny banged on the glass. "Starboard. I can see the fin."

"Weir, it's too risky. Can't we outrun it in this?" I asked. "This must have more power than the *Tukino*. Can't we just..?"

"It worked before, it will work again. Shallow water. That's the only thing we can do to beat it. You've seen the size of that thing, closer than anyone else on board this ship. We get to shallow water and it'll disappear. We'll run out of juice before we outrun that thing."

The mention of shallow water immediately made my brain turn to Gills. He had been killed in the shallows and Chelsea had almost died. We had grounded the boat and almost killed ourselves in the process of escaping the shark. Was it such a good idea to do the same? "Weir, what if..?"

"It's coming back around!" yelled Manny. He turned to us. "Dead ahead."

"Brace yourself, monkey," grunted Weir.

I caught Manny's eyes. There was a hopelessness in them that I hadn't seen before. The fear and amazement was something I had gotten used to. But this time was different. How could we beat it? We couldn't outrun it, we couldn't kill it, and we couldn't hide from it; heading to shallower water was the only option, and yet it carried as much danger as doing nothing.

"I have to warn the others. I have to find Pippa and Ava. Where are they, Manny? Where is..?"

The impact sent all of us flying. I landed on my back with Weir next to me, scrambling quickly to get back to the controls. I waited for the onrushing water to drown us, for the jaws of the shark to clamp around the boat and drag us down, but they never came. The yacht began to tilt and then it righted itself.

"Just a glancing blow," said Weir. "We're okay for now. She's probably testing us, seeing what we're made of." He looked at me. "You can rely on me when I say she'll be back. Third time *won't* be lucky."

"Manny, how much farther?" I asked. He glanced out of the forward windows.

"Liberty Island is coming up. We're close. Another few seconds and we'll reach Lower Manhattan."

"Hold on," said Weir. "This is going to get tight. You might want to go find the others and hold on. This ain't gonna be pretty."

"Can you handle this yourself?" I asked, hoping Weir would confirm he could. I had no knowledge of how to operate a huge ship like this, and I really wanted to get to Ava.

"Manny can stay and be my eyes, right?"

Manny nodded.

"Then go," said Weir. "Get going. If you find Douglas tell him I need him up here. He can mourn later."

I raced to the exit and rushed outside. The ship was large, but there were only so many places they could be. Outside in the fresh air I could see we were almost back home. Governor's Island was on my right, and the drowned remains of Brooklyn passed us by in a flash. I made my way down the deck to the rear of the ship carefully, wary that the shark might attack again at any moment. I didn't doubt Weir when he said that next time it would take us down. I had seen it up close, seen just how nasty it was. If it wanted us, it could open up its jaws and bite the ship in half. Below the helicopter landing pad, I found the dining area where the glass doors were open. I had to go into the bowels of the ship to find my friends and family. Before I went back inside I looked back at the ocean. Trailing behind us was the fin of the Megalodon. It almost appeared to be following us, as if drawn to us out of curiosity. By entering the bay had we already scared it off? I remembered leaving the apartment and what had happened to old Mr. Johnson. No, it wasn't scared. It was just picking its moment. Even in the close and shallow streets of New York it could still attack. It might struggle to navigate, and we would have an advantage at last, but would it be enough to ward it off before it took a bite out of the hull? The fin was tremendous, as large as the sail on any boat I'd seen. The rising sun hit it and sent a huge black triangular shadow across the stern. The colossal hunter was trailing us at a distance, seemingly following us but not coming in for the kill. Perhaps it just wanted to let us know it was there. Perhaps its food tasted better when it had been tenderized by fear and terror.

I wished we had something to defend ourselves with. There wasn't so much as a harpoon on the boat as far as I knew, and no flare gun was going to do anything. We were utterly reliant on Weir this time.

The shark suddenly veered away from the boat, its fin sinking beneath the surface of the water and I ran to the safety rail. I saw the outline of the monster beneath the water, its bulk incredible. It swiftly darted to the side and disappeared. Was it preparing to attack? I nervously watched the water and waited but it had gone. Just as I thought it might have gone for good there was an almighty booming sound and I looked across to the west. The Megalodon's head reared up out of the sea just as the flock of gulls took to the air. For many of them, they were too slow. The shark's jaws opened wide and revealed a dark abyss. It must have swallowed a hundred or more of the gulls alive before it crashed back down into the water. As it did so, it took out the statue's torch, smashing it to pieces and destroying the last visible sign that the Statue of Liberty was still standing. The masonry fell to the seabed and the icon was gone forever. The Megalodon vanished beneath the water, its appetite only sweetened by the appetizer the gulls had made. I saw the monster thrash around briefly, perhaps caught on the statue, but then quickly it resumed its hunt for us. I saw the fin turn right toward our boat and then disappear. There was no more time. It was coming.

"Ava? Pippa!" I yelled, running into the boat. "Where are you?"

I frantically ran down the upper corridor and began banging my fists on the doors.

"Chelsea! Estelle? Douglas?"

I heard shouting from below and raced down the interior stairwell. Reaching the bottom, I skidded to a halt and found Pippa standing in a doorway.

"Luke, what the hell is going on? Are you okay? Did we hit something? It felt like—"

"*It's back*. The Megalodon is back. We have no time, Pippa. Is Chelsea with you?"

Pippa frowned and nodded. She ran her hand across my brow. "Christ, Luke, I thought I'd lost you."

"We were just preparing breakfast. There's a whole kitchen in here," said Ava, emerging from the room behind Pippa.

Beyond her I saw Chelsea.

"Everyone come with me up to the bridge. I think we're better off up top, where we can see. The bridge has almost 360 degree views around us. The shark's back." Ava's face fell. I felt almost guilty for bringing them bad news, but there was no way of disguising it. "Weir's going to try and navigate a path through the streets, hope we can put it off."

"New York? We're home?" Pippa almost smiled. "Too bad we can't go back to our apartment and away from this nightmare."

I grabbed her hand and led them all back up to the bridge. If we were going to die, I wanted us all to be together. There was little point in hiding down in the bedrooms, waiting for the inevitable. I wanted to see New York for one more time. I hadn't realized how much I missed the place. It seemed apt that we had gone full circle. The shark had destroyed our home days ago and now it had returned to finish the job.

"Manny, how are you?"

We entered the bridge and Pippa rushed forward to greet Manny. Chelsea gave me a passing hug and did the same.

"Where is it, Weir?" I asked, as Ava slipped her hand in mine. "You got the drop on it, or what?"

Our speed had dropped considerably and we had sailed into Manhattan. Somewhere beneath us was the city: homes and stores, people and animals, vehicles and death, all waiting for us to join them. Somewhere below was the Megalodon.

"No sign," said Weir. "I've got my hands full getting through these streets. I can't do it all. I need eyes. I need you out there."

The buildings around us were getting closer, the shattered frames of skyscrapers bludgeoning the sky and squeezing in on us.

"I'll take the starboard," I said, dragging Ava with me to the open door. "Pippa, take the port. Chelsea, stay here and help Manny with Weir. Any sign of it, holler as loud as you can."

I made my way out back onto the upper deck and looked back into the bridge. Chelsea seemed content to stay inside with Manny which is where I wanted her. It was probably the safest place for her right now. I was reluctant to ask Pippa to help, but Weir was right. We needed as many eyes looking for the Megalodon as possible. I could see through the tall windows, past the controls and out to the other side, where Pippa was nervously pacing back and forth.

"Look at this place, Luke," said Ava, squeezing my hand. "Look at what's become of it."

Her eyes were drawn to the remains of New York. Brooklyn Bridge was behind us now, the dappled sunlight striking its brilliant arches. The Hudson and the Atlantic were as one now, and there was no distinct separation between the land and the water. The parks were gone, and it was an odd sensation to be sailing above the city. So many of the buildings were submerged, yet so many were still visible, their rooftops poking out trying to claim one last breath. We passed one covered in blankets and clothes, a few fishing poles lined up along the southern end of the building. There was no sign of anyone still living there. I looked down at the water we were cruising through. It was dirty and oily, and I'm sure I saw a mangled body drift close by.

"You wouldn't know it, but we're somewhere over Chinatown," I said. "There used to be a great little restaurant on Mulberry Street. Best wontons in the whole state."

"Gonna have to take your word on that."

Ava seemed mesmerized by the place. It was like a ghost town, like something out of an old western, except dust and sand had been replaced with icy cold water. As much as I would've loved to reminisce about my home, I knew we had to stay focused. "You think we've lost it? I thought it would have found us by now. What's keeping it?"

Ava peered around her, looking up and down the avenues and streets. "I don't see it. You?"

I looked back at Pippa. She caught my eye and shrugged. "No, maybe we lost it." I noticed that Estelle was in the bridge now, sticking closely to Chelsea. "Maybe Weir was right about the city being too shallow for it. There's a whole heap of shit down there. If it has any sense it'll head back out to deeper water and—" I paused. Movement caught my eye. It was just a shadow, a vague shape from where Confucius Plaza used to be. I pointed to Ava. "There. You see it?"

There was a ripple in the water and then suddenly it appeared. Ava screamed and I refrained from joining her as she squeezed my fingers to breaking point.

"Weir. It's coming!" I yelled. The massive shark was heading for us from the east. Its giant body was rising up out of the water, perhaps because Weir was right about it being unable to navigate through the shallows. It was bigger than the boat, and its massive jaws were bearing down on us, slightly agape. I could clearly see its black eyes as it bore down on us and we had very little time to avoid it. "Weir, for Christ's sake, do something."

Suddenly, the engine burst into life and the boat turned rapidly toward the AT&T building. Many of the upper floors were still above water, and then suddenly we turned away from it again. A huge apartment building, its shiny exterior glistening in the morning light, rushed to meet us, blocking the approach of the shark.

"Shoot." I pulled Ava back from the edge of the yacht as we flew by quickly, perilously close to the apartment. I could have reached out a hand and touched it as we sailed past.

"Where is it?" Ava pushed her back against the windows to the bridge. "Where is it, Luke?" she asked anxiously.

I had to admit I wasn't sure. Weir seemed to have thrown it off, sailing us so close to a building that it couldn't follow us. We began to leave the apartment building behind. "I think we lost it. That was close."

A door on the lower deck suddenly flew open and Douglas appeared. He began to march up the metal stairs toward us. He looked terrible, as if he had been crying non-stop for hours. His eyes were red and puffy, and he still wore the same clothes covered in his wife's blood.

"Douglas? Where were you?"

"Sorry, I… I couldn't face it," he said, as he ascended the stairs to us. "I was going to hide. Without Honey, I didn't want any part of this, but when I heard Ava screaming… I'm sorry. I should've come sooner. I just—"

It sounded like a rocket going off. The apartment building behind us exploded as the Megalodon tore through it, destroying one corner of it as the shark's massive body ripped it apart like paper. I watched in amazement as the building began to crumble and the shark splashed its way toward us. Huge clouds of white dust billowed up and across the water, obliterating the faint sunlight, as the giant shark zipped through the water. It parted its massive jaws, revealing those powerful jagged teeth I had seen all too closely, and then it pointed its snout down, disappearing under the water. There was a brief moment of quiet, and then the shark reappeared. Its giant jaws opened up and smashed into the stern of the boat, ripping off the rear of the boat, tearing through fiberglass and aluminum with ease. The monster's wake slammed into us like a hurricane hitting a 747.

"Ava!"

We were all knocked off our feet as the boat was thrust forward suddenly. The shark's jaws sliced off chunks of metal and the lower platform, where we had earlier boarded the yacht, collapsed in on itself. As I fell to the deck I saw huge swathes of the lower deck disintegrate and the Megalodon's jaws close as the monster slid silently back into the water.

"Luke." Ava was on her back and reached a hand to me. I took it and she looked at me as she regained her breath. "We're going to die, aren't we?"

I wouldn't admit it out loud, but the thought was forefront of my mind too. We would be lucky to survive another attack. The Megalodon had one half of the boat down its throat and we were about to be dessert.

CHAPTER 22

I hauled myself up using the handrail as the boat steadied itself. Glancing into the bridge and across to Pippa, I could see she was all right. They were all shaken, but as far as I could tell, unhurt. I helped Ava up. "No, we're going to beat this. But we might need a bigger—"

As I helped her stand Ava yelped with shock, and she pointed over my shoulder. Suddenly the shark was at our side. Its silvery skin bashed against the starboard of our creaking ship, buffeting it from side to side. I was worried we were taking on water at the rear, but there was no time to look into it. The shark had wedged itself in between us and the nearest building, and was ramming its thick body against our hull. Whether it was trapped or simply using its massive bulk to dislodge us, the effect was the same. I could feel the boat tearing itself apart as the monster repeatedly slammed into it. Ava slipped away from me once more as she skidded across the deck. A smell of what I can only describe as rotting fish wafted up from the churning ocean, and I reeled away from the side of the boat. Letting go of the rail I turned to help Ava.

"Luke?"

It was Douglas' voice. I had forgotten about him after the emergence of the shark, and I heard Ava shriek as we turned to look at where he had been standing. He had been thrown off the stairs and over the side of the hull. I saw his hands clinging desperately onto the safety rail as he tried to pull himself back up, but he was too weak and tired. His eyes told me he only had a few seconds left before his lack of energy would loosen his grip on life.

"Douglas, hold on." I jumped to the top of the stairs, trying to remain upright as the giant beneath us thrashed around in the confined space. Its massive tail struck a brick wall that collapsed immediately. Another building followed it to a watery grave as the shark rammed into us, forcing our boat to collide with the corner of another high-rise. The outer hull was scratched and torn as the dying building dragged its concrete claws along our boat. The ruins of New York were dangerous enough without the shark, and in the close confines of the flooded streets I couldn't imagine how we would escape with our lives.

"Luke, we have to help him," said Ava.

I reluctantly pushed her back. "Go to the others. I'll help Douglas. Get to the bridge, Ava."

I raced to help Douglas, but as I turned back to the stairs the shark suddenly twisted violently and spun away from us. Its huge girth forced a plume of water up into the air that crested over the deck, drenching Ava and I.

"Douglas, hold on!"

The shark slapped its huge tail against the hull, diving down and sending the boat once more careening toward the AT&T building. The towering building loomed over us and I knew if we hit it straight on we'd never survive. The crash would certainly destroy our vessel and I just hoped that Weir knew what he was doing. I had to trust him to steer us to a safer path. I slipped and grabbed for the upper rail of the metal staircase. As the saltwater showered down over me I reached a hand out to Douglas. "Take my hand," I shouted.

"I can't—"

Douglas's feeble reply was sucked into thin air as he let go of the rail and bounced off the side of the hull into the water below.

"Douglas, no!"

I stretched to reach him and leaned over the rail, dangling my hands futilely. He was gone. I saw him hit the water as masonry rained down around us. He sank beneath the surface of the foaming water and I shouted for him. Scanning the water, I saw a submerged car float past and a red wooden door bobbing along, brushing past the hull. A yellow cab struck the hull and then Douglas resurfaced. He floated up silently, his body motionless and far from the boat. His eyes were open and there was a huge gash across his head. I knew there was no chance of rescuing him. He was gone.

I rapidly turned away from his dead body, feeling sick. The Megalodon had done this. He might have drowned or broken his neck, but Douglas had been killed by the shark and I was sick of it. With the boat still ploughing toward the AT&T building I dragged my aching body to the bridge. The ocean had been churned up by the frenzied shark and the deck was covered in water.

"Luke, thank God." Ava pulled me inside. She was soaked through. "I thought—"

"He's gone." I let Ava hold me. Everyone was looking at me, their eyes and faces full of unanswered questions boring into me. Manny was in the opposite doorway, while Pippa and Chelsea were cowering behind Weir, watching him work the controls. Estelle was at the windows, watching the outside world drift past. "I couldn't get there in time," I said guiltily. "Douglas fell. I couldn't—"

"Brace yourselves!" yelled Weir.

The yacht clipped the corner of a building and the bow crumpled. Bricks rained over the deck and a shadow spread over the bridge. We were all struggling to maintain our balance and stay on our feet as Weir turned the boat away out into a wider street.

"Weir, we have to get out of here. The shark isn't going to back down. It's determined to bring us down."

"You got any ideas, monkey?" Sweat poured down his face. "Now's the time."

Suddenly Estelle screamed and staggered back from the large windows. "Hay peligro—"

The windows shattered as a huge chunk of the building we'd hit pounded the deck. The windows blew in and I instinctively pulled Ava into my body to shield her from the flying glass. It was all over in a second and when I opened my eyes I saw open space in front of me. All of the windows were broken. The city beyond rose up ominously. Glass littered the floor and Estelle had some bad looking cuts on her face and hands. Pippa rushed to her aid.

"Weir, this is madness," said Manny. "We have to do something. We've already lost Douglas. What are we going to do?"

I had never felt more determined in my life. If we did nothing, eventually the shark would bring the boat down. If it didn't manage to get us itself it would force us into another building. We were in dangerous territory, yet I didn't feel afraid anymore. I was concerned for the others, for my family and Ava. But I had a sense that this wasn't a one-sided fight. We didn't have to let it be. The shark had wasted its opportunity to bring us down when we were out in the open water. Here, in the compact streets, surrounded by tall fragile buildings, it wasn't so sure of itself. We had to start believing that for once *we* had the upper hand. I knew this city. I knew the layout like the hairs on the back of my hand. As Weir slowed the boat and kept us in a relatively open expanse, away from any further collisions with something that might fall on us, I saw the upper floors of the Empire State. The morning sun was dazzling, shining like a beacon, drawing us in. I realized Weir had brought us onto Broadway, heading north. We were going to end up above Times Square. It was too risky. The shark would have more room to maneuver, and more space to get itself into a position where it could take a bite out of our hull.

"Weir, these streets are too wide. We need to get to where it can't follow us," I said. "Shallow water and narrow streets will block it in. It'll give us half a chance."

"We need to know where it is first." Weir wiped the sweat from his brow. "Manny, make yourself useful and take a look. It won't have gone far."

As Manny left the bridge and stepped onto the portside deck, there was a strange rushing noise. It sounded like a wall of water bearing down on us, yet the water was calm and looking out of the open windows I could see nothing apart from the silent buildings and hopeful sunshine. The noise grew in volume quickly. My eyes caught Weir's and then I understood. He figured it out a moment before me and frantically thrust the engines into life. It was beneath us.

"Manny!" I yelled. "Get inside before—"

The shark struck somewhere at the back of the boat, no doubt rising up out of the ocean like a mountain. There was no time to do anything but hold on and hope the boat would hold together. We were shunted forward and up into the air. I imagined the bottom of the boat was lifted right out of the water and we were propelled forward with such velocity that Weir had no control over where we went. The direction was determined by the shark as it pushed us, and I saw Macy's looming up ahead. We glanced off the side of the empty building which rattled and shook as we gouged out several windows and half a floor. Pippa and Estelle were tossed around the bridge, their bodies rolling around in the broken glass, and Ava clung onto me. Chelsea screamed and I realized she had been behind me the whole time. Her fingers were digging into the doorframe and I reached out a hand to her, hoping to keep her on her feet. The door that led to the interior of the boat was swinging violently behind her, and she looked terrified.

"Manny!" I called for him, but there was no answer. I wondered if he had gone over the side like Douglas. "Manny, answer me. Where are you?" Whilst the boat was still charging forward, pushed along by the shark, there was nothing I could do.

I looked at Chelsea, trying to reassure her, knowing her mother's screams would haunt her dreams. As the boat began to settle, finally, I let go of Chelsea's hand. "Ava, stay with her. Please."

I staggered forward, glass crunching underneath my feet, and helped Pippa and Estelle up. "Go to the back of the bridge, behind Weir. Stay with Chelsea." Pippa was covered in numerous cuts and she was already plucking tiny shards of splintered glass from her palms. I winced with her, knowing the pain she was in. She said nothing, but took Estelle and carefully went to Chelsea.

"Manny?" I stood in the open doorway, reluctant to step out onto the deck. It was awash with masonry and water. There was no sign of him. I was going to have to go out there and find him. He could be hurt, perhaps unconscious but still on the deck. I couldn't just leave him and assume the worst when there was still a chance to save him. My friend had been there for me, helped me with Chelsea, and would do the same for me. I wasn't going to let him be taken like Douglas. "42nd street," I said to Weir. "Get onto 42nd and head east. I've an idea how we might be able to beat this thing. We'll be killed if we stay on this course. We need to move while we still can. Head east for about three blocks and then back north."

I heard Weir call for me, but I ignored him. I had to know that Manny was okay. The boat turned as I stepped over the threshold onto the deck outside. Weir could question me all he liked, but I knew from the direction the boat was going that he was listening to me. I took a few steps and looked around for Manny. The boat was a mess. I could hardly believe we were still afloat. How much more could she take? I called for Manny but got no reply, so I gingerly felt my way to the bow. There was wood and bricks, window frames and even a couple of mannequins scattered across the deck. The safety rail was a mangled mess of metal, twisted like a heap of frozen spaghetti. If Manny had been thrown underneath all of this he could easily have been killed. Equally, he might just have been knocked out. With so many objects flying around us he could also be bleeding and I had to find him. I began to pull bricks up with my hands and toss them overboard. My hatred for the Megalodon only grew as I found no sign of my friend.

"Damn it, Manny, where are you?" I made my way to a piece of the safety rail and peered into the water. We were heading east now and the water below was clogged with thick detritus and garbage.

"Uncle Luke?"

I whirled around, surprised. "Chelsea? Get back inside. It's not safe out here."

Ignoring my advice Chelsea hopped across the deck, and I grabbed her as she reached the rail.

"I saw him fall," she said quietly. "I saw him."

My heart leapt. "Are you sure?"

She nodded. "I don't know if—"

A groan reached my ears and I looked down at the lower deck. It was covered in masonry too, huge chunks of concrete and the remnants of Macy's. I heard the groan again and noticed a hand sticking out from underneath a sheet of plastic.

"Manny! It has to be," I said excitedly. "I have to—"

"No," said Chelsea firmly. "You *don't*. I'll go." Chelsea unclipped two straps that hugged her shoulders and swung a plain black backpack around. She held it out in front of her. "Open it."

I hadn't even noticed the pack and as I cautiously took it from her, I unzipped the top. What I saw inside made my eyes widen.

"I found it. After Lance and that other man, you know, died. They never got a chance to use it, but now maybe you can. I'll go to Manny. You go do what you have to do."

Ava and Pippa appeared in the doorway, and Chelsea smiled. She reached out a hand and helped her mother across to us. Ava followed and I tried not to be mad with them. It wasn't safe out here in the open. If the shark struck whilst we were standing out on deck we could end up anywhere.

"You know, I'd really prefer you to stay with Weir and—"

"This isn't your show, Luke," said Pippa. She pushed Ava toward me. "You can't make us hide and hope this goes away. Weir has control of the boat for now. Estelle's hurt but she'll be okay," said Pippa, wiping tears from her eyes. "So, *monkey*, listen to Chelsea. Stop trying to do everything and let us help."

I was reminded of the time my mother had scolded me for ordering Pippa to tidy up her toys. I had tripped over a doll or something she'd left in the kitchen, and couldn't understand why my mom hadn't told my sister to clear up. I guess I had always wanted to be in control, reluctant to let anyone else tell me what to do. I guess I couldn't tell Pippa what to do any more than the rest of them. I had their best interests at heart, but Pippa was right. I couldn't do this alone.

"So, what do you suggest, *mom*?" Pippa's eyes flickered but she ignored my barbed comment, as I did hers. There was nothing sinister, just the friendly sort of dig that two siblings did to each other from birth to death. I assumed that's how it was anyway. Pippa never let up on me, and I never let up on her. I think we would've been disappointed if either one of us had.

"Manny," said Chelsea. "He's down there, mom. We're going to get him. Luke is going to let Ava help him take care of the... shark."

"Shark?" Pippa shook her head. "Call it what it is, Chelsea. It's a Megalodon. It's a badass, but when it takes on my family, it's going to find out how much of a badass *I* can be."

I watched my sister and Chelsea walk back to the staircase to go down and help Manny.

"Call up to me. I want to know how he is," I shouted after them. I was proud of them both. I was irritated to hell, of course, and I hated letting Pippa get the last word, but sometimes I just had to admit I was wrong.

"What's that?" asked Ava, looking at the black backpack in my hands.

"This?" I took in a deep breath of fresh air. "This is going to help us win."

Crossing the deck, I stuck my head in the open doorway to the bridge. Through the vast window frames the cold air was rushing in, exposing the skeletal remains of New York that had become a silent graveyard. "Weir, make a left here. We're over Little Italy right now. You remember where you and Jonah picked us up?"

He nodded and looked at me with skepticism. "Sure, but if you're hoping to stop by and pick up your old Levi's you can forget it."

"When you reach where the apartment was, slow right down. I'll come up soon. When I tell you, cut the engines."

"Are you dreaming?" Weir rolled his eyes. "Boy, we are not best friends yet. You think I'm going to cut the engines and just wait for that bitch to eat us, you can think again. We need to be ready to move. We're going to—"

"Stop arguing with us, Weir and just fucking do it."

Even I was shocked by Ava's tone. From the look on Weir's face, he was either about to explode with rage or spend the next month arguing with her.

Ava grabbed the pack from my hands and stuck a hand inside. She pulled out a gun and brandished it in the air. "You know what this is, Weir? It's a start. A way of killing that thing. Luke knows this city. You might know the ocean, but this isn't your domain now any more than it is that damn shark's. So, for once, please, pretty fucking please with sprinkles on top, *do what Luke says*."

Ava turned and marched around me, toward the bow. I looked at Weir and shrugged. "What she said."

I followed Ava and together we clambered over the wreckage to an open area of the deck. "How did you know there'd be a gun in the bag?" I asked her.

"I didn't. Just took a guess that whatever that smug look was in your eyes earlier meant you actually had a plan."

"Smug? Me?"

We'd gone as far as we could. The front of the yacht had been smashed to pieces. We stood there looking out over New York. The city was so quiet that I almost forgot what we were here for. There were still a lot of buildings standing, and several of the skyscrapers I had grown up with were surrounding me now, like old friends come back to say hello. We were exactly where I wanted us to be, and I spun around to face the bridge.

"Stop here, Weir."

I took the pack from Ava and let her keep the gun. I pulled out another one and tucked it into my pants. Then I pulled out three grenades and threw the pack away.

"Hmm. Where did you get those?" asked Ava, the look of surprise on her face almost bringing a smile to my face.

"Your brother, believe it or not. Mckade ordered him to blow the yacht up. This must be how they were going to do it. I can think of a better way of using them, can't you?"

Ava reached up and kissed me, her warm soft lips pressing on mine. If it was my last kiss on Earth I couldn't have asked for anything better. Ava murmured quietly as she let me go.

"Why here?"

"It's the only spot I could think of that gives us a chance." I pointed over to the right, to an open expanse of water. "That's where my apartment used to be. There's a thousand tons of rubble right below the surface. No way can the shark get past it. All around us actually. The Stamford collapsed a while ago. You might think we're a sitting duck out here, but don't let the water fool you. These streets are congested and narrow, and there's no way it can get to us. The only way is from the west. Right there."

I saw a sight then that I didn't think I would see again. The uppermost tip of one of the spires of St. Patrick's Cathedral. There were only a few feet visible, but I knew what it meant. I was home again, hearing the buzz of the people below my apartment and the sirens at night. I missed New York.

"What is it?" Ava checked her gun and mine, and I handed her one of the grenades.

"St. Patrick's. Half of it is still standing, I think. When she comes for us, that's where she'll come from. It's the only way through. We'll see her coming and when she does..." I looked at the two grenades in my hand. "Boom."

Ava smirked. "Hope you're right, monkey. I truly do. If you—"

I grabbed Ava. "Later. It's here."

The water in the west was rising, pushed up by an invisible force. I knew what it was. The Megalodon was coming for us.

"Already? Sheesh." Ava steadied her feet and pointed the gun at the water, close to where the spire was sticking up out of the water. "Luke, I'm not sure about this. What if we're too slow? What if it's too fast? What if..?"

"I know, Ava, I know. If we miss there is no second chance or time to do anything else. We can't afford to mess this up. Just be sure with your aim and ready to go." I blinked away the doubt in my mind. "This will work, Ava. Just be ready. When you see it, unload everything you have. We've got one shot at this."

There was only a few feet between where we stood and the open water. If we missed, or if the shark was quicker than our bullets, then it would take us first. If I was wrong, then it would eat me and Ava first, and the rest of the boat just for the sake of it. I shoved the two grenades into my pockets and raised the gun. The fin was visible now, steadily rising up above the water. I estimated that the monster was directly above 5th Avenue. Its huge head began to rise up out of the water as it approached, unable to stay submerged in the shallow city streets. It revealed its teeth as it reached the cathedral and then suddenly everything happened fast. The shark was close enough to smell and its head was almost completely above the waterline. I looked into its jet black eyes, scared that I had misjudged it. The thing was huge and the cathedral did nothing to slow it down. I had hoped it might impale itself on the spires, but it simply crushed the cathedral as it swam toward us. As it got closer and closer, I noticed a long scar above its left eye. Someone had tried before, tried and failed to kill it. The thought that we might do the same crossed my mind, but there was no going back. There was no way Weir could move us out of its path now. It was time.

Both Ava and I instinctively knew this was our chance, and together we started shooting. The gun felt heavy in my hands and as I unloaded the bullets into the approaching beast I felt alive. I felt every single bullet rip into the shark's skin. I imagined the pain it felt as one of its eyes burst. The black eye simply exploded as Ava let leash a hail of bullets, and I heard her scream a yelp of delight as the eye was destroyed. The shark didn't slow down though. When our guns clicked empty we looked at each other and I frantically pulled the grenades from my pockets. I nodded at Ava.

We pulled the pins. The shark's gaping jaws opened wide and I felt my bladder weaken as it bore down on us. I could see right down its bloody throat, past the shiny white teeth into its belly. It extended its jaws so wide it could almost eat our boat whole.

"Now"! I yelled, and I threw the grenades as hard and as far as I could.

Ava let hers fly after mine, and when all three were airborne I grabbed her and pulled her down to the deck. I felt the boat tremble as the shark neared us, its head casting a shadow over us as I cradled Ava on the deck of the boat. The rippled explosions came barely seconds later.

EPILOGUE

Miles and miles of ocean. That's it. That's all there is now. I'm so sick of looking across endless stretches of water and having none to drink. It's been two days. The longest two days of my life. I can barely function anymore: no food, no water, and no hope. It all happened so quickly. It was over quickly, at least. Well, for most. Floating out here on what is left of the *Bella*, I keep going over in my mind where it went wrong. Leaving our apartment was the start of it. We should've stayed and gone down with old Mr. Johnson. It would've been over faster and been less painful. I wouldn't have had to watch the people I care about die.

I think about death a lot now. There's not much else to do out here. Baking sun and salty water that I can't drink; left with my own memories. Death would be one option. Sometimes it's a very appealing one too. But do I want to jump into the ocean and exhale? Fuck that. I'm going to make it. I'm not giving up.

The grenades caught the Megalodon, enough to give it one hell of a fright. We got her big-time. Blinded her at least and added a few more scars to her head. But it wasn't enough. The grenades fell short. They exploded in front of the shark, not in its jaws as I had hoped. We blew our chances when we blew off the side of its face, and from that point on it was over. I saw it coming. Standing up there on the deck with Ava there was nothing else we could do. I remember watching it bear down on us, its jaws just opening wider and wider, knowing that we were going down. I'd let Ava down. I'd let my sister and niece down, and everyone else on board the *Bella* that day.

When the shark struck the bow I thought it would swallow us whole. I swear those teeth were going to sink right into the deck and bite the yacht in half. It seemed to turn slightly at the last moment, which meant it sheared off one side of the boat. I'm not sure why. Maybe the explosion threw it off its game, or maybe it just changed its mind and decided it would have a little fun with us first. The result was catastrophic. The boat caved in and I was thrown into the air along with Ava. I heard screams and panic, screams that still reverberate around my head now. Sleeping doesn't come easy any longer.

The sound of the boat being mangled by the shark was louder even than the grenades. Metal and wood, fiberglass and aluminum, flesh and tissue: all were torn apart in a frenzy as the shark tore through the boat. I remember hitting the water and Ava's hands being pulled from mine. We were pressed right up against the shark, unable to control where we were thrown as the shark ripped open the boat's hull. It was like being in an underwater hurricane. I was repeatedly slammed into the side of the monster as I desperately tried to hold my breath. I tried to kick and pull myself toward Ava, but it was useless; like trying to swim against the strongest riptide you've ever experienced. I saw Ava pulled inexorably toward the monster's jaws. It had a force all of its own, and she screamed for me even as she was sucked toward its jagged teeth. Her blue eyes locked onto mine and when she slipped inside the jaws of death I felt my heart explode. I tried to use the shark to get to her, digging my fingernails into its skin to claw myself along its body until I could reach her, but it was impossible.

Ava disappeared from my vision as I was swirled around and around. I heard the sound of something snapping and when I managed to dig my hands into the shark's body, I saw its huge teeth crunching through the deck, the fallen masonry and anything that got in the shark's way. As I clung to the side of the monster I saw Pippa. She floated gently past me, not moving, one of her arms wrenched free from its socket, blood spewing out into the water. Her lifeless eyes swept past mine and then her body was propelled into the Megalodon's mouth. Her body was snapped in half. The monster's teeth ripped her apart like a rag doll, and her decimated body was the last thing I saw of my sister before the shark swallowed her.

Suddenly, I was thrust upward. The churning water forced me to lose my grip on the shark and I found myself emerging into the sunlight with pieces of the *Bella* all around me. There was no boat left. There was just a mountain of detritus and the shark swimming around it, determined to finish the job and pick us off one by one.

"Luke!" I heard a voice and frantically began swimming toward it.

"Luke?"

"Chelsea? Hold on." Her voice was close, but so was the shark. I saw its fin disappear beneath the surface and I swam harder, fighting back the tears as I remembered Pippa and Ava. I pushed aside garbage and a metal box, and then I saw her. Chelsea was lying prostrate on a piece of wood, her arms hanging limply in the water. "I'm coming, Chelsea." When I called to her she looked up, a bloody wound running down one side of her face.

"Luke, where's mom? I can't find her?" she sobbed.

"I'm coming, just hold on," I said, unable to answer her question. The city was silhouetted behind her, giant buildings reduced to shadows of their former selves. Up out of the water rose the shark and I screamed. "Chelsea!"

It rose behind her almost silently, opening its cavernous mouth to reveal a set of teeth that I knew could tear through anything. Chelsea turned when its shadow fell over her, and she screamed my name as it bore down on her. I saw her try to push herself off the piece of wood and begin swimming away from it, but the shark was too fast. Its jaws closed right around her and I heard a muffled scream from within its mouth before the shark devoured my niece and dove beneath the water.

"No!" I punched the water in frustration. "No, no, no." I hauled myself up onto an upturned wooden table and turned onto my back, the tears flowing freely from my eyes. I gasped for air, my hands idling in the water, blood and oil that surrounded me. The water lapped at me gently, and it was strangely silent. I lay there for a minute, waiting for the shark to reappear. I waited but nothing came for me, and I began to call out for help. I called for Weir and Estelle, but there was no answer. I called for anyone. I shouted until my throat was sore and my voice fading, but there was no answer. I think it was almost an hour before I saw their bodies. I was still on the upturned table, my mind numb, unable to comprehend what had happened, when I saw Weir. I wasn't looking for anything in particular, but when I saw the body in the water something clicked inside me. It was a few feet away and I watched him float closer. I slowly recognized Weir, at least what was left of him. His eyes were closed and he almost looked peaceful. His legs were gone and his torso was ripped to shreds. I let him go past me, drifting south toward the bay and wherever the current carried him. A few minutes later and Estelle followed him. Her body was a bloody mess, held together by a few nerves and veins, her flesh already soft and half eaten. Her body twitched, almost as if she was alive, as something underneath her nibbled at her rotting body. I was alone. I had been left alone. They were all dead.

"Why? Why me?" I slapped the calm water. I was angry and grief poured from my eyes once more as I began to punch the water. "Come on, you *bitch*. Take me. Come on, what are you waiting for? Scared? Come and take me." I remembered how Ava had pleaded with me right before she had died. The pain was unbearable. I wanted to be with her. I wanted to die and see her again. Her dying screams were all I could hear as I continued to slap my fists into the water. "Take me. *Take me!*"

The fin appeared first, swiftly followed by the Megalodon. It came at me from the west. I felt the water rising and then saw it. We'd done a good job in deforming it. One eye was gone and half of its head was a charred mess. The flesh was burnt and twisted, and when it finally came for me I stopped crying. I saw its huge jaws open up and then I closed my eyes. I smiled. It had won. I couldn't deny that. But I was going to see Ava again, and I felt a calm sense of relief wash over me as the shark neared. I wanted to hold her hand, to kiss those soft lips and look into those crystal blue eyes once more, to tell her how much she meant to me. I heard the shark's jaws snap shut and the huge beast slammed into me.

That was two days ago.

The *Bella* is my home now. All I have left is a single piece of wood that I cling to, until I don't have the energy anymore. It's not much of a life, but it *is* a life, and I'll take that any day of the week. I have to hope that someone, somewhere, is going to find me. I have a day left in me, and then I'm done. The shark, of course, never did eat me. I'll probably never know why. Maybe it just enjoys torturing me. Maybe fate intervened. All I know is that I woke up with a pounding headache several hours later to find myself drifting away from the city. The Megalodon was gone and so was the *Bella*. I was lying on a piece of wood that looked like it was part of the deck. I coughed up cold salty water from my lungs and watched New York fade away into the gloom of evening. I was still alive, yet I took no satisfaction in it. The Megalodon had taken everything I loved away from me and not even given me the decency to kill me too.

At least that's what I thought. By a miracle I floated past the wing of one of the upturned planes where I spotted a red hat in the water. I reached for it, but it was too far away. As I drifted closer I saw a body lying on the wing. A figure spread-eagled on the metal wing as if sunbathing. I summoned up my last reserves of energy and pulled myself to the wing, grabbing it with both hands. Ava said nothing as I pulled her to me. I grabbed one of her arms and her body slid down the wing effortlessly. I hauled her onto the wood I was marooned on and then the current took us. I tried to coax her back to life, to get her to say something, but I couldn't wake her.

I had no control over the current or where the ocean took us, so I let us drift. The city eventually disappeared and at some point I must have fallen asleep. When I woke the next morning the mainland was gone.

We've been drifting for too long and I have no idea where we are or what direction we're headed now. All I can see is the ocean. The Atlantic is a foreboding place, an endless world of blue and black. There is no land, no boats, nothing; I'd hitch a ride with a turtle if I could get us back to a boat. I don't want to let the Megalodon win. I don't want to give up. I want to fight back. I've had a long time on my own to think about it, and I want to find someone with the guts to take these things on. When they do, I'm going to be right there. I want to see one of these things die. I want to sit astride its dead carcass and laugh. I need to, for Pippa and Chelsea, and all the others these things have killed. This is about more than mere survival now. This is personal.

I still haven't coaxed Ava back to consciousness. I try to shield her from the sun, but I have nothing to shade her with except my own shirt. I guess she's in a coma. There's nothing I can do for her except make sure she doesn't fall off this piece of wood and drown. I keep checking for a pulse and it's still there.

Faint, but there. I wish she would wake up. I wish I could talk to her and hear the sound of something other than my own thoughts.

The world is a big place. There are others out there, other people who need help, and other Megalodons who will seek out and destroy every living creature on the planet. I can't let them. I can't stop. I'm going to find a way, but I need an arsenal.

The sky is blue and I'm starving. My lips are cracked and dry, and I'm quite sure that the cuts up and down my body are infected. But I'm *not* giving up.

"What?" The sound of my own voice is startling. "What was that?"

I raise my head and look to the south. Had I imagined it, or was there something there? I use my wrinkled hands to shield my weak eyes from the overhead sun and peer closely at the horizon. There it is.

"Uncle Luke, looks like you got lucky," I said. My voice is feeble and shouting is going to be nigh on impossible. I have to get their attention somehow, but I have nothing with me, just the clothes on my body and a will to survive.

"Ava?" I prop her head up. "Ava? What is it?"

Of course, she doesn't answer me. Her head falls limply back onto the wood and I slap the water in frustration.

The boat is distant, but large. I can tell from here that it's not drifting aimlessly either. It has power. There's a hazy gray smoke rising above it. The boat is headed north and if I can make it, I might just be able to hitch that ride I was looking for.

"Hey, over here!" I yell. The effort was almost too much. I have to wait until it's closer, close enough that someone might hear my cries.

I wait and watch the boat get closer, and as I do so, there's something else. I notice movement a little way behind it. Finally, I can make out that it's a triangular shape and although very large, it's smaller than the boat. It's a fin.

I let a smile creep across my cracked lips. "I knew you'd come back," I said. Blind or not, she wasn't going to give up. The shark would never give up. But, neither will I.

"Over here," I whisper. "Just a little closer. Come to Uncle Luke."

I'm going to turn the tables on these prehistoric sharks and hunt every last one of them down. I'm going to get Ava and me on that boat. This isn't the end for us.

This is the beginning.

THE END

Acknowledgements

Afraid of the water? You should be…
Please check out the numerous quality novels Severed Press have also have produced at www.severedpress.com.
Also consider leaving a review and pay a visit to my website www.russwatts.co or look at my other titles:
The Afflicted
The Grave
The Ocean King
Zombiekill
Devouring the Dead
Devouring the Dead 2: Nemesis
Goliath
Hamsikker
Hamsikker 2
Hamsikker 3
Jurassic Hell
Adrenal7n

CHECK OUT OTHER GREAT
DEEP SEA THRILLERS

LAMPREYS
by Alan Spencer

A secret government tactical team is sent to perform a clean sweep of a private research installation. Horrible atrocities lurk within the abandoned corridors. Mutated sea creatures with insane killing abilities are waiting to suck the blood and meat from their prey.

Unemployed college professor Conrad Garfield is forced to assist and is soon separated from the team. Alone and afraid, Conrad must use his wits to battle mutated lampreys, infected scientists and go head-to-head with the biggest monstrosity of all.

Can Conrad survive, or will the deadly monsters suck the very life from his body?

DEEP DEVOTION
by M.C. Norris

Rising from the depths, a mind-bending monster unleashes a wave of terror across the American heartland. Kate Browning, a Kansas City EMT confronts her paralyzing fear of water when she traces the source of a deadly parasitic affliction to the Gulf of Mexico. Cooperating with a marine biologist, she travels to Florida in an effort to save the life of one very special patient, but the source of the epidemic happens to be the nest of a terrifying monster, one that last rose from the depths to annihilate the lost continent of Atlantis.

Leviathan, destroyer, devoted lifemate and parent, the abomination is not going to take the extermination of its brood well.

CHECK OUT OTHER GREAT DEEP SEA THRILLERS

LOCH NESS REVENGE
by Hunter Shea

Deep in the murky waters of Loch Ness, the creature known as Nessie has returned. Twins Natalie and Austin McQueen watched in horror as their parents were devoured by the world's most infamous lake monster. Two decades later, it's their turn to hunt the legend. But what lurks in the Loch is not what they expected. Nessie is devouring everything in and around the Loch, and it's not alone. Hell has come to the Scottish Highlands. In a fierce battle between man and monster, the world may never be the same. Praise for THEY RISE : "Outrageous, balls to the wall...made me yearn for 3D glasses and a tub of popcorn, extra butter." – The Eyes of Madness "A fast-paced, gore-heavy splatter fest of sharksploitation." The Werd "A rocket paced horror story. I enjoyed the hell out of this book." Shotgun Logic Reviews

TERROR FROM THE DEEP
by Alex Laybourne

When deep sea seismic activity cracks open a world hidden for millions of years, terrifying leviathans of the deep are unleashed to rampage off the coast of Mexico. Trapped on an island resort, MMA fighter Troy Deane leads a small group of survivors in the fight of their lives against pre-historic beasts long thought extinct. The terror from the deep has awoken, and it will take everything they have to conquer it.

 SEVERED**PRESS**

CHECK OUT OTHER GREAT DEEP SEA THRILLERS

MEGA
by Jake Bible

There is something in the deep. Something large. Something hungry. Something prehistoric.
And Team Grendel must find it, fight it, and kill it.
Kinsey Thorne, the first female US Navy SEAL candidate has hit rock bottom. Having washed out of the Navy, she turned to every drink and drug she could get her hands on. Until her father and cousins, all ex-Navy SEALS themselves, offer her a way back into the life: as part of a private, elite combat Team being put together to find and hunt down an impossible monster in the Indian Ocean. Kinsey has a second chance, but can she live through it?

THE BLACK
by Paul E Cooley

Under 30,000 feet of water, the exploration rig Leaguer has discovered an oil field larger than Saudi Arabia, with oil so sweet and pure, nations would go to war for the rights to it. But as the team starts drilling exploration well after exploration well in their race to claim the sweet crude, a deep rumbling beneath the ocean floor shakes them all to their core. Something has been living in the oil and it's about to give birth to the greatest threat humanity has ever seen.

"The Black" is a techno/horror-thriller that puts the horror and action of movies such as Leviathan and The Thing right into readers' hands. Ocean exploration will never be the same."

www.ingramcontent.com/pod-product-compliance
Lightning Source LLC
Chambersburg PA
CBHW031947170626
46807CB00006B/2392